I0782123

HUNDRED PROOF

STORIES

SCOTT WOLVEN

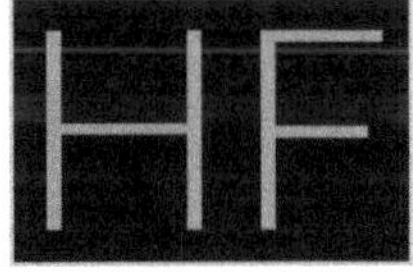

HIGH FREQUENCY PRESS

For Shanna

TABLE OF CONTENTS

PREVIOUSLY PUBLISHED WORKS INCLUDE THE FOLLOWING.

"Playboy" appeared in *Playboy Magazine* (2015, Vol. 62, #7)

Best American Mystery Story Series:

"Barracuda"—selected by Joyce Carol Oates (2005)

"Pinwheel"—selected by Carl Hiaasen (2007)

"St. Gabriel"—selected by George Pelecanos (2008)

Someday, in the presence of death, your verbal explanations will not be accepted.

—Yunmen Wenyan

HUNDRED PROOF

I WAS OFF-PAPER, LIVING IN A RENTED CABIN ON A LAKE in the Adirondacks when my old cellmate Jerry called. We had done two stints in county together, years ago. He was in for an assault charge. I ended up being in the state system for a couple years. He wrote me a letter while I was in. I wrote him back. He got my number from the boss at the shale pit where I used to drive a loader. It was April and raining. The call came way past midnight. I got up and answered. He sounded drunk.

"Hey," he said. "It's me."

"What's going on?" I said. I sat on the screened porch, looking out over the black lake and listening to the steady rain.

"I need you to do something for me," he said.

"What," I said. Thunder boomed in the distance. The line crackled.

He gave me an address about an hour south of where I was. A small town west of Albany, close to where he lived.

"Can you be there tomorrow?" he said.

"Yes," I said. "I don't work Sundays."

"What are you doing for work now?" he said.

"Running a Wood-Mizer on a commercial site up here," I said.

"Least you got work," he said. "Be there tomorrow morning around nine."

"I will," I said.

"I'll be there, too," he said. "Drunk." Then he hung up.

I got up early, drank some coffee and got on the road. Drove through the forests to the highway. It was easy to find. A rundown neighborhood on the edge of town. Jerry was already there when I pulled into the driveway. Two cop cars were in the driveway. The house was one level, red-brick. All the windows were busted out and stuff was strewn around the yard. I picked up a little muddy stuffed rabbit as I walked over to Jerry. There was yellow police tape around the house and the cops were inside. The front door was open and I heard their radios going off. I stood next to Jerry in the front yard.

"What happened?" I said.

"The landlady said when my daughter moved in, there was stuff—furniture and shit—left by the previous tenant. She told my daughter that my daughter could have it," he said.

"Yes," I said. I dropped the stuffed rabbit to the grass.

"Apparently they came back and wanted their shit," he said.

"Oh," I said. "Is your daughter okay?"

"No," he said.

"Jesus," I said. "How bad is she hurt?"

He turned and looked at me. "Dead," he said. "And we can't find her son."

"Oh Christ," I said.

One of the uniformed cops came out of the house and looked over at Jerry. "You're not thinking of doing anything, are you?" the cop said.

"What do you mean?" Jerry said.

"You're not going after them, are you?" the cop said.

"No," Jerry said. "That's up to you."

"We'll find 'em," the cop said. He walked to his cruiser.

Jerry shook his head. He knelt like a catcher in the grass, looking down, talking to someone who wasn't there about how much he missed and loved them. He picked the rabbit up and turned it over in his hands. Crying. Shaking.

"He was such a good boy," Jerry said.

"I'm sorry," I said.

He pointed at a tire hanging from a tree. "I put that swing up for him."

We walked around the house, looking at the broken windows. There was a lamp in the side yard. Next to it sat an empty bottle of Southern Comfort. Jerry picked up the empty bottle. We walked around to the small backyard and there were a bunch of things in the grass—a hammer, a big kitchen knife, two rolls of duct tape and a plant in a broken ceramic vase. Jerry lit a cigarette as we slowly walked around. When we had made a full circle and were back on the driveway, he spoke to me.

"What do you think I should do?" he said. He took the empty bottle of Southern Comfort and put it on the front seat of his pickup truck.

"I have no idea," I said. The cop radios were still going off. It looked like it might rain.

He nodded. "If you think of something," he said, "let me know." He held out his hand and I shook it.

"You want me to come to the funeral?" I said.

"Nah," he said. "My wife's family is coming from Binghamton and they'll just ask who you are and I'll have to hear about what an asshole I am for doing time, even though it was almost ten years ago."

"Okay," I said. "Keep me posted."

He opened the glove box on his pickup and we came up with a pen that wrote and a scrap of an insurance envelope and I gave him my mailing address. On the way back up to the Adirondacks, I stopped for gas and picked up a twelve pack of beer. I sat on the screened porch, sipping from those cans, staring at the lake. Thinking about that poor little boy's stuffed rabbit. I tried to remember what animals I had, when I was a kid and for some reason, the combination of the beer and those memories made me cry. As the rain came down and filled the lake.

Two weeks later, I stopped at my mailbox, on my way home from work. There was an envelope with messy handwriting on the outside. Inside was a note from Jerry. The cops used a sniffing dog and found his three-year-old grandson dead in the woods, a mile from the brick house where his daughter had lived.

The site I was working on got cleared. I milled the logs into boards for some rough-cut fencing, sent loads to the kiln for the finer work. The crew I was with put up the barns and houses. I went home every night and drank alone and stayed out of trouble.

At the end of August, the Adirondacks was as dry as a bone. The foreman shut the site down—a stray spark in the woods under those conditions was a risk he didn't want to take.

The phone rang, deep in the night. I answered. It was Jerry.

"Hey," he said. "You still working?"

"No," I said. "Too dry right now."

"I figured that," he said. "Come down to my house and get drunk tomorrow."

I was sitting on the screened porch. I could hear the faint echo of my own voice off the pitch-black lake. "Okay," I said. "What time."

"Late afternoon," he said.

I could hear the liquor on his voice. "How's your wife holding up?"

"Sheila's gone to Binghamton to be with her mother," he said.

"Okay," I said. "Should I bring some beer?"

"Bring whatever you like," he said.

We sat in lawn chairs in the back of Jerry's house, drinking beer from a cooler full of ice and bottles and cans. He was smoking a cigarette. He had some brown liquor in a glass over ice going at the same time as his beer. The charcoal was heating up and we were getting ready to put some sausage on. Next to his little shed where he kept his motorcycle and mower and snow blower, there was a small beat-up wooden penguin lawn ornament. He pointed at it. Next to it was a glass liquor bottle.

"What's with the penguin?" I said.

"That's from my friend's brother," he said. "My old friend Brian." He pointed at the thin woods behind his house. "He used to live behind me, beyond those trees. His brother gave me that penguin years ago."

"What happened," I said. I swallowed my beer.

"Brian used to hunt and fish with me. Talked about buying a motorcycle. He was a prison guard. I came home one day and there were cops over there," he pointed at the woods. "He'd blown his brains out in the backyard," he paused. He sipped his beer, then his liquor. "Sheila called me at the plant and told me."

"You guys were married then?" I said.

"Yes," he said.

"Oh," I said. "I thought you and Sheila just got married recently."

He nodded. "We did. Sheila was married to him at the time and I was married to someone else. That's what I meant by married."

"Okay," I said.

He hit the liquor, draining his glass and finished his beer. He flipped the ice by the penguin. "He likes that," Jerry said. "Reminds him of home."

He got another beer from the cooler and went inside the house and came back out with a fresh rocks glass full of booze. "She's been gone for a week," he said. He sat in the lawn chair next to me.

"You think she'll come back?" I said.

He shook his head. "I wouldn't," he said. "Given a choice, I'd get as far away from me as possible."

"What makes you say that?" I said.

He shook his head again. "It ain't worth talking about," he said. He turned his beer up so it caught the sun. "Did you ever fire a gun at a woman?"

"No," I lied. "I never did."

"I have," he said. "So there you go." He drank his booze. "I haven't been right lately."

"Oh," I said.

He lowered his voice to a whisper. He pointed over toward the penguin. "See that bottle?"

"Yeah," I said.

"That's the bottle I took from outside my daughter's house in the spring," he said.

"Yes," I said. "I remember."

"She didn't drink Southern Comfort," he said.

"Okay," I said.

"So after it happened, I talked to Brian's brother about it. He called me, actually. He's a corrections officer, too. Hadn't spoken with him in years. And yesterday, he came over here and talked to me."

"What did he say," I said.

Jerry held up one finger and went into the house. He came back out with a full bottle of Southern Comfort, and poured himself a fresh full rocks glass. He reached into his pocket and dropped a handful of bullets onto the picnic table. They were round nose bullets with gray heads and copper-colored shell casings. He picked out five of the bullets and put them in the rocks glass full of booze. Then he spoke.

"Brian's brother told me he heard three guys talking in lockup, bragging about how they got away with something in the spring. About how all they drink is Southern Comfort."

"How do you know it's them?" I said.

"I don't," he said. "But I'm going to talk to them tomorrow morning."

I stood up. "Jerry," I said. "I know you're hurtin', but I'm not getting in that kind of trouble again."

He looked at me. He held out his hand and we shook. "That's alright," he said.

I started to walk to my truck.

"What if he's setting me up?" Jerry said to no one. "I've prayed for my own death. You're a liar if you say you haven't."

He was sitting in a lawn chair by the picnic table, drinking a glass full of booze with bullets and ice in it.

OCTOBER

I'M LIVING ONE DAY WHILE THINKING ABOUT ANOTHER.

Greg and I are driving south to Boise, trying to track down a missing girl who might be living with some meth heads on the outskirts of the city. We've been getting more of these types of jobs—missing persons— and lately they seem to be girls who just vanish for what appears to be no reason.

Greg's driving. The glare off the road is making me close my eyes. To keep last night's booze from kicking the inside of my skull too hard. Last night, the girl's parents gave us her journal. They couldn't bring themselves to read it, but they wanted us to have it, in case there was a clue that could help us find their daughter. As we all sat around their kitchen table, each with a beer, the father put his glasses on and got a pen and checkbook from a drawer. He had a faded green tattoo of a girl on one forearm and an anchor on the other. He wrote Greg's name slowly on the check and then filled in two hundred fifty dollars for the amount. He signed it and handed it to Greg. As we stood on the cinder block stoop, after his wife had gone back inside, he spoke.

"Wait till Friday on that, okay? Give it a little room to clear." He sipped his can of beer.

"How's Monday morning?" Greg asked.

"Better make it late Friday, and don't wait till Monday," the father said. "If I know there's extra money in the account over the weekend, I'll drink it."

"Okay," Greg said.

The father stepped back inside and the porch light went out. It was dark. The fall air, right at that moment, with the smell of alcohol, took me back years.

"Makes me think about my Uncle Jim," I said out loud.

"You can think about him all day tomorrow," Greg said. "We'll have a long drive to Boise."

I remembered my Uncle Jim and the girl's journal he and I had used to track her in the fall years ago, back east. Catskill Park is seven hundred thousand acres of state preserve, about two hours north of Manhattan. The reservoirs in Catskill Park supply most of the water for New York City. Almost half of the park belongs to the state's conservation department and Jim was in charge of a satellite office of Department of Environmental Protection cops. In New York, the DEP has more power than the state cops—they just don't have as many men. For thirty years, if something happened in the portion of Catskill Park covered by Sullivan County, chances are Jim Thorn investigated it. That fall, I helped my uncle look for two missing persons, two girls. Jennifer Flint and Patricia Fineman.

You can never see someone's whole life, unless something has gone terribly wrong. The first time I saw a person's entire life, it was in a cardboard box that someone had written Jennifer Flint on the side of in black magic marker. I rode back to Catskill Park with my uncle Jim and the box was on the back seat of his department cruiser. He used me on cases with him, back then, because he wanted me to earn some money and get a direction in my life.

In the middle of the summer, the state cops quit working the Jennifer Flint case. They stopped looking for her and turned over everything they had—the entire case file—to my uncle Jim. The box had a couple pieces of clothing. A computer. And a journal she had written in, with passages

I never forgot. My uncle had me read her entire journal, looking for clues, and the things she wrote stuck in my mind, as I tried to replay her thinking, hoping for anything that would help us find her.

There are no shadows on the sun. The burning, brilliant, flaming light is everywhere, consuming any shade and scorching the darkness. Making everything it touches, through terrible, uncontrollable combustion, into light. Subsuming all things into its brightest beacon. Making all things, by force of hellfire, into itself. Anything the sun touches becomes part of the sun.

Jennifer Flint was a smart girl, a sophomore at Cornell. An athlete, a standout member of the track squad. A long-distance runner. Her parents had a summer home in Catskill Park, near the Neversink Reservoir and Jennifer used to stay at that house and run around the reservoir, twelve miles or more, during the summer. Preparing for her college track and field season.

We used a good dog to sniff the clothes and see if we could come up with any sign of her. We posted pictures, the parents offered a reward. For all of August and September, we looked for Jennifer Flint. We got nowhere, no real leads, and by October, we stopped looking.

I sat on Jim's back porch having a beer with him, on the day he called off the search. He wore a blue ball cap over his crew cut.

"There's nothing to be done," he said.

"Sure," I said. "Her poor parents."

"It must be terrible," he agreed. He swallowed some beer. "But here's a real lesson about detective work."

"What's that?" I said.

"Victories and defeats," he said, "look exactly alike and it can be hard to handle either one."

"How do you figure?" I said.

"The last victory I had," he said, "a man's in Sing Sing now for twenty years. Doesn't make me feel good, although I'm glad he got caught. Last defeat I had, I shot a guy. Maybe the wrong guy, who knows. But that didn't make me feel too good either."

"I don't really follow you," I said. "It's part of the job, isn't it?"

Jim shook his head. "When you've done something for as long as I have, the job is all you have. Life seems to evaporate." He looked up at the sky and we sat there on the porch until dark, drinking. Jennifer Flint's parents could keep searching for her, but we wouldn't be an active part of the investigation any longer. I started to concentrate on making sure I had enough wood for the long winter that would eventually arrive. Jim said he would get me some more work as soon as he could. Before my money got too thin.

August and September didn't bring any rain to the forests of Catskill Park, but a dry storm hit the first Sunday in October. The black clouds threw lightning at the ground and the wind tossed the trees all around my rented cabin near the reservoir. The phone rang, as I was falling asleep. It was Uncle Jim and as soon as I said hello, the storm crossed the lines. A woman's voice was in the phone. Then Uncle Jim came back on.

"In case I lose you," Jim said, "stop over at my office in the morning."

"Okay," I said.

The storm took over and Jim's voice cut in and out. The last words I heard before he hung up were "another missing girl." The phone rang again, a minute later and I picked up. No one was on the other end.

I got up the next morning and started to drive my truck around the twelve miles of the reservoir, to my uncle's office at the Department of Environmental Protection station. As I approached the long hill leading to the southern end of the reservoir, a pickup truck was behind me, then passed as I climbed the grade.

As I topped the hill, the pickup truck was about two hundred yards in front of him. It swerved, quick, and continued on. I didn't see it at first, but there was a deer dragging its hind legs, trying to reach the reservoir side of the road. The deer crawled under the retaining wire, into the woods that sloped sharply down the water. I pulled over and got out. I reached under the seat and took out my pistol. The deer was still dragging itself through the woods. Now I could see the State Police divers and boats out on the water, obviously looking for someone.

As I approached the injured deer, it made a painful noise. I took the safety off my pistol and delivered two fast shots right to the head, through the eye. The report of the pistol made the State Police and DEP cops look over at me. I waved and they recognized me and waved back. I picked up the shell casings. I popped the magazine on my pistol and replace the two shells with ammo I carried in the glove box. Then I got back into my truck and continued around the reservoir to see my uncle.

There are no seasons on the sun. The sun can cause seasons, by its distance to an object. But the sun itself is eternally burning, a flaming summer that no one can escape. Seasons allow for change and renewal. The seasons allow time to be transmitted through the air, with the cool crisp fall and winter cold. Nature's clock. Looking forward to seasons still to come. When you are close enough to the sun, there is no future. Just an oppressive burning now, blotting out and destroying anything that is not itself.

You never see someone's whole life, unless something has gone terribly wrong. All I saw of Jim's life was work and tremendous drinking and that seemed like his whole life. He could drink himself sober. I'll never forget watching him at my grandmother's funeral. He came in from the front porch of the funeral home, slightly bent and unsteady. He was putting a pack of cigarettes inside his suit coat. He looked like he had all the booze in the world inside him. He drew himself up, ramrod straight, in the back of the room. He had on an old black suit, with his crew cut. He walked forward, past the small crowd of family and friends, in a pointed line to the coffin. He didn't use the kneeler. He crossed himself, said his prayer, and moved on, as straight as he'd come in.

"He was decorated for bravery, in the service," my father said, as the line of people moved past us, paying respects.

"He drinks a ton," I said.

"Don't judge people," my father said. "He came today and that's what matters to me, not how much beer he had."

"He has a tough job," I said.

"Not a lot of people could do it," my father said. He looked around. "None of the people in this room could even begin to do Jim's job," he finished.

As I pulled up to the station house, Jim was outside smoking a cigarette, dressed in his green DEP Police uniform. I watched him very carefully drink from a stainless steel thermos cup.

"I want you to get Richard and his dog over here," Jim said. "I'm short deputies today because all my guys are helping the State Police over with the water operation. You're going to be my right-hand man for the day on this missing girl search."

"Sure," I said. "When did she disappear?"

"We're not really certain," Jim said. "Could have been last week. Her family is coming up today. She was fifteen." He took a drag on his cigarette. "She is fifteen. I have no reason to think she's dead." He tossed the cigarette away. "Patricia Fineman. Her mother has a rental up here, just west of the reservoir and she and Patricia were at that house last week."

"That's two girls this summer," I said. "Jennifer Flint, was the college girl's name."

"Jenny," Jim said. "Jennifer Flint."

"Did they find her?" I said.

"Not that I know of," Jim said. "Richard worked that case for me with his dog for a while too, until the state cops basically took over again." He paused. "I got a little more information out of them, but not much."

"Any idea what happened?" I asked.

"No idea," Jim said. "The only reason why they were even looking around here was that Jenny had mentioned to someone she had a friend around here and that she used to run around the reservoir on weekends. You knew she belonged to the track club at Cornell."

"Sure. That's a strange case," I said. "All I knew were those passages from her journal. There were no clues, other than the stuff they gave us."

"Yeah," Jim said. "Apparently she had a boyfriend on campus, but she used to take off every weekend. This summer she was on campus during the week doing a special study. Every weekend, she left and no one knows where she went. She might have come here to her parent's weekend house, but we just don't know."

"Was she pretty?" I asked. "All I ever saw were those couple of pictures."

"She seemed good-looking from her pictures," Jim said. "I saw a couple different sets and she looked good. They don't let any dummies into Cornell, so I don't think she'd mess around with any of the guys from around here."

"Thanks," I said.

"Except for you, Einstein," Jim said. "Now go get Richard and that dog he uses, so we can get on this."

I drove to Richard's house, about two miles away. The dogs were howling as I eased into the yard and I could see the kennels next to Richard's trailer. The howling set off other dogs in the valley and from far away, I heard the howls and barks answering the kenneled dogs. Richard was out in front of the trailer in jeans and a denim work shirt with a ball cap on. A pistol was holstered in plain view on his right side. Richard put a dark tan bloodhound into the back of the truck and climbed in.

"What's his name again?" I asked.

"That's Shane," Richard said. "Your uncle asked for him specifically."

"How come?" I asked.

Richard shrugged. "He had me sniff around with Shane for that other girl a couple weeks ago and I think he liked him."

"Oh," I said.

The sun shone brightly as we drove back to the DEP station. The leaves were all orange and fiery in the fall light. Dry leaves scattered along the road as we drove past.

"Hard to believe it's October," Richard said.

"I never liked October," I said. "Never liked Halloween. It scared me as a kid. October usually meant that the Red Sox had either already lost or were in the process of losing."

"Everybody was always out in the woods deer hunting," Richard said. "I liked it."

"Hunting was fine," I said. "I just liked November better."

I pulled into the parking lot of the brick DEP station. Jim was standing outside talking to a small woman dressed in new jeans and boots, with a barn jacket on. Richard and I got out of the truck.

Jim indicated the woman. "This is Cathy Fineman," he said. "These are my two deputies for the day—John Thorn and Richard Schmidt."

They all shook hands with Cathy.

"Don't you have," Cathy said, "regular deputies?" She made a motion with her hands toward me and Richard. "No offense," she said.

"No problem," Richard said. "I do a lot of the search work for the department, because of my dogs. I just don't wear a uniform."

"John's my nephew," Jim said. "He helps me on the tougher stuff. All the guys I've got today are at the reservoir, helping the State Police divers search the shore and woods." Jim pointed vaguely at the reservoir. "That's a big operation."

"I just wondered," Cathy said. Tears came to her eyes. "I just want to find her."

"Of course you do," Jim said. "We're here to help."

Cathy wiped her eyes with a white tissue from her purse.

"Can I ask you some basic questions?" Jim said.

"Go ahead," Cathy said.

"Where's your husband?" Jim said. "The girl's father."

"He lives in Florida now," she said. "We're divorced."

"Has she been in touch with him?" Jim said.

"I have no idea," Cathy said. "She's probably just confused, but why would she be in Florida?" She shook her head. "Her father's out of the picture, she wouldn't have anything to do with him."

"Kids are funny," Jim said. "Did she keep a journal?"

"Yes," Cathy said. She pulled a small purple journal out of her purse and handed it to Jim. "But it has a lock on it and we respect that in our house."

Jim took a knife out of his pocket and popped the kiddie lock with the blade. He opened the journal. He flipped some pages.

"She must be a very advanced girl," Jim said. "I didn't think like this when I was fifteen."

"She goes to Hunter High School," Cathy said.

"That doesn't mean anything to me," Jim said. "The only place I've ever been to in New York City is the bus station and Yankee Stadium."

"Hunter is a remarkable high school," she said.

"She seems very intelligent in her thoughts here," he said. "We had a college girl disappear up here a couple months ago and I got to read her journal. The school gave it to me, thought it would help. That was incredible. You never know what people are thinking about and how they see the world."

"If it's any help, let's use it," Cathy said.

Jim stared at her for a minute. "Don't think I'm dumb," Jim said. "You opened this up and it was left in a place for you to find and open."

"As long as it was locked, I would never read it," she said. Cathy was stunned.

"Those lies might be the nails in her coffin," Jim said.

"I'm not to blame for this," Cathy said. "I didn't make her run away."

"Nobody said you were to blame," Jim said. "How come you haven't called her father?"

"It's not his concern," Cathy said. "He's out of the picture. I can handle this. Women are just as capable as men, you know."

"I didn't know that," Jim said. He took a drink from his thermos cup. "You must think we're a bunch of hicks up here and that's fine. I don't care. But in order to help find your daughter, I might need you to be honest with me. Do you and your daughter get along?"

"I'm never less than honest," she said. "And yes, Patricia and I get along well."

Jim indicated the journal. "It doesn't say that here and you know it. You're fooling yourself," Jim said. "You lie so much you don't know when you're telling the truth." He drank the last of his thermos cup. "What did you and Patricia argue about when she was up here?"

Cathy started to sob quietly. "Her nose," she said finally. "She pierced her nose without telling me."

Jim looked at the journal again. "Did she threaten to run away when you started yelling at her?"

Cathy looked up into the sky and then back at Jim. "I was very upset by it," she said.

"I think Patricia was too," Jim said. "Let's go over to the reservoir and see what we can make out with this dog."

There are no days on the sun. Day requires night and the sun has burned night away. The sun never sleeps. It lives its entire life awake, burning. When the burning stops, it will be dead. But you will not be the one to pronounce yourself dead. Someone who is alive will do that. Someone outside of yourself.

At the reservoir, Cathy gave Richard a piece of clothing from Patricia, which he in turn gave to Shane. The bloodhound sniffed several times around the small tourist pull-off overlooking the water, the last place Cathy had seen Patricia. It was a great view of the water and everybody went there. I remembered that the state police had searched there for the Flint girl with no luck.

The dog started to veer away from the water, into the woods and up the hill.

"He's got something," Richard said.

"Let him run with it," Jim said.

Richard loosed the dog and Shane took off up the hill. We followed as best we could. Jim called out to us.

"I'll take Cathy in the truck and catch up with you."

We waved to him and headed deeper into the woods after the dog, howling ahead of us. I could feel my pistol grinding into the small of my back as we ran, but I was moving too fast to change its spot right now.

After we cleared the woods, the brush thinned. We stooped and went under the rusted barbed wire, into an open field. At the far end of the field was a group of cows gathered around each other. Richard read the posted sign.

"This is Zimmer's property," he said. "Do you know his son, Ted?"

"I went to high school with him," I said. The road was about fifty yards away and after a minute, Jim pulled up in the truck and leaned out the window.

"Okay," Jim said. "Let's go to Zimmer's."

"We were just talking about Ted," I said.

Jim turned to Richard. "Yeah, Ted was a little intense, wasn't he?"

Richard nodded. "Something might be wrong with Ted."

There were three ponds in plain sight. The dog started to bark at the water on the farthest pond. Richard calmed the dog down. A man in a baseball hat and denim coveralls came out of the barn. An old green tractor sat in front of the barn. A red pickup truck was in front of the farmhouse.

"Hi, Charlie," Jim said.

Charlie Zimmer walked a little closer. "Jim," he said. "What are you doing?"

"We're looking for a little girl," Jim said.

"Patricia Fineman," her mother said from Jim's truck.

Charlie nodded. "Well look around," he said. "There's nobody here but me." He paused. "I hope you find her."

"Where's your boy?" Jim said.

"Camp Lejune, North Carolina," Charlie said.

"You must be proud of him," he said.

"The farm isn't very exciting," Charlie said. "Do you need me? I've got some work to do in the barn."

"Thanks, we're just looking," Jim said.

Charlie stood there with his hands in the pockets of his coveralls.

A big buzzard flew overhead.

"Sometimes," Jim said, looking up at the bird, "they flap their wings once in the morning to get going and not again the whole day."

"How long are you going to be?" Charlie asked.

"I want to get him tracked on a new scent," Jim said, pointing at Shane.

Charlie nodded.

Richard tried to lead Shane off to the other side of the farm. The dog wouldn't leave the pond. It sat there, right on the edge. When Richard gave the command to relax, the dog laid right where it sat, staring at the dirty water of the pond.

"What's he after?" Jim said. He stood by Richard and the dog.

"No idea," Richard said.

"Do you think there's something in there?" Jim said.

"Could be," Richard said.

"You guys want a beer?" Charlie asked.

"Yes," Jim said. "Bring three beers."

He turned to Cathy Fineman, still sitting in the truck. "Do you want a beer?"

"No," Cathy said. "I do not. Does the dog think something is in the pond?"

"Maybe," Jim said. He walked over to the truck and spoke privately with Cathy. Then he walked back to Richard and me.

"Keep everything here calm," Jim said. "I'm driving Cathy back to the station and I'm coming directly back here."

Richard and I both nodded and Jim drove away in the big pickup, down the hill of the farm road. The dog didn't move from the pond.

There is no smoke on the sun, despite all the fire. The sun would burn the smoke, like the most efficient stove. There is no noise on the sun, because of the vacuum. The most intense flame in the universe blazes silently, consuming itself in front of everyone. But no one knows. They can only see the light coming off, for to look directly at the sun causes blindness and after a while, people stop trying. The sun can't take care of itself, all it can do is burn out. That's its job.

Richard and I waited at the pond. Charlie Zimmer wandered down from the barn again. The three of us stood, looking at the surface of the water. As the sun hit the surface, the water looked almost dusty. I couldn't see below the surface at all.

"Where do you think Jim went?" Charlie said.

"I have no idea," I said. "I guess he took Cathy back to the station."

Charlie nodded. "Yeah, I guess you're right."

Richard skipped a stone across the pond.

"Don't do that." Charlie said.

Richard looked at him.

"Bothers the cows for some reason," Charlie said.

Richard shrugged. "Okay."

Jim was coming back up the dirt farm road with a big pickup truck and he had something in the back of it.

"What's he got?" Charlie said.

"I don't know," Richard said.

"Looks like a pump," I said.

Jim and I lifted the pump out of the truck and put it next to the pond. Jim pushed the hose that was going to suck out the water beneath the surface.

"Can I just direct the water down the hill?" he asked Charlie.

"Sure," Charlie said. "That's fine. Do you really think you're going to find something in there?"

"The dog thinks we will," Jim said.

"Suit yourself," Charlie said. "You guys want another beer?"

"Yes," I said.

Charlie went up to the house and came back out with three beers. He handed one to Richard and myself, each, and the last one to Jim.

"I just got off the phone with my lawyer from over in Phoenicia," Charlie said. He cleared his throat. "Unless you've got a warrant, get that pump out of my pond."

Jim shut the pump off. "Do you want to talk, Charlie?"

Charlie shook his head.

"Because," Jim said, "I made some phone calls too. Long distance. Your son isn't at Camp Lejune."

"Maybe he got deployed and didn't have a chance to let me know," Charlie said.

"I've got to do this and you know it," Jim said. "I'm not going to bullshit you and say I could help your son, or lighten his sentence. It might ease your mind a little, that's all."

"I don't know what you're talking about," Charlie said. "Get that pump out of here and get off my land."

Jim had his pistol in his hand. He wasn't pointing it at anything or in any special direction. He just held it.

"Richard, John," Jim said. "Empty the pond."

Richard and I put the hose back in the water and started the pump again. The muddy water cascaded down the hill, into a growing puddle that drained everywhere.

"Sit down," Jim said to Charlie.

Charlie stood there looking at Jim. Jim pointed the pistol in the air and fired a shot. Charlie sat down on the grass. The report of the pistol echoed.

After half an hour, the level in the pond was steadily going down. The water now rested over halfway down the drainpipe. Areas that had been covered were dry now, drying out in the sun. A small turtle crawled in the mud. There was something red underneath the water. It looked like a red sneaker or a red running shoe. The gas engine of the pump kept roaring. Now we could see an ankle, white as a fish belly. Now we could see a leg. There was a dead girl in the bottom of the pond.

There is no water on the sun. There is no air either—water and the sun have that in common. The burning energy of the sun has no air in it either, which makes it like water. Washing over everything with a flame so intense everything, even water, is gone. Nothing is left once the sun has been there.

"Watch him," Jim said, as he got back into the truck. "I'll only be gone a minute. I want a state cop up here."

"Okay," I said. Richard nodded as he watched the pump. Charlie sat on the ground.

As soon as Jim was gone, Charlie started in with me.

"Hey John," he yelled over the engine. "I've got to piss."

"Go ahead," I said.

"I don't want to go in front of you," he said. "I want to go in the woods."

"Fuck you," I said. "Sit your ass right there and piss yourself."

I think he started to stand up. I will always say to myself, he started to stand up. Maybe if he was going to stand up, maybe he was going for a weapon. Maybe he had a pistol in his coveralls.

The first shot hit him directly above the heart and spun him around. Blood flew everywhere, as if somehow he was under pressure that had been released. Blood spattered onto my face and clothes. I kept squeezing the trigger of my pistol and Charlie's body kept jumping on the ground, as blood leaked all over the grass. I was snapping empty metal when Richard shut the pump off and shouted at me to stop. I had shot Charlie twelve times. He was twitching on the ground as the blood left him. Then he stopped.

It was the first time I had seen the very end of a person's life.

There were small problems when Jim got back with the state cop. It turns out I had drank three beers during the day, which the state cop smelled on me. Jim knew him and took him to one side and when he came back, he didn't ask me about the beer anymore. Only about how Charlie had started to come at me. Which he hadn't done. But Richard and I both swore to it and that was how the statement stood. Shane must have locked on to the old scent when we were at the pull-off by the reservoir. When the clothes from Patricia Fineman didn't give him a scent, he went back to his other scent. Jenny Flint. Dogs work, they don't always distinguish. Shane had found his quarry.

I had found Jenny Flint after all, only she was dead. I had shot and killed Charlie Zimmer. Except Charlie didn't kill Jenny Flint. The state cops found the body of Charlie's son Ted in the reservoir. The body showed evidence of a fierce struggle. It appeared that Charlie had killed Ted, probably after finding out that Ted had killed Jenny. And to be honest, I had killed Charlie before I knew it was Jenny Flint in the pond. If there were any victories, I couldn't find them.

A couple days later, I was sitting in a cubicle at the DEP office with Jim.

"Hey," he said. "Guess what?"

"What's that?" I asked.

"They found Patricia Fineman," he said.

"Where was she?" I said.

"At her grandmother's house in Maryland," Jim said. "She took the bus back to New York City last week and the grandmother came and picked her up and brought her to Maryland."

"The father's mother?" I asked.

"That's right," Jim said. "Mother just talked to her on the phone." Jim lit up a cigarette and started to walk out of the building. I followed him. "She's fine," he said.

"Thank God," I said.

"Trust me," Jim said. "By the time you're done with your life, you'll get to see a whole new map of hell."

"I believe you," I said.

There is no truth on the sun. The sun consumes and burns all things to produce light. Light is not truth, although it may help you find it. To the sun, everything is fuel to be burned. Truth. What is real. Lies. The truth about lies. It all burns. This life that I'm living now will be nothing but a memory, trapped inside my head. My days on earth will be eaten by the sun and others will have to pronounce me dead, outside of my own life.

Greg and I can't find the house. There were some likely meth houses, from the look of them, but not the one we want. We drive around, on the outskirts of Boise in the dark, for almost an hour. The house we first thought was it wasn't it. Wrong street.

"Let's get rooms," Greg said. "We'll hit it again in the morning."

"Fine with me," I said.

We got some burgers at a diner after Greg found us a hotel. I went back to my room and tried to go to sleep, but couldn't. I sat up drinking, watching TV. Waiting for today to turn into tomorrow. I drink a lot more than I should.

Late that night, I dialed my uncle's old number. It must be six in the morning back east. He's been dead for at least two years. It's ringing and an older woman answers.

"Hello?" she says.

"I'm sorry for calling so early," I say. "I'm calling for Jim Thorn."

"That's alright," she says. "I was up. But you have the wrong number. We get a couple calls every year for Jim, but we just ended up with his number somehow. He's passed on."

"Oh," I say.

"Where are you calling from?" she says.

"Idaho," I say.

"What time is it out there?" she says.

"Late," I say.

"You should be asleep," she says.

"I'm looking for someone," I say.

"Are you looking for Jim?" she says.

"No," I say.

"Well that's good because he was kind of a rough customer around here," she says. "Who are you looking for?"

"John Thorn," I say.

"Oh," she says. "Well that was Jim's grandnephew or some such relation."

"Okay," I say.

"But you wouldn't want anything to do with John. He's a drunken killer." She paused and I listened to her light a cigarette. "I think he's in prison or somewhere, maybe a mental hospital." She yells into the background. "Harry, whatever happened to Jim Thorn's relation there, John?"

"How the hell should I know? He killed Charlie Zimmer, I think," came the voice from beyond. "Jesus Christ, it's a little early to be calling, don't you think?"

"My husband Harry says he's a drunken killer," she says. "John's probably dead."

"Good to know," I say.

"Stay the hell away from him, if he's alive," she says.

"I'll remember that," I say.

"Now go get some sleep," she says.

That cool fall breeze from Catskill Park comes right through the phone line and I can smell Charlie Zimmer's blood on the air as if I shot him all over again right there, in a hotel room in Boise, Idaho, twenty-four hundred miles from where they buried him on his own farm, fifteen years ago.

My hand is shaking as I hang up. Waiting for the burning sun to rise.

MASTODON

MAKE A FRIEND.

Just one. That's how you have to begin. Because friend's talk to each other and one might be enough. We all know what making a friend looks like from the outside. That's what I focus on. What does it look like I'm doing from the outside. Because the stakes are high, when I start an operation.

Ten thousand years ago, mastodons vanished. But in subzero conditions off the coast of Siberia, in the East Siberian Sea, is an island the size of Delaware called Invisible Land. Where a population of roughly five hundred of the mammoth wooly creatures survived another seven thousand years. It wasn't until man penetrated the polar fog and found out where the mammoths were that the massive prehistoric beasts became extinct. Hunted by men from five hundred to zero.

They claim the Devil has people to do his work and I am one of those people. Talking to me is like to helping the cemetery worker dig your own grave. There are only about twenty people in the whole country like me—high-level professional criminal informants—and as the old saying goes, it's already later than you think. In the shadow world of drug dealers, killers and corrupt cops and district attorneys, I'm the only king.

But in any situation, there is never one king. And that's always a problem.

Gravel parking lot and I'm standing next to my truck at 4 a.m. in early July in upstate New York. Everything is blue right before dawn. This is the west side of the Hudson River, the land of Rip Van Winkle and caves and mountains and the sea of trees. The land of prisons and drugs.

I went to high school here, which should allow me to talk to the target—he knows me a little and might trust me. The target might talk about the immense amount of cocaine and oxy and pills he's selling across upstate New York and Western Massachusetts. He might talk about his connections. About Tim Decker, the man I'm really looking for. The dirty cop. I tighten my black breath mask and stretch the black balaclava up over my nose. Dark blue ball cap worn low.

The investigator is there and he puts the wire on me—thin transmitter, lower middle of my back with duct tape, two-way microphone the size of a half toothpick attached below the back collar of my zip-up track jacket. I have a Kimber K6S with a shrouded hammer in my right front jacket pocket, in the event of any misunderstandings. The investigator checks the wire—gets a clear signal, the high sign from his audio tech— and gets back in his van.

I walk through the brush and trees, up the slight incline and am standing on a quarter-mile oval surrounded by trees as the sun starts its sky-journey, a black cinder running track with a clipped green soccer pitch in the middle. I start to walk the oval, headed toward the massive iron train trestle that dominates the view. Following the oval, gently curving around on itself, until the trestle is in front of me again. One lap.

I suffer from a condition that's not a medical disease. More a disease of the mind. I have lived these days before. Not in the sense of déjà vu. Rather, being on the brink of a very powerful epiphany that hovers ghostlike at the edge of my perception. Yet never arrives. It causes me to live in the land between life and death, because I never feel fully alive. I'm constantly beyond awake, from the danger being an informant and yet everything seems like a horrible sleepwalking nightmare. Are all our secrets the same, simply because they are secrets? Are there people somewhere, keeping happy secrets? If they exist, I have never met any of those people.

Years ago, when I stood here on that morning in high school, there was a man hanging from the trestle, rope around his neck. Maybe twenty feet below the rusted iron superstructure and the passing northbound freight train made it seem as if he was dancing in the air. Bouncing. His arms moved, his legs moved. His head. He slowly rotated—suspended— as the heavy freight cars and diesel engines rolled over the tracks on the trestle. I knew someone would come and cut him down and I wondered if he wished he could stay there, dancing with the passing trains. I wondered if when they cut him down, would they catch him and bring him up onto the tracks or would they just cut the rope and let him fall a hundred and fifty feet to the ground. He was already dead—what would it matter.

That man on the trestle was the first dead person I'd ever seen by myself, alone. There were others before that, but always with other people around.

Here comes Ben Kinney the target. He wears a mask and scarf and he walks next to me on the cinder oval. We went to high school together and we start talking back and forth about the long funeral procession of life. It's all a funeral to me. A giant shared history of sadness. Talking about death and dead people always lulls the targets. Always. All death is a single, giant event all connected, it just happens to every one of us at different times and different ways, but that's just death fooling you—it's all the same. As if the times and ways matter. Like children, we make things that are supposed to last forever—marriages, careers, genders, days, summer days of no school and bright sunshine and ice cream. Pets. We think we can put the magic inherent foreverness into all things. Death is the only all-connector. When I mention the man hanging from the trestle to Ben, it takes us both back, connects us to where we both were on another day.

I've made a friend.

We talk about our old friend Kurt. Kurt's mother—Anna—had died the year before—when he was twelve—and he didn't act like himself anymore. His family came from Germany and were farmers, about two miles outside town. A hundred acres that they dusted themselves with a small plane. In the late fall, when the leaves were crisp and on the ground, Kurt's father Luka would flood the cow pond and the clear ice became thick and solid and anyone who wanted to could play hockey or just skate around. Anyone. If you didn't have skates, over the years, extra skates were put in the barn in several old milk crates. Old hockey sticks were in the corner, near the tiny plane that rested under a tarp. Pick out a pair of skates and get on the ice. Use your legs, Luka would say in his accent. Do something—live. It doesn't cost anything to live, does it. This is America, he would say. It's free to live. And it snowed and froze and froze and a bunch of us shoveled the pond and played hockey.

Ben and I were on the far end of the ice—we didn't have enough kids for a proper goalie, so Kurt was our hang back defenseman. We turned around and Kurt was gone. We skated down and there he was— under the ice. Luka ran from the house, slid down the hill to the pond, moved much more quickly than we thought he could and grabbed someone's skate and began using the sharp end to try to chisel into the thick ice. Chips flew but that's all it was—chips. A hole the size of a thimble. Kurt and Luka were looking at each other through the wavy clear ice, warped like a funhouse mirror, and Luka began to sing in German—*Guten Abend, gut' nacht, mit Rosen bedacht*—it was a lullaby. He sang louder, put his mouth almost on the surface of the frozen pond. He was screaming by the end and Kurt was beginning to turn blue under the ice. There was no air. Kurt drowned before he froze. We found out later that Luka had used an ice saw the night before to cut a big block of ice out of the pond. He had cut it and thought no one would skate there. That it would refreeze. It snowed a little overnight and obscured the square of the block and Kurt fell right through.

For a few years, people said that at night during the winter, they saw Luka standing, looking over the pond, singing in German. A few years later, on Christmas Eve, the fire department arrived to the whole pond in a raging inferno lighting the night—flames forty feet high—and there was Luka, ablaze, skating on the ice, singing in German, spinning, jumping, screaming. He had poured straight gasoline all around the edge and surface of the pond. He had pumped as much wide-cut jet fuel—color of straw, volatile, non-freeze—as he could under the ice for two days. And then, on Christmas Eve, set the whole farm on fire. The big house on the hill burned with a hellfire only accelerants can produce. That Jet B mix under the ice reached the point of autoignition after about half an hour, when Luka—burned beyond recognition from the gas fire, falling through the now-melting ice into the fuel mix trapped beneath—helped the process along—took a road flare, lit it, and stuck the lit end directly under the ice into the pond. The force of the explosive blaze shot what was left him over half a mile into the night sky and he was gone, violently incinerated. Reunited with his wife and son. The fire department applied spray foam, to try to control the fumes. The structures burned to ground and the spot where the pond stayed hot for a week, with a department truck on-site, monitoring the crater the whole time.

Ben and I talked about Billy Ward, a kid in our class. Coach Frank made him run the track even though Billy had a heart condition. His blood was probably still mixed into the cinders. Died right here, coughing on his own bright red life in front of us. Ben says he had a dream about Billy and I was in it and I realize for the first time that all the dreams you show up in are not your own and Ben says that's true, he had never thought of it that way. Another lap.

And then we got around to business.

"Why are you here man," Ben asked.

"I'm looking for someone," I said.

Ben nodded.

"Tim Decker," I said.

"Well now you're out of your mind," Ben said.

"Do you move stuff for him," I said.

"I sit home and watch Jeopardy," Ben said.

The cinders crunched under our feet.

I tried a different route. "Do you get hold of him or does he get hold of you."

"You're trying to buy something that's not for sale here," Ben said.

I nodded. This was it. Never pressure a friend.

Ben kept on. "I might know him," he said. "That guy comes around once in a while." He shrugged. "He's a cop, you know."

"I know," I said. "Maybe we could all meet."

"You looking to move weight," Ben said.

"That's it," I said. "Does he have a spot he likes. Somewhere safe."

Another lap. Of silence. The crunch of cinders. Our breath, double-filtered by masks and scarves.

And Ben whispers. Because friend's whisper sometimes. A location. The next step on the ladder. Closer. More danger, but closer.

In the Franco-Cantabrian region, in the highest mountains in Basque Country, Spain, there is a cave. On the left, as you enter, the wall is covered with human handprints thousands of years old. From the size and apparent bone structure, the prints—hundreds of them, all on a 25-yard stretch of cave wall—are all women. The women made a compound of special mud and chalk and put it on each other's hands and made sure all their hands—from the oldest to the youngest child—touched that wall. It appears to have been a ritual. I am here, I am alive, you are here, you are alive—we give birth to each other and we give birth to ourselves and we are here.

Forward, as you proceed deeper into the cave, there are another set of drawings. There appear to be the work of a single, lone man. Of giant elephant-like figures—mastodons—with spears protruding. Line drawings of men with spears. Line drawings of men prone. And of an individual standing upright near the prone figures. One man appears to have sketched all this.

I want to be that man. Before death. He thought the other men were sleeping or had just stopped for a reason that he could not fathom. He did not know what the death of men was. He knew killing—what they did to mastodons. I wonder when he realized it was being done to his friends by some invisible, outside force. That they were being somehow hunted.

I want to be that man, doing the right thing by sheer ignorance, I want to stand next to all the people I've ever known who have died— until my living day is occupied with death. And I arrive one day to discover animals have eaten my friends and a body is missing—dragged away and I question my duty but I mark the spot with a stone and I visit the stone every day. And the number of stones grows and then grows beyond measure.

And I decide to make pictures on the wall because there is danger in visiting my prone friends and I stay safe and I want to be that man. Before we knew what death really was. Before evil.

But I'm not that man.

I watch Ben walk away from the cinder track oval as I slowly walk through the woods, down the steep embankment, to the parking lot and the van.

I turn to the investigator and say "What do you want to know."

"The BCI is picking up Ben right now," he says. "Are we closer to Tim Decker? Something solid?"

I shrug. Cops going after cops with criminals. Like a pit of snakes eating each other. They're not different. They're all the same. Can't tell them apart. "Maybe," I say.

Mastodons vanished over ten thousand years ago. There are scientists who believe the extinction of the species was caused by a cataclysm—a mass extinction event, a single blow. There is a larger group of scientists who believe the giant creatures were devoured one-by-one, hunted by men with spears, until the mastodon existed no longer.

I know where Tim Decker is.

YOU BETTER RUN

THE WORLD CAN CHANGE OVERNIGHT. IT DOESN'T NEED to sleep and hot and cold don't bother it. It creates the seasons, not the other way around.

The northbound freight train sat stopped on the tracks, baking in the noon sun. Boxcars and a string of tanker cars linked together. Three sheriff's patrol cruisers and a local cop SUV were all pulled off to the right, in front of the train. The chest-high reeds and marsh grass moved in the breeze and on the other side of the dead train, less than a mile, was the Hudson River. Catskill was two miles north and the cement plants were less than half a mile south. Beyond that was Smith's Island, the hamlet that used to be called Cementon. 9W ran parallel to the river, and continued all the way to Albany. Embought Road made this tee off 9W and headed through the marsh and toward the river, eventually snaking into Catskill. My brother and I sat in his pickup truck, in a line of about ten vehicles that had been stopped by the train. The track gates were down, but the warning bell wasn't going off. The one gate was crooked and damaged. On the left hand side of the road was a sheriff's car that looked like it had been hit by a giant steel rhino. The front passenger tire was torn off and the cylinder and brake mechanism were visible and chewed up. Part of the engine showed through the torn hood. Two sheriffs were looking at the damage. A local, older cop and a young sheriff's deputy were walking slowly along the line of vehicles, on the passenger's side.

"What is this?" my brother said to me, quietly. The window on his side was open and he rested his arm on the truck door.

I was in the driver's seat, with my hands on the steering wheel. "Nothing," I said. "We've been fishing." I didn't look at him as I spoke.

The cops stopped at the blue car in front of us and motioned the driver to make a U-turn out of the line and get back on 9W. The young sheriff took down the plate number as the blue car drove away. Now the cops were looking at us.

I leaned over toward the passenger side window. "What happened?" I said.

The older, local cop shook his head. "Escaped convict," he said.

"How did that happen?" my brother asked.

The young sheriff was writing down our plate number and walked over to stand next to me.

The older local cop was sweating in the sun. "He was being taken to court up here in Greene County for an additional hearing before his sentencing and when the officers stopped their car for the train, he forced it onto the track somehow. He must have got out after the train hit it," he said.

The younger sheriff looked at me. "You're John, aren't you?"

The sweat ran down my back. "That's right," I said. The small automatic pistol I had in the pocket of my fishing vest seemed to gain weight and give off heat that I felt on my right side. The lever-action rifle behind my head in the gun rack shifted like a ghost had touched it.

"My father was good friends with your uncle," he said. His name badge had SINNOTT on it. "I'm Tim Sinnott," he said. "You probably don't remember me, but we bought a dog from you once, years ago."

"Oh, Jesus, yes," I said. I held out my hand and we shook. "A black lab. I remember that."

"That's right. Skeeter was that dog's name." He paused. "Your uncle was a DEP cop, for a while, wasn't he? I think that's where my father knew him from," Tim nodded.

"Yes," I said. "Uncle Al knocked around there with the DEP for a couple years."

"Is he dead?" Tim asked.

"Yes," I said.

"I remember him drinking beer in our back yard," he said.

"Al liked to drink," I said.

He nodded across the hood at the local cop. "You remember Al, used to work out of Sullivan County with the DEP?"

The local cop took his hat off and wiped his brow. "Yeah, of course. I remember him."

Tim pointed at me. "This is his nephew," he said.

"Okay," the local cop said. He nodded through the windshield at me and my brother.

Tim turned back to me. "You won't believe who it is that escaped," he said.

"Who?" I said.

"Remember Fred Burnley, his father owned that service station in Cementon for years?" He pointed south, in the direction of Cementon.

"Sure," I said. "I remember Fred."

"This is Tony Hall, the guy that raped Fred's sister."

"Oh my God," I said.

"Yeah," Tim said.

"But he raped her right here, didn't he?" I said.

Tim nodded. "Tony and another guy raped her a little closer to the river, but she got away and started up here," he pointed to the road beyond the train, "on Embought Road." He motioned at the field of high grass. "Somehow, they found her in the grass. She had a knife that we think she took from one of them and in the course of the struggle, she fatally stabbed the other guy. Or Hall stabbed both his buddy and Fred's sister. We could never really figure that out. We picked up Hall walking on 9W well after midnight, covered in blood. Never found the knife," he stopped. He looked at the side of the road—a raised five-foot bank that went down into the marsh. "Too much mud. That was five years ago."

"Now he's out there somewhere," I looked over the grass toward the river.

"Yeah," Tim said. He took a step back and checked the bed of the truck. "You both got waders?"

My brother nodded.

"Yes," I said.

"Pull up behind my cruiser there on the right and get your gear on. You can help us look for him. The state cops are bringing the dogs, but that might take a while." He raised his voice and asked the local cop. "That's okay right?"

"As long as you vouch for them, it's okay with me," the local cop said. He swatted a mosquito on his arm. "I just want to find Hall and get out of here and go home." He walked towards the car behind us, as I eased in behind the sheriff's cruiser.

"What are we doing?" my brother whispered.

"We're stuck here," I said. "No numbers today."

"They'll be pissed," my brother said.

"I can't help that," I said.

We both got out of the truck and put our waders on. Tim opened the trunk of his cruiser and brought out a pair of green waders for himself. He took the riot gun off his center console and racked the slide.

"Better bring that rifle," he said to me.

I took the rifle from the rack and checked it. Clicked the safety on and off and back on. Once I climbed down the bank, I clicked it off again.

We pushed out into the grass, that was over our heads. The mud sucked at our boots on almost every step. We walked up, over the gravel road into the active cement processing facility. We headed for the abandoned cement plant, following the train tracks. We had walked over half a mile in the slop. When we got to the abandoned silos and aggregate yard, Tim stopped us. He covered us both with the shotgun.

"Toss the rifle away from you," he said.

"How's that?" I said.

He flicked the safety off and motioned with the barrel of the shotgun. "Do it now."

I tossed the rifle into the high grass.

"So what the fuck are you two doing out here, every day?" he said quietly.

I looked at my brother.

Tim kept on. "I think you're casing the payroll truck that comes to the plant, but I really don't know. All I do know is that I want in." The grass shook with the hot breeze.

"I don't know what you're talking about," I said.

"I patrol out here every day. I drive 9W every day. I sit places and watch things. I look in the quarries and all along the river. And for the past month, you've been out this way," he said.

"Fishing," my brother said.

Tim swung the muzzle to my brother. "You're missing my point. I want to kill you both right now. You're alive because of me right now. I want to be part of this job. Or you can go away. Forever."

"Okay," I said. I nodded. "We're looking at the payroll truck. How can you help?"

"I can help a lot," Tim said. "I can stop the truck on a DOT violation, I can pull them over. How much are they carrying?"

There was a man standing in the shadows of the old aggregate belt conveyor. He had an orange jumpsuit on and he was cuffed and shackled. He was covered in mud and bleeding.

"There's Tony Hall," I said quietly.

Tim turned and both my brother and I were on him.

I kicked Tim Sinnott as hard as I could in the balls. He fell to the ground, dropping the shotgun and rolling around. My brother swiftly unholstered Tim's pistol, and shot Tim three times with his own weapon. The force of bullets pushed Tim back, into the grass. My brother's breath came out hard through his mouth.

I picked up my rifle and worked the lever. Fired two shots in the air.

We didn't even make an effort to follow Tony. Just trekked out through the mud, across the abandoned cement plant, and finally reached the wide river. Behind us, I heard some dogs baying. The staties must have finally arrived. My brother wiped Tim's pistol on his shirt and and threw it as far as he could into the river. Then we walked back up Embought Road, to the still-dead train. And asked if anyone had seen Officer Tim Sinnott.

They shot Tony Hall about an hour later. He had apparently surprised Officer Tim Sinnott by the abandoned cement plant and wrestled his weapon away from him, fatally shooting Officer Sinnott. On the premise that Hall was armed and a cop killer, they didn't take any chances.

The last time I saw my friend Mike was in the county visiting room, before he got transferred. His girlfriend has told me to go see him. The stainless steel tables had round seats welded onto them and the tables were bolted to the floor. Mike had on a blue jumpsuit.

"It's a huge job," he said. "A lot of people are doing different parts of it. I need this money."

"Who should I give it to?" I said.

"My girlfriend," he said.

"How will I get paid?" I said.

"Put a crate out on your back porch with some newspapers and wood in it. The money will be in there every week."

Taking the numbers off the tankers and calling them ahead. To an unnamed voice at the Port of Albany. My brother and I found an observation spot in the abandoned cement plant and sat there every day, out of the rain. Every morning, there was three hundred dollars tucked in among the wood and newspapers on my back porch.

But after the day with Tim, we never went back. And we both traveled armed all the time. The guys who had been stealing the chemical tankers probably weren't very happy.

When I was a kid one winter, my father was driving with me north on the Thruway, headed to Albany. From a ridge overlooking Coxsackie, the two facilities there—a medium and a maximum—were clearly visible in the snow.

"All around them, it looks like no snow," I said.

"The guys inside are angry," my father said. "Bad men kept in a bad place. The heat from their anger probably melts the snow before it hits the ground."

I think about Tim, lying face down in the cold mud and I think about Fred's sister. She must have gotten cold. Nothing possesses its own temperature. If the sun stops shining, your body wouldn't be ninety-eight point six. It would be zero. Then lower. Fire—distant fire—provides the life that we see pass by us every day. You're watching the result of fierce combustion from a million miles away. But you think it all has something to do with you and that somehow you control it. The sun seems like a benevolent light to your eyes, but only from so far away. Too much and it would all burn, even the air. Too little and metal would freeze solid. The molecules would stop moving and it would shatter from the touch of a leaf. Concrete would become brittle and the ice would form, two miles thick.

The summer passed, the fall came and then the brutal winter. But my brother and I are still alive. So it's not that day yet.

BARRACUDA

THE BAG OF CLEAR LIQUID HUNG SUSPENDED ABOVE ME, hooked to a metal pole and ran into my right arm through a clear plastic tube. A nurse came in and looked at me, adjusted the flow of my drugs, and left. There were two other beds in the room, one empty and tightly made. The other bed had an old guy in it, rigged up to more bags and machines than me.

"What's your name?" he asked.

"Paul," I lied.

"Paul, you're in a bad way, but you're going to make it."

"I'm hurt," I agreed.

"Pain is just weakness leaving the body," the old guy said. "Learned that in the service."

I was silent.

The old guy indicated the empty bed. Next to it was a table full of surgical tools, bright and shiny stainless steel. I saw the raw rows of teeth of what I took to be a bone saw.

"There was a cop in that bed five hours ago," the old guy said. "Had some emergency operation, right there on the spot."

"Really," I listened. The bed was freshly made with clean white sheets showing, and a white pillow. It looked as if nobody had ever been in that bed, ever.

The old guy kept going. "He had gray hair and didn't want to tell me he'd been a cop, when he first came in. I introduced myself and he didn't say anything, really, so then I heard the nurse taking insurance information from him and when she left I said 'Insurance? That must be nice'. And he said 'Well I earned it', and I said 'What did you used to do?', tryin' to be friendly, get a little conversation going while I'm waitin' to kick off and he didn't answer, so I said it louder: 'Hey, what do you do?' and he says 'Private security', and that put me onto it, right there."

"Really," I said.

"I said to him 'That's a job they give off-duty cops. You a cop?' and he mumbled some shit about being an MP in the service and coming out and getting a job as a radio patrol car officer years ago, in Jersey and then coming up here and being a uniformed cop up here for thirty years."

"Sounds personal," I said. "On your end."

The old guy didn't let up. "Don't give me that crap, that you like cops. Come in here beat the hell up like you are and tell me you haven't been around." He moved around in the bed. "When I came out of the service, I got a job making parts on an assembly line. I got in a couple scrapes, more than I should have, but I worked there till I retired and I'm lucky I got a pension. The collection agency still calls all the time from when I was in the hospital four years ago. And don't tell me somebody didn't take a tire iron to you. I know what I'm talking about."

"I don't know what you're talking about," I said. "This was a work accident."

The old guy raised himself up on one elbow and looked over at me. "I've been around," the old man said. "You look like you've been around."

"Sure," I said. To shut him up.

"Don't kid yourself," the old guy said. "You're always all the men you've ever been." He quieted down as a nurse came in to check on him. She fed him some pills and water and left. The old guy pointed at the surgical tools on the metal table by the empty bed.

"Think those tools are sterile?" he asked.

"That's what they tell me," I said.

"You can't sterilize the inside. Those tools remember where they've been. Saving a life one day, killing someone the next," he said. "Those tools are playing a little game with the doctors. The doctors think they control the tools, but it's the other way around."

"Okay," I said.

"The cop started to have some type of fit and they all came in and rushed around him and put up a movable curtain, but there was a space between the curtain panels. Right through that space I watched that saw and it bit too deep and I knew it as soon as it happened and I knew he was getting' it back, getting done to him what he did to somebody."

The drugs the nurse had given him must have relaxed him too much to make him a good roommate anymore.

"Hey," he said. "If I asked you a question, would you tell the truth?"

"Sure," I lied again.

He stretched his neck up toward the dark, blank TV mounted from the ceiling in the corner of the room. He lowered his voice. "Whenever I'm in the hospital, I see a man in a black suit with a hat on, inside the TV, when it ain't on. He's looking out at me." The old guy paused. "Do you ever see that?"

"Yes," I said, to help him. "Sometimes."

"Bull," the old guy spit. "If you saw something like that, you'd shit the bed."

Two nurses and a doctor came into the room and began wheeling him out the next morning. I thought he was asleep, but as he passed my bed, his eyes were open.

"Watch yourself," he said to me. "They don't save everybody here."

After sixty-five days, I was allowed to leave the hospital. The doctor saw me during morning rounds and signed off on my discharge paperwork. One of the blonde nurses I'd flirted with stood next to me and whispered in my ear. Goodbye, Mister Whoever-You-Are. They'd seen enough loggers float in, the facility being so close to the Adirondacks. Sixty-five days without a visitor and no phone in my room, no calls, Paul Wagner wasn't going to be paying any hospital bill or following up with occupational therapy. The insurance cards I vaguely referred to would never arrive and I'd sell the pain pills to my buddies, if I could make it through the day on a shot or two of straight hard booze. Paul Wagner died the minute I hit the exit door.

My truck sat in the parking lot with tiny deltas of mud near the tires, left there as the rain flowed into the lot's sunken storm drain. A layer of dirt and fine grit covered the windows. Dirty rain, over the largest forest in the Northeast. People talked about whole lakes being ruined, far to the north, but you hear a lot of things in the woods. The toughest trick in the mountains and valleys was telling where the shot came from, what was the echo and what was the original report, what was reaching your ears and eyes. The shape of the land gave birth to lies of sound and the same was true with people. The shape of their lives led them to lie. Sometimes they had no choice. That's what I told myself about being Paul Wagner for sixty-five days.

The truck started on the third try. It stuttered. The brakes were stiff, they groaned and creaked a little. I jammed it in gear and left. The foot long ceramic spike that had caused some of the damage to my right arm and head after my saw hit it rolled around on the passenger's side floor. I was on a job and spotted a chance to make some extra money with a stand of straight maple, fifty yards off a landing site. Seven thousand dollars covered in bark and leaves. It was coming down. I ran the metal detector over the trees and nothing showed on the meter, so after the crew left, I took a saw to the lead tree in the group. Two things happened at once. The chain snapped and the saw kicked out of the cut with so much force, it broke my arm and slammed into my head, digging deep into my helmet as the chain shot one last revolution through the orange plastic housing, like a deadly silver ribbon, flashing and slicing its way to my bones. My Kevlar pants finally stopped it, but I was on the ground, bleeding.

Someone had been protecting those trees. There are only two reasons to spike trees. If you're an environmental whacko, who doesn't realize that loggers need to eat too. Or to protect something you own that's valuable. I doubt they were protecting the trees against me specifically, just people like me. Because in the world of the woods, there are a lot of people like me, who steal good timber and once it's on the ground, it's long past late.

The landowner and his son drove up in a king cab rig and the old man must have puzzled out what happened right away. He grabbed a ten-pound rubber mallet out of the lock-box on the truck and hit me in the head and spine like I've never been hit before. I went unconscious from the pain and woke up in the hospital. The doctors thought a tree had fallen on me, that's what the two guys who brought me in said. They'd left my truck in the parking lot. A broken eardrum and severely bruised spine with a possible cracked disc was thanks to that mallet. At least they left me my truck. As I drove out of the parking lot, I reached under my seat. The old forty-five I kept there was gone.

I drove around the reservoirs, south, into my own territory. The western edge of Catskill Park, the Pepacton Reservoir. Mostly Department of Environmental Protection cops, state police. If something serious happened, the Bureau of Criminal Investigation, the BCI handled it. They were the detectives of the state police. No local law. Once in a while, a Sheriff's patrol. When I got behind a long yellow school bus, with kids giving me the finger through the back emergency exit window, I realized it must be the first week of September.

My rented cabin smelled. Bad. It was chilly, because the temperature had been dropping at night and I hadn't been there to light the fire.

Ladybugs clustered on the ceiling, trying to stay warm. Two months of bills sat in the mailbox, some of them soaking wet. The phone was cut off. Before I went on the job that day, I'd meant to pay the bill. I always meant to pay all my bills, but I never did.

It looked like a good time to start skimming timber. In my honest life, I was a timber appraiser and a good one. I gave people prices based on all the usual formulas. Felling and bucking, skidding cost, making sure all the wood was merchantable, all the current stumpage rates on standing timber. Landowners needed that information for tax purposes, to make a buy or sell decision, for due diligence valuation. Any number of reasons. I loved the job, being out in the woods, working. Weather never bothered me.

But when I was short money, truth and honesty rested outside of me. My relationship with money was more important, like most people. I would skim. Skimming timber is an unteachable skill. In the course of evaluating standing timber, I would mark a few trees—prime trees, like tiger maple, or northern white ash—and cut them, the day before the big crew moved in. It meant working alone with a fast saw, no hangers, nothing stuck or tipped or fucked. Straight trees on the ground, limbed up and ready to go and my buddy Dave would come in with his cherry picker and load up, maybe twenty trunks depending on the size. Off he'd go. Usually to Maine, where we knew a specialty furniture maker who always bought from us. Always no questions asked, always cash. You didn't want to skim too much, because people noticed and you couldn't truck it out. Most timber companies know that appraisers make a little extra money on the side and nobody kicks too much. Most timber companies hand out cash themselves, to appraisers. The difference between a hundred-thousand-dollar appraisal on a hundred and twenty-five-thousand-dollars-worth of wood is usually worth a thousand dollars to the timber companies. A low appraisal gives them leeway. In case some trees aren't straight enough for high-grade lumber, or if gas prices go up, or if weather beings to eat paydays for the crew. There was more than one way to skim and all of it was dangerous, lying work.

I drove to a gas station, picked up a calling card and went to the payphone. I started calling all the big outfits I'd ever worked for. There was no work right now and I think a couple of them were skeptical that I was even calling. I put in a call to Molly Johnson at Hayes. I made it a point to know these people and had even taken her out to dinner once when I was in Canada and treated her to a Tim Horton's after. She seemed glad to hear from me.

"John, I'll tell you. You're welcome to this guy. I'll note it on the file that you're the one doing the work. But it has to be done right. He's got a couple friends up here and he's a big deal, know what I mean?"

"Sure," I said. I strained to hear her as trucks pulled into the gas station. "Molly, I appreciate it."

She paused, then went on. "They haven't assigned a supervisor to this project yet, we haven't even officially taken it, but I'm sure it'll go through. We're just waiting on the appraisal. We're actually holding his check," she said. "So do a good job, because there will be people up here who will listen if he yells."

"Thanks for the heads up," I said and wrote the name and number she gave me on a slip of paper. Theodore Morrison. He had called Hayes to have his land in upstate New York logged off, but Hayes didn't operate that way. They liked to have an independent appraisal, in case the landowner changed his mind midway through the cut. I'd seen it happen. Change of heart, mixed feelings, a broken business deal. Half the trees were gone, and it was impossible to get an accounting from the sawmills. The appraisal was a smart thing. It was supposed to keep everybody honest, but the added layer just allowed for more skim. I called the Manhattan number Molly had given me and a secretary answered.

"This is John Thorn calling. Is Mister Morrison available?"

"One moment, please. What's this regarding?"

"His upstate acreage," I said. "Logging it. I'm calling from Hayes Canada."

"One moment," she repeated.

Morrison got on the line. He sounded like an older man with some kick left in him. "Mister Thorn, you're with Hayes?"

"John's fine," I said, "and no. I'm the independent. Molly Johnson at Hayes told me you were hiring an independent appraisal of standing timber in order to complete a clear-cut job and that I should call you. I work independent, call around every week or so, to see what jobs are available."

"Where are you located?" he asked. In his background, in the concrete woods of Manhattan, a faint siren moved closer, then further, then gone.

"Northwest of Roscoe, outside of the Catskill Park area. Do you know where that is?"

"I can find it on a map, I'm sure. Listen, what kind of credentials do you have and how fast can you get on this thing?"

It started to look good for me. "You can call Hayes, if you like, and get hold of Tom West, he's a supervisor up there and has seen my work and my clients."

"Okay," Morrison said. "I'll do that." He paused. "How fast?"

The necessity of speed always works on the side of the skim, never against it.

"What's the parcel and what are you doing?"

"Almost five hundred acres, and I've got two offers on the table right now, one from a condo developer and one from a lawyer in Albany with Indian connections, who wants to build a casino when that new legislation passes."

"And you want to sell the timber rights off first?"

"That's it. I haven't been up to the property in twenty years, my wife and I used to go camping up there years ago, but she enjoys warmer weather now, so it's Florida and the beach. Twenty-five years, I bet. We even put in a foundation. Never did anything with it. Taxes are all paid and I used to have a local guy look it over, a guy named Nolan, who I originally bought it from. But he's passed on."

I considered. "I can go get the survey map today, if you had it done local."

"The map is at Menden's, do you know them? Are you going to bill me or do I need to have a check sent to you?"

I was in the driver's seat now. "Wire transfer me two thousand dollars. I'll give the routing numbers to your secretary. I don't take checks anymore. They take too long to clear." I waited and controlled the pace. "I know where Menden's is, fine. I'll get the map."

He knew he was a passenger. "Fine. Just get in there and get it done. I'll put you back on with Karen."

"Nice to do business with you, Mister Morrison."

"It is nice to do business with me," he made himself laugh. The secretary was on the line and I gave her the bank instructions and numbers. I drove to Menden's office, twenty miles to get the maps, and then parked in front of my bank. I told the head teller I was waiting for a transfer and I sat there. She came out from behind her desk an hour and a half later to tell me I was two thousand dollars richer. In the skim, checks are no good. You can't put a stop payment on a wire transfer. And you can't get it back, either. I withdrew all but two hundred of it and when I got home, sat and figured my bills. Three hundred was left when I got done paying. I was trying to live low. I was lucky. I went to sleep and dreamed of the site. Tried hard to dream myself up some tiger maple, a whole straight stand of them. My arms and legs hurt from the accident and beating and that night my back seized once. The pain pills helped, with a chaser. It wasn't going to be easy cutting trees.

The next day on my way to the site, I stopped and phoned Dave, my cherry picker man. He was home.

"Hey," I said.

"Shit," he said. "St. Peter hand you the phone or what?"

"I got hurt and ended up in the hospital." He didn't say anything. "Look," I went on. "I've got a job."

"It will have to be within the next three days," he said. "Where is it?"

I told him.

"I've driven past that for years, used to be posted under the name Nolan, I've been up there hunting."

"That's the spot," I said.

"Park your truck where I can see it from the road," he said. "If I can't see your truck, I'll figure it's off."

"That's good," I said.

"See you then," he said as he hung up.

"See you then," I said to nobody.

Part of working in the woods means being able to see things and knowing how those things will impact the operation later. What soil will give way after a rain and heavy tonnage load of logs, bogging down equipment. I drove my truck up an old dirt path, so I could come back down within sight of the road when I was ready for Dave. I took a can of Hi-Vis orange marking paint and drew myself a landing site on a slight hill and started to look the place over. Within ten minutes of walking, I'd found what I was looking for. Some of the best maple I'd seen in years. At least twenty of them, all straight up to the sky like God meant them to be. I tied some yellow area tape around them, then some orange and when I got done walking the site, at least a couple of them were coming down today. I kept walking and making notes in my weatherproof book.

It was always strange to me, to be doing an honest appraisal and keeping an eye out for trees to steal. I crossed a small stream and started up a rocky hill that had more timber behind it. This was a great spot and why Morrison wanted to sell was beyond me. It was funny that I hadn't seen any deer yet, but I figured they must be deeper in the woods. I got to the top of the rocks and it looked like there was a trail ahead of me.

The man leaning against one of trees held a rifle. It was a stainless steel, wood grip lever-action, with a short barrel. He wore a black work jacket.

"I'm up here on a timber appraisal," I said. "For Morrison. He said anybody who knew Nolan was okay with him." I tossed in the only local name I knew.

The man nodded. "Come here," he said.

I didn't move.

"Come here or I'll shoot you and leave you there," he said. I walked toward him and we started down the trail together, with me in front. As we went forward, I heard noise. I'd heard the same noise once before, in a logging camp in Quebec. Dog fights.

There was an old barn, half falling down and a bunch of guys standing on an old concrete foundation, looking down in. I could hear the dogs ripping into each other, low growls, yelps, then a sound like strips of Velcro being yanked apart. Bodies hitting the concrete walls. And the scraping of claws on the concrete slab floor. They had a long handler's stick set up and it looked like they yoked the dogs into a crate and then used pulleys to haul it up to the rim of the foundation. Nobody went into the pit except the dogs. That was the fight area.

A couple of the guys standing around were state cops, I sort of recognized them. A DEP cop stood right there in his uniform, giving his bet money to a man behind a makeshift desk in the barn. My escort with the rifle took me over to a fat guy sitting on stool near the barn entrance. There was an old car there, a Plymouth Barracuda, light blue, and as I walked past, a pit bull slammed with everything he had against the window trying to get at me. I jumped back a few steps and the fat guy laughed at me. I looked at the chrome fish emblem on the car and thought about how barracuda are supposed to have rows of sharp teeth and the chrome brought me back to the surgical tools from the hospital. Fear made my mouth taste like hot metal.

"Christ," I said.

"He's in the car," Fatman said. "He ain't gonna hurt you."

"What's his name?" I asked.

"What's his name?" Fatman said. "What are you, five years old? Want to name your doggy? His name is bite-the-living-shit-out-of-anything-that-moves. He's a fighting dog. What the fuck does he need a name for? He'll be dead in a month." He coughed. "Call him Barracuda."

"I found him walking through the woods," my escort said, pointing the rifle at me.

Fatman shook his head. "What the fuck do you need a name for?" he asked, pissed, looking around. "Do you know anybody here, can you help yourself out of this? This is a serious fucking hole you're in."

I looked around. A guy with a ball cap on, near the foundation, I swore I had gone fishing with his brother years and years ago. I think the guy had just got out of prison. I pointed at the guy, "I used to go fishing with Russell Work and I think that's his brother Jimmy over there, the big quiet guy with the baseball hat on straight." Men were handing him money, so his dog must have just won the fight. They were starting to load the dog from the Barracuda into a crate, two big guys with the full-length leather gloves and another guy with a neck harness made from a belt wrench. The dog looked to be around a hundred pounds of pure black and white muscle. Once they had him in the crate, they lowered him into the pit.

Fatman yelled. "Hey Jimmy come here."

The guy I thought was Jimmy Work walked over to us.

"Know him?" Fatman asked.

His brother Russell and I had driven through a snowstorm once to visit Jimmy up in Dannemora. I think after he got out, he'd done more time somewhere. He was at least ten years older than me and I hadn't seen Russell in over five years. He looked at me hard. The scars on my face and the way I held myself after the accident and the beating. I must have looked totally different. His mind tried to place me.

"John," he said. "You're John, but I can't get your last name." He turned to Fatman. "He's okay. Friend of my brother's."

I started to breathe again. "How is Russell?" I asked.

Jimmy Work was already walking back to the dog pit. "Passed on," he said over his shoulder. My guard walked into the woods, as sweat rolled down my ribs under my T-shirt. I sat on a plastic milk crate for a minute to cool down. It happened then.

The DEP cop shoved Jimmy Work over the edge of the concrete pit. I heard Jimmy hit the floor and the dog was on him. I got to the edge of the pit and the dog already had hold of his leg, clamped on, and had bit Jimmy in two spots on the arm. He was bleeding and the floor of the pit was covered in shit and blood and it smelled. Somebody shot the dog, and we all hit the deck, the ricochet buzzed out of the pit through the woods, sizzling through the leaves. Two guys jumped into the pit and cut the dog off Jimmy, they had to practically skin the thing to get at the jaw and get that loose. Blood was everywhere. The fucking DEP cop was next to me.

"Saw man," he said. "He just got hurt in logging accident and you and I are taking him to the hospital."

"Fuck you," I said.

"Yeah," he said. "And the next time we see a cherry picker with a single load going around the reservoir, we'll stop it. And the next time. And the next time. Until your eighteen wheeled friend loses his license. You must think we're stupid, running single loads up here before the big crew shows up."

At the hospital, a different one from the one I'd gone to, closer to Syracuse, the doctor took me to one side, behind a curtain. He was obviously from India, very serious looking. Concerned. His English was a little tight but good.

"These wounds, sir," he said to me. "They are from an animal, probably a dog. Not a chainsaw, as you told me. As the officer told me."

In his world, you called people sir and expected them to act accordingly. With truth and honesty and human concern. I wanted to act like someone who deserved to be called sir, but I couldn't.

"It was a saw," I said. "He was climbing, way up, with the small limb saw and he fell, with the chain going, and really did a number on himself." I nodded to myself and him.

"Yes," the doctor said. "That is what happened in the lie the officer told you to speak. This man could die from his punctured arteries. Be honest with me now."

I wondered if in India they had trees and chainsaws and men who fought dogs in the afternoon. "Chain saw," I said.

"Yes," the doctor said again. "Never." He shook his head and walked past the curtain back to the emergency room. The DEP cop hung around, to make sure Jimmy Work lived, then took off. It took Jimmy almost two months to recover. The cop had bet a hundred to one against Jimmy's dog and lost. I missed my rendezvous with Dave, I never turned in the appraisal. I knew Molly at Hayes wouldn't work with me again. If any Hayes crew ever came down to the site, they saw the marking tape. They're not stupid. I visited Jimmy Work twice and he stayed at my new apartment for a month. I had to move out of my old cabin because I couldn't make rent.

The first time I saw the DEP cop after that was in a bar, Cody's, a one-pool-table joint a mile off the reservoir. It was night and snowing. The DEP cop was parked behind my truck when I came out.

"Hey," he called out his window. "Where's your friend Jimmy?"

Jimmy had moved in with this woman he knew, not far down the road. "I have no idea," I said.

"Tell him I'm trying to get some money together," he said. "In fact, why don't you give me what you've got in your wallet?"

Nobody else was in the parking lot. "Piss on you," I said.

He took his foot off the brake of his patrol car and tapped the back of my truck. "I could total it," he said. "You're drunk, and this car isn't going to hurt me."

I couldn't afford a new truck. I took fifty dollars out of my pocket and handed it to him.

"You're a good boy," he said. The cruiser spit gravel at me as he sped into the night.

I was off, headed to this girl's house, when through the park, behind me came a DEP cop. He followed me for over a mile and then the flashers went on. I pulled over.

When he got next to the truck, I recognized him and he had his gun in his hand. "Hey," he said. "You were speeding and weaving and out of control and then we had a high-speed chase." He was grinning from ear to ear as he said it. Behind him it was pitch black.

"Here's my license," I said.

"I don't want your license," he said. I could smell booze on him. "I want two hundred bucks." I reached into my wallet and brought out some twenties and handed them to him.

"I bet you didn't know this was a toll road," he said.

I didn't say anything.

He took out a knife and stuck it in the sidewall of the front driver's side tire. I listened to the hiss as he yanked it out of the split rubber.

"Front tire's flat," he said. "Flat flat flat. That's too bad." He had his gun in one hand and a knife in the other.

"Come on man," I said. "Give me a break."

"Sure," he said. He started to walk back to the patrol car, stopped at the end of my truck and kicked out a rear light. The whole truck rocked. "Got a back light out too," he said. "That's a violation. Better get that fixed." He slammed his door and swung around me. I watched his taillights get smaller in the dark as he drove off.

A couple months later they found his patrol car empty on a logging road near the reservoir. The door was open, the cop radio was turned on. There was money and blood all over the place, like green and red leaves blowing in the wind, and as the investigation went on, the BCI determined it was his money. He came to that spot to pay someone for something. But they didn't take his money. They took him.

NEWS ABOUT YOURSELF

For EJS

THE FALL BROUGHT SOME COLD NIGHTS AND THE POND had the thinnest sheet of ice I'd ever seen. I pointed it out to Richard as we walked around the old farm, eighty acres, talking about how he wanted me to tear the buildings down and how fast I could get the job done. We looked inside the first two barns, then just walked around. We spooked some deer that were bedded down in a field near some old apple trees. The barns all looked the same inside, I was pretty sure of that. We passed by the pond again.

"Ice melts from the bottom," he said. "I never knew that till a couple years ago."

We stood on the point, where you could see across the Hudson River. Richard worked a farm on the other side, up in Greene County. This farm, outside of Red Hook, had been a project his younger brother was going to start, before he passed away in late summer. No illness, no warning. Richard was going to have the barns and outbuildings torn down, to make it a neater parcel for developers. He didn't have a choice. He couldn't very well run two farms. The fall had been very slow for my logging business and I was more than happy to help Richard complete the demo and keep my machines working. I hadn't talked to Richard or his brother since high school. His brother and I had been in the same class, with Richard a couple years ahead of us. The three of us had been great friends when we were kids. I knew his brother had gone on to college, been a fraternity man, and come home to work. He was an officer in the fire department. The past ten years or so, I just waved to them while they were working out in the fields if I happened to be in Greene County visiting my folks. I'd been out of prison about five years at that point.

"I can do it," I said. "It will take me a week. I'll leave the stub-ups in place for the utilities, so if you decide to bulldoze below grade you won't hit anything." Only four of the seven barns were electrified and only two of those had water.

"The electric is dead back to the pole," Richard said. "How much?"

"Twenty-five hundred," I said.

"That's not enough," Richard said. "You have to make money too."

"I'll make money at twenty-five hundred," I said. "My trucks are sitting right now. I've got to get them on a job. Might as well be this one."

Richard nodded. "My family will appreciate that."

"How's everybody doing?" I said.

"It was a real shock," Richard said. "We're watching out for each other." He looked around at the old farm. "I almost never came over here, unless he asked me to. I don't know what he planned on doing with it." He swallowed his sadness. "But I know he had plans for it."

I nodded. "Please give my best to your mom and dad."

"I will," he said. We started to walk back across the property, toward our trucks. "Remember we used to play so much basketball?" he said.

"Sure," I said. "You guys had the only court that was dry in the rain, inside your barn."

"Once he got into the fire department, that was a big part of his life," he said. "He was a good judge of men and fires."

"I bet he was," I said.

"Time goes so fast," Richard said. "Time is not watches and clocks and calendars." He opened the door to his pickup truck. There was a shot in the distance. "Muzzleloading season opens today," he said. "I'll see you, Ray."

"See you Richard," I said. I stood there as he drove away. He had work to do on his own farm.

I started right away the next day. Brought my two big trucks up, along with a skid steer. Two of my regular guys were working with me. We ran the work in an orderly fashion. One of the guys would climb into the rafters of the barn with a logging chain and hook onto the main beam. We'd hook the other end to the skid steer and pull, which usually made the barn collapse. Then we'd load the wood and debris into the trucks with the skid steer and haul it back to my woodlot, about ten miles away. We drove with the flashers on and I followed in my pickup truck, to grab anything that fell onto the road. Three barns fell that first day and we were able to haul most of the stuff off.

The next morning at the farm site, there was a man in an SUV parked by the big house. He got out of his truck as I parked. He started talking before I opened my door.

"What are you doing?" he said.

"I'm handling a job here for the Broderson's," I said. My two guys were there already, and I waved at them to go ahead.

"This isn't going to developers," the man said. "You can't do that. The town won't allow it."

"I think you're trespassing on private property," I said. "Hit the road."

He shook his head. "I've got people coming from the town with a Dutchess County Sheriff," he said. "We're going to put a stop work order on you."

I looked down the dirt road toward the barns. My guys were hustling, already had the big chain hooked up and were ready to tear down another barn. I gave them the thumbs up and the skid steer lurched forward. I turned back to the man as the barn collapsed.

"Wait on the road for your people," I said. "Get off this property." The man looked at me like I was kidding. "I can hook a chain on your truck and drag it to the edge of the property," I said. "Or you can drive it there."

"Do you know who I am?" he said. "I'm Cal Sheely."

"Like I give a fuck," I said.

"Who are you? Some tough guy?" he said.

"Find out," I said. "If you want to get in a fight, I'll help all I can."

Cal sized me up and must have decided I was tipping the scales too much to mess with. He got back in his SUV and drove to the edge of the road, off the farm. I kept my eye on him. He sat there for almost an hour, before he pulled away. We had loaded up the truck at that point and were ready to make a haul back to my woodlot. I called the guys over.

"Let's make a change today," I said. "Let's put all the structures on the ground right now, as quick as we can. Then we'll load and haul them. It will make for a messy worksite, but that's how I want it done."

They agreed and we ripped down all but the last barn when I saw some trucks coming into the farm entrance. I stopped working and slowly walked up to see who it was. Two men from the town, a sheriff, and the man, Cal Sheely, I had seen earlier. I recognized one of the men from the town. It was Ernie Pickens.

"Hey, Ray," Ernie said to me. He pulled me to one side. "This guy's got everybody in an uproar, says the farm is covered in asbestos shingles. Says you've been hauling it near town. It that true?"

I pointed at the remaining building. "It's tar paper, Ernie, with regular shingles. There's no asbestos here."

"Okay, okay," Ernie said. "Will you let us inspect it?"

"It's not my property," I said. "Call Richard. If you get the okay from him, it's okay with me."

Ernie walked up to the other men and got on his cell phone. He walked back to me next to the last barn after a minute.

"Richard says okay," he said.

"Do what you want, then," I said.

He motioned at the last structure. It was the largest barn, the only one still standing. We opened the big swinging doors. It smelled like wet hay.

Inside was an old fire truck.

"Maybe he was restoring it," Ernie said.

The truck must have been brought in on a flatbed. All the tires were flat. It was a dull red and most of the gold lettering had been scraped away. The axes on the sides showed rust. I climbed up into the cab. There was a yellow legal pad sitting on the front seat. There was a list of things that needed to be fixed on the truck. Along with a list of names. Richard's name was on it, his dad's name. It was a list of guys that he would have wanted to be on the truck with him. Some of the guys were already long dead, like his grandfather. My name was there. It said Ray Cooper, my good friend.

I stepped outside, into the sunlight. The sheriff was there, smoking a cigarette. I walked over and stood next to the big farmhouse. My two workers were there and we waited until the town was done. Ernie walked over to me.

"There's no asbestos here," he said. He said it loud enough so Cal Sheely could hear him. Sheely walked away and sat in his truck while we worked. Finally, he took off.

After they all left, we chained up the fire truck and dragged it out of the barn. We chained up the main timbers and the beams snapped like matchsticks as the structure collapsed. The guys got busy putting the debris into the big dump truck and hauling it. They cleaned up the site pretty well and we were done a day early, as it turned out.

I called Richard to tell him I was done and about the truck. The next day there was a check in the mailbox from him with a note that just said: Thanks. A couple cutting jobs turned up over the next couple weeks and I ended up being busy into October and beyond.

It must have been a year later, in the late fall. I was having a bad time of it, for several months. I had a dream and woke up suddenly in my own bed, my heart pounding. The dream had been that the old fire truck was running, with lights and sirens going. I got into my truck and drove over to the farm property. The truck sat in the field where I'd left it. It was too old a model even to have lights on it. Rifle shots came across the morning air and I thought about how much the hunters would hate it if I somehow got the siren to work. I got back into my truck. Something kept me from walking into the woods and fields in my tan jacket and taking my chances. Among the trees and the evergreens and the deer.

It was a couple summers after that when something came my way. It was late August. I was sitting at the garage to escape the heat, downing beers with Jimmy Work and he started to talk about this guy that owed him money.

"Who is it?" I said. Jimmy had tattoo sleeves. He'd done about eighteen years overall and I met him inside after knowing him outside, which is pretty rare. He was a big guy, walked like a biker and had a lot of biker friends. Sometimes he hooked people up with drugs, if the buy was big enough and he was sure it was safe. He made sure the rent was paid. Cash.

"This guy, used to be on the Town Board around here, till he moved," Jimmy said. "Now he owns a store and used car lot over by Saugerties. Cal Sheely and his oldest son."

I drank a beer like it was water. "You don't say," I said. "How much is he into you for?"

"He's owed me eight grand for over six months," Jimmy said. "I just thought about it today and started to get angry."

"Do you know where he lives?" I said.

"Yeah," Jimmy said. "I know where he lives."

I emptied another beer and so did Jimmy. "Let's go talk to him," I said.

"Yeah," Jimmy said. "Let's go talk to him."

We got in Jimmy's truck and Jimmy drove over the bridge, into Kingston and headed north. He cut off the main road, until we were riding north right along the Hudson River, with big houses and huge lawns on either side of us. It was almost dusk on the river. Isolated by at least two miles from the other houses was a white, Italianate fake mansion with an attached garage.

As soon as we were in the driveway, a black German Shepherd mix came out and started barking at us. Jimmy pulled a silver whistle from his pocket and I knew it was a dog whistle, but I couldn't hear it. The dog put its tail between its legs and lay on the driveway. Jimmy and I got out of the truck and walked through the open garage. I was carrying a claw hammer that I'd picked up off the floor of the truck.

We walked through the garage, through the house and ended up out back by the pool. There was a young girl and boy there, probably neither of them more than fifteen. The girl was in the water and the boy was sitting under a big umbrella, talking on a phone. He stopped talking when we came out of the house, through the back screen door.

"Hi," the boy said. "My dad isn't here."

"Is he at the car lot?" Jimmy said. "He's selling us a car."

"Oh," the boy said. He looked at the hammer I was carrying. "He should be home any minute." The girl kept swimming in the pool, glancing at us.

"Where's your brother?" Jimmy said. He pointed at the phone next to the boy and the boy tossed it to him. Jimmy tossed the phone in the pool.

"Cape Cod," the boy answered. He picked his head up and listened. "I think that's my dad," he said. A car door slammed from the front of the house and we heard the dog give some friendly barks. The boy was smarter than he looked. "Don't hurt my dad," he said, very softly. The girl stopped swimming.

After I smashed his arm and shoulder with the hammer, Cal opened the floor safe in his bedroom and paid Jimmy what he owed him, plus the rest of the contents of the safe. We brought him back downstairs, out to the pool. The boy still sat under the umbrella and the girl was wrapped in a towel next to him. The dog lay on a chain run in the back of the yard.

Cal got up off the grass and started to run for the trees at the edge of the property. He was trying to carry his right arm, the one I'd smashed, with his left. He was limping. He was overweight.

Jimmy drew a pistol with a silencer out of his coveralls and drilled Cal once in the back and then again in the side of the head. The blood flew, like a red shadow coming out of Cal's head in the last of the fast-fading sunlight. Then Jimmy shot both of the kids, the girl and boy, twice each, through her towel and through the baseball shirt the boy was wearing. We got back into Jimmy's truck and left. We didn't speak, all the way down the road and across the bridge. When we stopped at the garage, I got out and got into my truck. I might have waved as I left. I forget.

The outrage in the community, not for Cal Sheely, but for his children, was tremendous. The BCI questioned Jimmy twice, at his garage. Nothing ever came of it.

I didn't see Jimmy for a while after that, but I was out in the woods working in the spring and I turned around and there was his blue beat-up truck.

"Hey, Jimmy," I said.

He waved. "You were never there," he said. "Sleep easy."

I nodded. He got back into his truck and rumbled down the logging road I had cut.

I thought about the list of men in the old fire engine. I didn't belong on that list. Maybe I had never belonged on that list.

FTW

FIVE FIFTEEN IN THE MORNING AND THERE WERE MEN on my porch. I went to the door. It was my parole officer, two sheriff's deputies and a man I didn't recognize. The man is wearing a badge that says Department of Corrections Investigator.

"Ray," my parole officer said, "step onto the porch." I opened the door and stood on the porch. The two deputies are tossing my house. I keep the stuff that I move in a garage behind the house. This could be bad. Today was supposed to be my last day on parole.

The DOC investigator shows me a booking picture of Mike Strong. "Do you know this man?" the DOC investigator says.

"No," I lie.

"Well he's dead," the investigator says. "He had this street address in his cell when he died. So he knew you." The investigator stands there, as if I'm going to say something.

"You have conditional release," my parole officer said. "It takes thirty days for the paperwork to come through. We're going to let this investigation continue, but as of right now, you're been granted conditional release."

I went to the mailbox. A razor slice on the envelope, invisible tear. There's a tiny note inside. A kite. I need to go see Ahmed, Mike's cousin. Bring the duece duece, the note says.

I woke up, drank coffee and got dressed. I walked to the house and red barn that sat back off the road in the field. Kevin was working, repairing a chainsaw he had stripped down on the floor of the barn.

"What can I do for you?" he said.

"I need some twenty-two long rifle shells," I said.

He stood and opened a workbench drawer. He brought out a box of bullets. "How many do you need?" he said.

"Two," I said.

"You're a good shot," he said.

"I don't want to waste them," I said.

"I saw the cops at your place the other morning," he said. "Is everything cool?"

"Everything's cool," I said.

"Well that's good," he said. He handed me the shells.

"What's that?" I said. There was a small wooden box, about three feet long, on the workbench. It was made from brand new pine.

"That's that little kid's coffin," Kevin said. "You know the one that died near the state road two days ago? Car just came along and hit him out of nowhere."

"Oh," I said.

"Jimmy Samson," Kevin said. "He was four. My wife knows his mother and they don't have much money, so I made the coffin for them. Funeral's tomorrow, but I'm having a hell of a time getting the lid right." He opened and closed the lid and I saw that it was uneven and not quite flush on the sides. "I think I might have to put the hinges on the inside. I don't know if I can get it right in time."

"That's too bad," I said.

"I truly can't bear to work on it anymore," Kevin said.

We stood there and looked at the small coffin. I started to walk away, back toward my place.

"How can I make a box good enough for heaven?" Kevin said to the air. He kept talking, low and soft and I kept walking. To my house and then back out to my truck.

The drive to the Wende Correctional Facility in Alden, New York took three hours. When I stopped for gas, I left the fuel door open. I parked facing away from the facility. I knelt to fake tie my sneaker and put a twenty two shell on top of the tire. As I turned and walked toward the facility, I stopped to shut the fuel door and bent to look at it, putting the other shell on top of the rear tire. The facility is a maximum classification and the sun shone off the triple razor wire and gun towers. The rest was all concrete and steel. There was a two-guard K-9 unit in the parking lot, walking their dog and watching him. Armed with an automatic rifle and a shotgun.

Inside, I went through visitor in-processing. Name, signature, identification. Two metal detectors and an X-ray machine. It took me half an hour to get to the visiting room and fifteen more minutes to be called.

Ahmed sat at one of the metal tables bolted to the floor in the visiting room. He was wearing a cream-colored knit kufi and a blue jumpsuit. The visiting room was filled with inmates wearing jumpsuits talking to people in street clothes. Ahmed shook my hand and I sat down.

"I was sorry to hear about Mike," I said.

"We got that covered," he said. "Did you do that one thing?"

I barely nodded.

"I might get moved," he said. "So keep an eye out."

"Yes," I said.

We made small talk for half an hour. Maybe it's not small talk—Ahmed has eighteen felonies and once gunned down two bank guards in front of at least ten witnesses. Nothing about his criminal life is small.

I leave the facility. When I open the front door of my truck, I bend down. There is a brown envelope on the top of the front tire. A thousand dollars. A jailhouse fortune. The stuff that I move used to go through Mike. I guess it will go through Ahmed now.

Two weeks later, I get another kite from Ahmed. Come back up, it reads. I burn it when I'm done reading it.

Early Sunday morning, Kevin is knocking.

"Do you want to go to church?" he said. "My wife and I are going."

"No thanks," I said.

"Sure," he said. He turned to leave, then looked back at me. "Praying doesn't have to look like praying," he said. "It can be private. You could do it anytime."

"That's good to know," I said.

"I prayed for you while I was eating breakfast, before I came over," he said.

"That's nice," I said.

"I prayed for Jimmy Samson too," he said.

"I thought you said Jimmy was in heaven," I said.

"He is," Kevin said.

"Then why do you have to pray for him?" I said.

"It's just a nice thing to do," he said.

"Oh," I said. "Thanks I'm all set."

"What are you doing today?" he said.

"Driving out to Alden," I said.

"To the facility?" he said.

"Yes," I said.

"You should come to church with us," he said. "You don't want to go out to Alden."

"No thanks, Kevin," I said.

"Okay," he said.

When I get to the facility, I park like I did last time. As I walk through visitation in-processing, two guards come and took me out of line.

"Ray Cooper?" the guard says.

"Yes," I say.

"Come with us."

We walk down a different concrete corridor and make a few turns, ending up in front of some holding cells. The DOC Investigator who was at my house is in front of one of the doors.

"What are you doing?" he says.

"Visiting William Ahmed Burke," I say.

"He's dead," the investigator says. "He killed a guard with a homemade zip gun and died during the struggle." He opens one of the holding cells. "Said he was avenging his cousin." Inside the room are two other guards with riot batons and a plainclothes State Police Officer. There are some chairs and a metal table. Far off, I can hear the voices of inmates. "We sent you the kite to come up here."

I nod.

"Get in the room," he says, motioning into the holding cell.

I stand there.

"Get in the room," he says.

The two guards with the riot batons step out of the room. The guard closest to me smashes my right shin and I go down on one knee. The other guard hits me in the face and I feel a front tooth being tugged out by the wood of the baton. The other guy hits me again. And again.

There are only four ways to leave the earth—death by natural causes, accident, suicide, or murder. Is there one death, the same for everyone, visited upon everyone? Or is everyone's death—like their life—a different and unique thing. Who is the king of tomorrow. Were these men waiting all these years, to deliver my death to me—them carrying it and me, seeking it. Had I been someone's death, waiting for them and now they would be spared.

The path of lies had led me to the room of hard truth. Hell is empty and all the devils are here.

JOHN THE REVELATOR

SILENCE DOESN'T ECHO. THE INITIAL SOUND HAS TO happen and then, carried through the atmosphere, the echo can live. It is the original sound, changed by everything it has come into contact with. Sound is absorbed and reflected differently by objects. All of those things impact the echo. They can make the origin of the original sound difficult to pin down. An echo is the original sound, dying on the air. The life of the echo is your life. Not present at your own birth, changed by everything you've come in contact with, weakening the longer you go on. Turning into silence.

I didn't want to go in tonight. I have a feeling. I always go in and pick up the drugs, but not tonight. I got a note that said my aunt died and it put me on edge. I opt to stay in the truck.

The night is deep black. A fall moon is hidden behind dense clouds. Soft rain. Early September in rural, central Vermont and I'm sitting behind the wheel of the truck in someone's dooryard, with the engine running and no lights. Mike is inside getting the drugs. From people I don't know. We've got to make a run to Maine this morning. A big delivery. The digital clock on the dashboard moves ahead one minute, to 3:50 a.m. When I close my eyes, I see wicked things, so I'm trying to stay awake and focused. There is a flash and a single flat crack from inside the house. Mike comes out of the house and gets into the passenger's seat.

"Got it?" I say.

"Got it," he says. "Go."

I ease back onto the logging road and don't turn my lights on for a solid mile. The dirt and gravel become blacktop and we're headed east. We're in New Hampshire when I realize Mike isn't talking anymore. He has bled all over the seat, his life spilling out of him. He has stopped living.

In the dark, I stop at a house when I see a cinder block wall next to the road. I take ten cinder blocks and toss them softly into the back of the truck. At a pull-off next to a lake, I drag Mike through the brush to the shore. I had some wire coat hangers in the back of the truck and a few short bungee cords. I wire and tie the cinder blocks to his wrists and feet and drag him out in the water as far as I can. He sinks from the weight. I go back to the truck, soaked and shaking.

People die at four a.m. It's the most recorded hour of death in the world. No blaze of glory. No massive battle. Go to bed at night, don't get up in the morning. Not much different, from one person to another. If I had gone in the house, it would have been me.

Ten years ago, I was incarcerated when my uncle died, so I didn't get to attend the funeral. His wife died today and I won't get to go to her service either. She lived in Florida and I live in Vermont and am headed to Maine with a truck full of drugs. I know exactly what the funeral will be like without being there. I can see it. The cousins, making runs to the Goodwill store to find dark, used little sport coats so the children can attend this first funeral wearing dress clothes. I know what happens at funerals.

A prophet is man with a job who has no references. He hears a voice that other normal people can't. Things come together in a different way for him. Events are foretold to him. His dreams are a film of reality yet to be. He moves through the world guided by something bigger than petty concerns.

The ride goes by. Driving toward morning. The sun has to rise. The easternmost point in the US is there. Looking over the ocean. Maybe I'll ride right into it.

Prophets don't have dreams. They have visions. Someone—God or someone like him—provides the vision. Dreams come from the person dreaming them. Visions come from outside or originate from outside the person who has them. Dreams happen. Visions come upon you.

I can't take the truck on the ferry. I park in the tiny lot and stand on the dock, waiting for the local guy who always comes to take us to the island. I get into his boat and head out.

Thunder is the sound lightning makes. Thunder does not exist on its own. Things in the physical universe—sounds, objects, events—are always connected to other things in some causal way or relationship. A wonderful net of occurrences, that are tied into time or perhaps help create time. Lightning itself is silent. Discharged in a vacuum, the bolt happens—a flash—and is gone, leaving only an echo of light on the eyes of the observer. The sound of thunder is the actual rent of the atmosphere. All the molecules and particles torn from each other. Forcible, physical displacement of air, through extreme speed and heat. The impossibly rapid burning and crushing of all the air's constituent parts. All of it amplified by the choppy water, the rain and black rocks, as I stood soaked on the rough beach of a Maine island and listened to Eli, the guy who is buying the drugs, tell me about the ills of the world and how he was doing so well.

"I've never been better," he says. He is smoking some weed and gesturing at the ocean. "This is my backyard," he says. "It's awesome."

The ocean is dangerous. No human can live in the ocean for long. Men and women measure the ocean. The tide. The depth. People tend to think of death as an isolated, singular event. But it isn't. That's just death playing its game. Pretending to be something else, something small. Something that fits into the eyes of your brain, something you fool yourself into understanding. Allowing you to see a small part of it and in seeing that part, arriving at an acceptance. As the ocean will, for anyone. The ocean contains death and is death itself at the same time. Just like all of us. Carrying our end inside us, somewhere.

Another guy from the island, a captain, walks over and joins us. He's got a six-pack of beer and Eli gives him a hit of the joint.

"I saw a great white shark," the captain says.

"When," I say.

"A couple days ago. I had a fishing charter, two guys from Rhode Island and some dippy girls they brought with them and all of a sudden, about fifteen miles out, holy shit. Fucking fin through the water, and it was huge."

"How big," I say.

"Bigger than my boat," the captain says. "Apex predator. A floating school bus with teeth."

"Wow," I say.

"I thought I saw it again, a couple hours ago, before the storm."

"Where," I say.

The captain reached under his rain slicker and brought out a waterproof notebook with small charts and graphs. He flipped a couple pages and then pointed. "That dark spot is us and my finger is the shark. Approximately." He drank his beer.

"Do you think he'll still be there?" I say.

"I don't know that much about great white sharks," the captain says. "What I see on TV. That's about it. I have no idea how much they move. I do know there's a bounty."

"How much is the bounty?" Eli says.

"Twenty thousand dollars," the captain says. "Ten thousand just for a verifiable photo."

"That's a lot of money," I say.

"It is," the captain says. "It's fall now, but soon it will be winter. That money might let you skip winter." He pointed, at a distant house. "The guy that lives in that house knows about it. He's an old man, with a lot of friends on shore, a lot of connections. Ask him."

The storm trapped me on the island for the night. I slept in a little shed behind Eli's house. I knew that staying on the island for the night made me a target for the police. I should have gone back.

In my dream, Mike is alive, thrashing in the water, trying to get the cinder blocks off his hands and feet. Churning the water and screaming.

In the morning, the sun came as usual. Everyone was gathered at the dock, watching a small boat headed in. Two men in blue uniforms were on the ferry, but they turned out to be paramedics. The old man who had the information about the shark bounty had died during the night. His wife found him in the morning, dead in the living room. I head back on the ferry. The one paramedic knows what I'm up to. I can see it.

I stop making the trips. But I don't stop using drugs or drinking. I have two thousand dollars from Eli. I try to stretch it. I go back to my old job, cutting firewood, and running a chainsaw.

Late one afternoon, I pull into a driveway. There's a sign that reads "Camp Wood" and under a small lean-to, bundles of wood are tied together with twine. Ten dollars a bundle. I stick a twenty in a white plastic bucket with a slit cut in the lid. Toss two bundles in the back of my truck. Even the thought of an evening bonfire doesn't lift me at all. I know I'm in a bad spot. That night, I have a dream. I have cinder blocks tied to my hands and feet and am drowning. I can't get back to sleep.

Two days later, we're in the field hunting, my old friend and myself. Talking about another friend, who died a few days ago. My old friend describes how the other man, now dead, had a heart attack and how his car went off the road.

"That isn't what happened," I said. "He killed himself."

"I never thought of that," he said. "What made you think of that?"

"I didn't," I said. "I didn't think of it. It was given to me."

"Given?" he said. "Given how?"

"I listened to what you had to say and I know that stretch of road. You can see three states from there. To get out there in the air. Death knows your name. For some people, it's comforting to make themselves their own killer," I said.

"So as he's having a heart attack, he doesn't take his foot off the gas pedal," he said. "That shit happens. I've read about that."

"How the hell should I know what he did. I'm just telling you that's what been given to me," I said.

"Given?" he said.

"Shown," I said.

"I think I have to go," he said. "Wouldn't you leave a note? If you were going to kill yourself, wouldn't you leave a note?"

"His whole fucking life was a note," I said. "All the failure, the mistakes. The self-induced problems. One long note. He wanted to kill himself his entire life."

"How do you know?" he said.

"Because," I said. "Things are shown to me."

"Future events?" he said.

"Maybe," I said. "Maybe something like that."

"I just can't listen to that anymore," he said.

"Sure," I said. "No problem."

"I'm sorry," he said. He shook his head. "I just can't do it."

"Okay," I said.

I watched him, in his blaze orange vest and cap, walk slowly along the edge of the field. Back toward the trucks. As he reached the woods, a good size buck rose out of the grass. I brought my rifle to my shoulder and flicked the safety off. I sighted the animal. I couldn't shoot it. The big deer was directly behind my friend. I stood there and watched as the buck slowly walked behind my friend, keeping an impossible line to fire on.

I started to climb the hill. I knew there was a flat plateau there, a small meadow, a hundred yards along and the deer felt safe. I'd sit on the edge of the meadow in the cover of the trees all afternoon. I never wanted to leave the woods again. The roar in my ears is my heart slamming, pushing blood. I am listening to the echo of life rushing through my body at an incredible pressure. Bending and twisting, and everything I've come into contact with, pushing me closer to death.

HIGH LIMIT

STRIPERS SWAM UP THE HUDSON EARLIER THAN USUAL that spring and right away, the fishermen were talking. I was working near Woodstock, hauling shale and aggregate for my cousin and every day, the other drivers would bring back stories about who caught what. Describing the good fishing spots on the river in detail, or lying about them—to keep the good fishing to themselves. The truth depended on who you were talking to. Baseball scores came first, then the fish stories. As far north on the river as the Athens lighthouse and as far south as you felt like sailing, although most of the guys didn't go below Poughkeepsie. My cousin's materials outfit was acting as a subcontractor on a state job, so we weren't hauling weekends. Saturday and Sunday were good days to be on the river. I was simply glad to be out in the world and earning money at the time. I got involved with the wrong side of things up in Canada—moving meth on the northwestern border of Maine—and had just come back after four years away. It was my first stretch and I wanted to put it behind me. Listening to the guys talk about fishing made me want to get out there and put a line in the water. They were catching some big ones.

I was living on an old run-down farm—thirty acres—between Saugerties and Catskill, that had been in my family for years. My great-grandfather's brother George had owned the property. Nobody remembered what George had done for work, but he must have enjoyed his privacy. The farm was set way back off the road—the dusty dirt trail that led to it was close to a mile and the mailbox on the road had never had a name on it—with the two-story main house on a slight hill. The main house was white and blue, with a wraparound wood porch overlooking the pond. A couple large sturdy red barns and two buildings just about to fall over. The property had three little gray cabins on it, facing the mountains. Someone, years ago, put the cabins up and tried to get people to stay there. It hadn't worked. The cabins each were equipped with a sink and a stand up shower, in addition to flush toilet, which was probably illegal given the size of the property. The cabins had black phones in them, hanging on the wall and when you picked them up, they rang to a single phone in the main house. For the guests, I imagined. There was still a gas pump and buried tank next to the one barn. I suppose if I went through the trouble of having someone come out and inspect the pump, I could have had my own gas on-site. It was an empire of dirt, but it was paradise to me.

I drove the truck up the road that Friday and my father's silver truck was parked in front of the house. He was sitting on the front porch in a lawn chair with his ball cap on, drinking a soda. He'd retired two years before from a local lumberyard.

"Hey there," he said.

"How's it going?" I said. "How's retired life?"

"Can't complain," he said. "What are you doing tomorrow?"

"Nothing," I said.

"You're going fishing with me and Rich, okay? Be the best thing for you."

"Sounds good," I said.

He was getting in his truck. "See you at six a.m. Catskill dock."

"See you tomorrow. Say hello to Mom for me."

"Will do," he said. "She's going to visit her aunt."

"Wish her a good flight," I said.

He waved as he drove away from the house.

Rich had a new boat he kept at the Catskill dock. It wasn't brand new, but it was new to him and he kept it shining. He was retired too, from a state conservation job. He made extra money running fishing charters out of Catskill and did pretty well for himself. Rich knew where the fish were. The other guy in Catskill who knew where the fish were was Tom, the man who owned the bait shop. Tom was a big, tall guy, an old basketball player. He owned the bait shop in Catskill for years, and it was the best bait and tackle shop on the Hudson. All the fishermen along the river knew to stop at Tom's before they went fishing, to get the latest report on conditions and fish. And to buy bait and everything else—reels, rods, the latest lures. Maps and charts. Tom could wind your reel with new line while you stood there and have you back out on the river in half an hour. Listening to Tom could keep you from getting shut out. No fish was no fun. When I passed Tom's on my way to the dock, I saw my father's truck in the parking lot. He pulled into the dock parking lot behind me and we headed out onto the Hudson River with Rich driving the boat.

"Tom says go north," my father said to Rich.

"We'll try it," Rich said.

My father turned to me. "I asked you here for a reason," my father said.

"Go ahead," I said.

"Do you remember Bob?" he said. "Bob Threepersons?"

"Sure," I said. "Still lives in Florida?" Bob had been in the army with my father and Rich. They hadn't been in the same units, but met back here in the states when their tour of duty ended. Bob had been a tunnel rat. He was originally from Idaho. His whole family lived on a reservation out there. He still had a sister who lived on the reservation. He came and visited, almost twenty years ago. He stayed in one of the little cabins on the old farm. I remember Bob kept an owl for a pet.

My father nodded. "He's having a heck of a time."

"What type of problems?" I said. We were moving north through the water. The great Rip Van Winkle Bridge was overhead, with its huge stone pilings diving deep into the water around us. Rich stayed in a channel and we passed underneath. Rogers Island was on our right and the train tracks ran along the bank.

"Money," my father said. "Drugs. Booze."

"Is he ready to clean up?" I said.

"He says he is," my father said.

"Does he need money?" I said.

"No." My father shook his head. "Having extra money is part of his problem right now."

"Are these the type of money problems that are likely to follow him up here?" I said.

"There's a chance of that," he said. "Anything can happen."

We let the conversation sit, because he'd hooked a fish. Rich and I watched him bring it to the boat, as the pole he was using bent around. Rich got the net and we wrestled a good-sized striper to the deck. The fish had bright colored scales and a white belly. After we removed the hook, my father tossed the fish back into the Hudson.

"You want him to stay in one of the little houses?" I said.

"Yeah," my father said. "That's a good plan. He kicked heroin there one summer, so he knows he can get clean there."

"I never knew that," I said. "I just thought he was visiting us."

"He was," my father said. "But he was having some problems at that time too."

"Why do you guys keep helping him?" I said.

My father tasted his coffee. Rich shrugged.

"You can't turn your back on people when you know what they've seen," Rich said.

My father nodded. "War loves young men," he said. "Those aren't my words, somebody else said them first, but I don't remember who. Anyway, Vietnam got hold of Bob and hasn't let him go yet. We're lucky," he motioned at Rich and himself, "that we don't have the problems Bob does." He drank another mouthful of coffee. "I can't watch TV anymore except baseball. The war coverage makes me think about those men and women overseas and how, even if they make it back and with all their limbs, it could still ruin their lives. I can't stand people—ordinary, average, everyday people—suffering the consequences of politicians. Bob is like that—he's nobody special, he's just special to us." My father finished his coffee and Rich nodded as he watched the water.

"And this time," my father said, "Bob's problems seem a little tougher and different."

"These new problems," I said. "Gun-type problems?"

"Yes," my father said. "He might need some help watching his back."

"I've got a brand-new shotgun," Rich said.

"I've already got a shotgun," I said.

"I meant for Bob," Rich said. "Do you have a dog?"

"No," I said. "I work too much to take care of one."

"I used to have a good German Shepard named Shane, but he's long gone. I can't help you with a dog," Rich said.

"Okay," I said. "When should I expect Bob?"

"Soon," my father said. "Tonight."

We caught another striper north of Hudson—Tom had been right—and headed back to the Catskill dock. After we moored the boat, Rich brought a gun case out of the back seat of his truck, along with three boxes of shells. I put the stuff on the back seat of my truck and shook hands with both of them before driving off.

I stopped and picked up some groceries on the way home. At the farm, I got things ready to have a guest. I cleaned out the cabin and put some food and a jug of water out there. I put a bar of soap and shampoo in the shower, a razor, shaving cream, toothbrush and toothpaste on the sink. I put the gun case Rich had given me and the boxes of shells on the bed. Next to the gun I put a case of cigarettes, two plastic lighters, four bars of chocolate and a couple candy bars. I started a fire with the coals and after it died down and the coals went white hot, I put some burgers on. I loaded my own shotgun, checked the safety, and leaned it inside the screen door. I sat on the porch and ate.

The sun had gone down when Bob showed up. He was driving an old beat-up station wagon with fake wood paneling and Florida plates. The passenger's side front tire looked low. When I got close to the car I could see a long, jagged crack in the windshield.

"Hey," he said. We shook hands. He wore his long hair in a ponytail with gray in it. He looked tired and thin. He was wearing a long sleeve shirt that he'd sweated through. "Well hello John," he managed. He was carrying an old tan suitcase and a blue gym bag. He set the bags on the ground.

"Good to see you," I said. "Do you want a hamburger?" I pointed at the grill, still glowing in the twilight.

"That sounds great," he said. "No beer."

"Yeah," I said. "My dad told me. No problem."

"I just need to relax a little," he said. He shook a cigarette out of the pack and lit it. "We need to hide this car."

I walked over to the big barn and swung the door open. "Bring it right in here."

He guided the station wagon into the empty space between an old Jeep under a tarp and a pickup truck. He shut the engine off and took out a big screwdriver.

"Got to get these plates off," he explained.

"Sure," I said. He was sweating. "Can I help you?"

"Work on that back plate," he said.

I laid on the rough concrete floor and sweated, using an oversized screwdriver to get the screws out of the license plate. I skinned my knuckles. We finished and put the plates on the front seat. I made Bob a burger with a roll and gave it to him.

"This is your cabin right here," I said. I pointed at the middle cabin. "Hasn't changed much since your last visit." I carried his two bags up to the small porch.

"I really appreciate your help," he said. He had taken a couple bites out of the burger.

"If you need anything, lift that phone next to your bed. It calls me in the house."

"Okay," he said.

"See you in the morning," I said.

"Thanks," he said.

I gave my father a call when I got back in the house.

"Bob's here," I said. "He ate and went to bed."

"Good," my father said. "Let's try some fishing again tomorrow. Bring him with you."

"Sure," I said. "See you tomorrow."

I shut the lights out and sat in a chair looking out the window. I could see the end of the driveway and the road and I watched for an hour. Cars passed in the dark, but nobody slowed down or stopped. I slept with my shotgun on the floor next to my bed. I didn't know how big Bob's trouble was and I wanted to be ready.

I drove Bob to the Catskill dock the next day. He didn't look well—he was wearing a light blue jacket despite the heat—when he got in the truck, but we stopped at a gas station and I bought him a coffee. It was good to watch him drink something.

"That's good coffee," he said.

"Nice," I said. "How're you doing?"

"I've been better," he said. "I've been much worse. This will pass."

"Sure," I said.

It smelled like gas and oil and fish at the dock. My father and Rich were already on the boat. Bob and I got on. Rich gave us all rods, all rigged up. My father and Rich shook hands with Bob and they both gave him a hug. Rich piloted the boat into the Hudson and nobody said anything. We were busy fishing. We were headed slightly south today. One of the large Hudson mansions sat on a hill on the east bank and we all looked at as we passed. Rich hooked a nice striper, brought it up into the boat and released it.

"I remember the last time I visited," Bob said. "We fished then too."

"I remember we caught a couple good ones," my father said.

"We ate those fish, didn't we?" Bob said.

"We did," my father said. "Things have changed in the river."

"That's too bad," Bob said. Less than a minute after that, he hooked one and fought it to the boat. After he released it, a large hawk took off from a dead tree close to shore. The hawk gained altitude and floated high in the blue and the clouds.

"The sky is part of the color of that bird," Bob said. "In a blue sky, the bird looks a certain way and in a gray sky, the bird looks another way. The bird doesn't pick the color of the sky, he just lives in it. He doesn't try to change it. I remember my grandfather telling me that." He was crying now. My father and Rich sat close to him and I watched the boat. I couldn't hear what they were saying. Rich stood up and took over, heading back to the dock. My father stayed close to Bob until we were getting off the boat.

"It's hard to be off drugs," Bob said. We were headed toward my truck.

"Everything's hard," my father said. "You can do it."

"Good luck," Rich said.

Bob and I drove back to the farm and when I came out of the house, he was sitting on the porch, looking at the sky. I fixed us some dinner and we both went to bed. I got up at two a.m., to take a look around. To be safe. The house phone rang and I picked it up.

"Hey," Bob said. "Are you awake? I thought I saw a light."

"Yes," I said. "Checking things out."

"I'm going back to sleep," he said.

"See you late tomorrow," I said. "I've got to work."

"Sure," Bob said. "I'll fix dinner."

"Sounds good," I said.

We went fishing as much as we could that summer. We went out on the river with my father and Rich. One time Bob's pole bent so much, we all thought he'd hooked a sturgeon. It would have been a once in a lifetime catch. Whatever it was spit the hook before he could land it. The next weekend, we were out on the river again.

"What did you do?" I said. Bob had been staying on the farm for five weeks and we were sitting on the porch, eating sandwiches.

"I counted cards at the high limit table," he said. He finished his sandwich. "More than once. At more than one casino, all along the Gulf Coast." He scratched his head. "I learned I could count cards when I was in the army," he said. "Wish I never had."

"How much did you get away with?" I said.

"Not enough to be worth this," he said. He inhaled his cigarette. "That's for sure." He took another drag and then went on. "It used to be like I couldn't tell if I was awake or dreaming. I had this big pile of chips and I'd cash out and the money would pile up."

I nodded. The sky was night-dark except for the stars and on the edge of the mountains, we could see the static charges of heat lightning, flashing.

Bob seemed like he was talking to himself. "I had that money and off I'd go, on a bender. I shot dope again. I drank all the time. I did everything I could get my hands on. Until it was like I wasn't real anymore. I came home to my house at one point and thought people had broken in, that's what a wreck it was."

"That sounds bad," I said.

"Then the pit boss at the one casino, he must have seen me doing something because the next time I went to play, they wouldn't let me sit at the table. So I went down the street and counted cards there and took them for all they could handle." He shook his head. "Men followed me out of the casino and tried to beat me up, but I got away. I realized they must have put a price on my head. That's when I decided to come up here."

"What would they gain by killing you?" I said.

"Nothing," he said. "Probably a couple thousand dollars from the casino management firm."

"Can you pay them back?" I said.

"I don't even know how many times I won off them, or what casinos I won it from. I took a couple loans from bookies to cover myself. It's an ugly mess."

"That sounds bad," I said.

"I came home one night late and turned on the TV and I think I fell asleep. I woke up and there was a cowboy and Indian movie on and I started to lose my mind. I thought that's all they show, is us being killed." He pointed at his head. "My own mind is my worst enemy." He looked over at me. "What did you do?"

"Got into a scrape up in Maine," I said.

He nodded. "Did your father ever tell you about the scrape I got into in the late seventies?"

"No," I said. "He didn't." The lights from planes moved slowly through the night sky, among the stillness of the stars.

Bob put his cigarette out. "I tried to make some money as a big game scout. Signed on with a guy out of Florida named Mackenzie, who arranged hunting trips to Africa for wealthy clients."

"What did you take them hunting for?" I said.

"When they signed up, supposedly it was for antelope. Large game deer, mostly. But we were really going over to shoot rhinos," Bob said. "Everybody knew that." He pointed through the darkness to the little cabins. "Imagine an animal the size of one of those cabins, faster than your truck and basically plated with armor."

"I've seen them on TV," I said.

"Well I saw it in real life," he said. "That last afternoon, a rhino came out of the grass after the truck and we all started shooting. Five men. I had one of those newer Mauser rifles, but it was still bolt action, and I'm slamming that thing home and firing and the rhino hit the truck like a fully-stacked freight train, wham." He made a flattening motion with his hands, then lifted them into the air. "Up I went and down I came."

"What happened?" I said.

"I couldn't fire anymore, because I was out of shells. The rhino stomped and gored everyone but me. Put a hole in Mackenzie that I could see through. The ground was so soaked with blood that the natives who rescued me were afraid the smell of death would bring other animals to the spot. The natives took me to a ranger station."

"Jesus," I said.

"Sometimes," Bob said, "I used to stay awake for days at a time, so I wouldn't have to dream about that stuff and what I'd seen in Vietnam. Drugs helped me keep the past quiet, in the short term. Till it got the best of me." He paused. "Did you ever try to wash someone else's blood off you?"

"No," I said.

"For some reason," Bob said, "it's hard to get it off. Almost as if blood holds onto your skin, because it knows your skin is still alive."

We picked up the plates and put them in the kitchen sink. I saw him smoke another cigarette on his small cabin porch before going inside.

It was about four a.m. when I heard the car door slam in the yard. I flipped the lights on downstairs and outside and opened my bedroom window. I put the barrel of the shotgun out first and racked the slide.

"What do you want?" I said.

The two men blinked against the light. "We're looking for somebody," the one man said.

"This is private property," I said. "I'm calling the cops."

"We'll be gone before they get here," the man said. He had a pistol holstered on his right side.

"Get back in that car or you'll need an ambulance," I said. "Last warning."

I hoped that Bob was awake at that point, ready to back me up if shooting started. They weren't sure where he was, so he could get off a couple rounds from the middle cabin before they knew what hit them.

Both men walked back to their car, turned it around and spit gravel going back down the road.

In the morning, I walked to the middle cabin and opened the door. There was nothing there. It looked as though no one had ever slept there at all. I went around to the back barn and found what I was looking for. Under the tarp that used to protect the old Jeep, was Bob's station wagon. A set of New York plates was missing too. Bob was on the road again. I called my father and told him.

I came home from work in the middle of the week and found everything torn apart. Whoever those men were, they must have come back while I was gone. The beds were out of the cabins, stuff spread across the lawn by the pond. The big barn door was open, exposing the cars. The tarp was off the station wagon and the doors were open. The door to the main house had been jimmied open and sat on bent hinges. But there was nothing to find.

The first letter I got wasn't really a letter at all. It was an envelope with an Idaho postmark and two photographs. The first picture was of a huge fish—what appeared to be a white sturgeon—half in the water, ready to be released back in. The second was a similar picture of the fish from a different angle and the photographer had allowed his shadow to fall out over the water and into the shot, along with the tip of his right boot.

The boot looked like Bob's, and the shadow looked like it had a ponytail.

Two months later, a postcard showed up in my mailbox. It bore a Vancouver postmark. "Still OK still sober" was all it said on it.

One night I was sitting there during a terrible lightning storm. The cabin phone rang. Scared the hell out of me. I answered the phone. Within the flashing darkness, it sounded like someone was there.

"Bob?" I said. "Bob?"

There was no answer. The lightning must have made it ring. I was alone.

The stripers were hitting in the Hudson in April and May this year. I caught my share on the weekends, with my father and Rich. I fished from shore some weekends during the summer and got a pass to one of the reservoirs. I saw some eagles early one morning and the fireworks got rained out on the Fourth of July, so they shot them off the following weekend. I watched them from the porch of the farm, what I could see of the lights above the trees. The shale business kept on and I drove every day and got dusty and dumped and hauled all the loads my cousin gave me. I was grateful for the work.

I pulled up the dusty driveway one Friday in late August and my father's truck was close to the house. He was sitting on the porch with his ball cap off. I got out of my rig and walked to the house and he didn't say anything. He was holding something and when I got closer, it looked like an envelope.

"Hi," I said. "What's going on?"

He just handed me the envelope. It had an Idaho postmark and my father's address handwritten on the outside. Inside was a newspaper clipping from a week earlier, from a newspaper in Spokane, Washington. I read it.

A man the Idaho State Police had identified as Robert Threepersons had died from gunshot wounds in a parking lot outside a truck stop casino near the Idaho Washington border. The police were investigating the shooting, although there were no clues at this time.

"I should have told him to stay here," my father said. He indicated the clipping. "His sister must have sent this from the reservation."

I didn't know what to say.

"Between the war and the drugs and the gambling, the poor guy must have been afraid of his own thoughts," my father said.

"He probably was," I agreed.

"And people coming after him," he said. "It was too much."

"Yeah," I said.

"I can't draw a straight line from the war to Bob's problems for you to see, but I know it's there," he said.

We sat on the porch till it started to get dark. My father headed home to his house and my mother. And I looked over at the middle cabin, to the place where Bob had been sober for a little while. To where my fishing buddy had lived for a summer.

What if it wasn't him that died in that parking lot? What if somebody got the drop on him but he shot them and put his identification on them, to throw the cops off? Or what if he were finally dreamlessly asleep and peaceful, delivered by violence into someplace else. Off this earth, with the beautiful blue sky coloring him forever.

EVERYTHING TASTES LIKE WHISKEY

DAWN. A DOZEN DARK BROWN EMPTY BEER BOTTLES stand on the kitchen table and a half-empty bottle of bourbon stands on the floor. My small, blockhouse rental smells like a cheap bar. I get up and get dressed. Put on a light black work jacket and a black ball cap. Strap the holstered stainless steel Colt Anaconda to my right hip.

Outside, the blue fall sky of Moscow, Idaho is crisp and bright. I follow the concrete sidewalk, walking across the University of Idaho campus, filled with students carrying books and backpacks. Talking to each other. Laughing. I killed a man in a gunfight a week earlier. No one seems to notice. I look up at some the etchings and stonework on the library, showing cowboys and Indians killing each other and I feel like I belong. I walk past the nameless WWI doughboy statue and give him the nod. On a September morning in France long ago, fifty-eight thousand men died for less than an acre of land. I'm not worried about killing one meth head who would have killed me, if I let him get to his gun. It happened so fast, I can only remember it in slow motion. I pulled the trigger and it was as if a giant invisible hand swatted him so he spun backward and fell, curled up, blood leaking everywhere. He made noises I'd never heard a human make before. The air he took into his mouth bubbled out the wet hole in his back. The first cop on the scene joked that I hadn't shot him, he'd been hit by a freight train. One of the cops puked. A .44 Magnum shooting at ten yards doesn't leave a survivable wound. Shut the lights and sirens off, because there's no rush when you're headed to the morgue.

Greg was already in the office when I got there. I sat behind my desk. He was talking into his cell phone. He finished his conversation and turned to me.

"How do you feel?" he said.

"Good," I said. "I feel good."

"Okay," he said. He sipped a cup of coffee.

"How do you feel?" I said.

"Fine," he said. "That's not the point."

"I know," I said. I sat down at my desk. "It doesn't bother me."

"It bothered me terrible when I shot that guy a couple years ago," he said. "I kept thinking my pistol would jump off my belt and start shooting people on its own."

"Nothing close to that," I said.

"How about sleep?" he said.

"Like a rock," I said.

"Would you do it again?" he said.

"Yes," I said.

He sipped his coffee. "What about two guys? Would you shoot two?" he said.

"Yes," I said.

"What if there were a hundred guys in front of you? And you had enough bullets," he said.

"This is getting stupid," I said.

"Alright," he said. "Serious. Five guys with three visible guns."

"All dead," I said. "Pine boxes all around."

"Good," he said. "Because I got a call this morning on a job."

"Whereabouts?" I said.

"Outside of Rexburg," he said. "On a ranch."

"What am I doing?" I said.

"A little bit of patrol duty," he said. "Some hunting."

"Working for who?" I said.

"An old friend of your uncle," he said.

"Who's that?" I said.

"Bill Warner. His son just called me and asked if I could send somebody to help his dad. I said you were available and he said that would be fine."

"Bill Warner's still alive?" I said.

"Apparently," Greg said. "And having problems with wolves. And trespassers."

"What's he got on the ranch now? Cattle?" I said.

"That's right," he said. "Why don't you head over that way, get you out of town for a few days while this shooting blows over." He took a drink of his coffee.

"What's to blow over?" I said. "The cops looked at everything. Nobody said a word to me."

"Sure," Greg said. "Except that's who I just got off the phone with," he pointed at his cell phone. "Larry Samms, chief sheriff's investigator. Asked me two questions. Did we know the deceased and why did you carry such a high-caliber pistol."

"We knew the deceased and so did the sheriff's department, if they were paying attention. Even during the time we were watching him, he must have made ten trips to Canada and Montana and been driving three different trucks. It was just a matter of time before he got caught," I said.

"Apparently, the deceased was also involved in a snitch program for the Mounties, so I don't know if anything is going to appear in the paper or on the news, but he just suggested to me that it would be good if you kept a low profile. Unofficially," he said.

"There's ten guys between Moscow and Potlatch who carry bigger pistols than this," I said. I patted the Colt.

"Yeah," Greg said. "But they're killing animals, not people turned into animals."

"It was him or me," I said.

"I'm glad it turned out to be you," Greg said. "And so is Larry Samms. He's just a little concerned."

"Fair enough," I said. I stood.

"It's the Steel Dust Ranch," Greg said.

"I know where it is," I said as I shut the office door. I walked back across the beautiful campus. Stopped at the gas station along the way and picked up as much beer as I could carry and made my way up the steps of my rental. Closed the door, took off my gun and started to try to clear my head with booze. The next morning, I went out to get more beer and the paper and the shooting was front page. FATAL DRUG SHOOTING IN MOSCOW. There were no pictures of me. Just the front of the meth head's house and a few cop cars. Larry Samms had a couple comments. I bought enough beer so I wouldn't have to come out again and walked back home.

Greg showed up on my steps two days later with fresh coffee. He handed me a cup when I answered the door and we sat on the top step together.

"You look like shit," he said.

"I'm not worried about it," I said.

"Would you please go see Bill Warner for me and help him out?" he said.

I took a drink of my coffee. It tasted good. "Yes," I said. "I'll be there by tonight."

"I'm counting on you," Greg said.

"Okay," I said.

I watched him drive away. I packed a small gym bag with clothes and a toothbrush. I opened my gun safe and brought out the short-barreled Remington .30-06 pump and two boxes of shells. I thought about bringing along a more powerful rifle, but I wasn't sure what was around the ranch and didn't want my bullets ending up on someone else's farm or ranch by accident. I put the packed bag in my truck and hung the rifle on the cab rack. Then I started south along the highway toward Boise and east toward Rexburg and the edge of the state.

On the way to the ranch, I stopped to see my uncle in the hospital. He was in Mercy Hospital, in Nampa. I parked and walked through the lobby. A large recessed statue of the Virgin Mary was on the wall. The hospital smelled stale. I don't know how long my uncle had been in. My father's brother. He'd been a ranch hand, working with cattle his whole life. Tough old guy with a kind heart. Probably eighty years old, twenty years older than my father. I hadn't seen him in two or three years. He was in a shared room, but the bed next to him was empty. He didn't recognize me when I came in the room. A tube was stuck up his nose and IV drips were in his arm.

"Uncle George, it's John," I said. His body barely wrinkled the sheets and that was hard to believe. George used to be as big as the rest of us.

"Oh, John," he said. "Sure it's you, how are you?" His head was shaved and covered with a white bandage and wound dressing.

"I'm doing fine," I said. "How are you doing?"

"Not so good," he said. "I'm so glad you came to visit. What are you doing around here?" He nodded at some of the plastic chairs against the wall. "Grab a chair."

I moved the chair over so I could sit by him and then I sat down. "Working," I said. "I got a job outside of your old stomping grounds over there near Rexburg."

"Oh," he said. "What are you doing over there?"

"You remember Bill Warner?" I said.

"Yes," he said. "I remember him." He nodded. "I worked with him for a while."

"He's having some trouble with wolves bothering his herd. So I'm going over to see if I can take care of it for him," I said.

"He's crazy, you know, or used to be," he said. "Drank like a fish." He looked up at the ceiling.

"When are you getting out, when are they going to let you go home?" I said.

He shrugged under his thin green gown. "They're not," he said. "Since they tried to take that tumor off my brain, I've been having seizures at night."

"Really," I said.

"It's awful. I'm asleep and then my whole body starts shaking and my heart pounds and bang! I sit upright and start grinding my teeth and I can't swallow," he said. "Never get old and sick, John, it's horrible." One of the monitors he was hooked up to beeped. "The morphine gives me bad dreams," he said. "I almost can't take it."

"Did they get all of the tumor?" I said.

"That's the other thing," he said. "They can't tell. I might still have cancer and be going through this."

"I'm so sorry to hear that, Uncle George," I said.

"What can you do," he said. "That's life." He paused. "Next time you talk to your father, tell him to get over here and see me." He reached a thin hand out from underneath the sheets and squeezed my fingers. "I'm not long for this world, John," he said.

"I'll tell him," I said.

"We had some fun when you were a kid, didn't we John?" he said. "Hunting and fishing."

"That's true, Uncle George," I said. "Lots of fun."

He seemed to go to sleep after that and I put the chair back where it had been and quietly left the room.

The Steel Dust Ranch was fifteen hundred acres of dream property, several miles east of Rexburg. The sign on the main road read Steel Dust Ranch and it was getting dark when I arrived. Bill Warner had run it since the day his father died. He was at the main house when I arrived. There was the big main house overlooking the woods and fields, with a full front porch and four barns spread around it. A couple of outbuildings. Some rocking chairs on the front porch near the door. Bill Warner was a short, older man, and it was hard to believe he was even close in age to my Uncle George. His silver-gray hair was slicked back.

"You must be John," he said. I smelled the booze on him the minute he opened his mouth.

"That's right," I said. We shook hands there on the porch and stepped down onto the gravel in front of the house. "Greg said you were having some problems out here."

He shrugged. "Look," he said. "I could go on a rant about wolves, like any rancher, I suppose. Why they brought them back and on and on. All I want to do is kill them. Can you do that?"

I nodded. "I think I can," I said.

"Thinkin' really isn't good enough," he said. "I had a guy here two weeks ago, thought he could hunt wolves. Told me he could hunt wolves. Didn't get anything. He isn't here anymore and I didn't pay him. Unless I see carcasses, I don't pay."

"Fair enough," I said.

"What are you shootin' 'em with?" he said.

"Remington," I said. "Thirty oh-six pump."

"Yeah, that'll do the trick," he said. "I got one of those Winchester short magnums, it's like an angry supersonic bee when it comes out."

"Flat shooting," I said.

"Straight-edge," he said. "Point-to-point."

"Nice," I said.

"You use a scope?" he said.

"Not with wolves," I said. "You might have to lead 'em a little."

"That's what I tried to tell this other guy, but he wouldn't listen to me."

I nodded.

He brought a flask out of his jacket pocket. "You want a drink?" he said.

"Not when I'm on the job," I said.

He unscrewed the bright silver top and took a pull, then screwed the top back on. "You separate that out? Living and your job, that's two different things to you?" he said.

"Yes," I said.

"Well, you must be wealthy," he said. "That's how rich folks do it."

"I'm not wealthy," I said.

"Preparin' to be wealthy," he said. "You're not wealthy now, but you want to be."

"Sure," I said. "That wouldn't bother me."

He pointed back at the porch. There were several rocking chairs, the one he had been sitting in still rocking a little. "That's all I ever wanted right there. That porch, those rocking chairs and that view," he said. "And to enjoy it in peace after a hard day's work."

"It looks like you have that," I said.

"I had a vision of myself, my last days. And it used to be of sitting on the porch. Then, about twenty years ago, it changed. I was sitting on the porch drinking. Can you believe that? Why would I do that? Then the picture changed again. Now it's me sitting on the porch, drinking, with my rifle across my lap. That's some change, isn't it?" he said. He drank from his flask. He tipped his head back.

"I guess it is," I said.

He wiped his lips. "You can stay over there in the bunkhouse," he pointed across the property at an outbuilding. "I've only got a couple day hands on right now, so take any room you like." He cleared his throat. "I got your license information from Greg, so there's wolf tags here on premises so you can hunt. I'll call in to the state ranger's office every morning, to make sure this area hasn't gone over the hunt limit."

"Is that how they do it?" I said.

"Yes," he said. "You don't need to worry about it—just shoot 'em."

"Greg told me you had some trespassers too," I said.

"They moved on," he said. "Gone, as far as I can tell."

"Okay," I said.

"Put your stuff in the bunkhouse and come back for dinner," he said.

"Okay," I said.

That night in the bunkhouse I had a terrible dream. In my dream, I was just about to shoot the meth head. He was reaching into his truck for something and as he brought his hands out, I realized in my dream that I didn't have to shoot him. That he didn't have anything in his hands. But I fired anyway.

It was cold that morning. I was out in the woods, sitting on the ground on a steep hill, probably a mile from the main house and barns. My position allowed me to be elevated and I held a clear view of the trees and the edge of the field. I figured the wolves would wait at the edge of the woods and rush into the field, to attack any cattle they thought they could kill. There was some movement. Maybe a wolf. Bright color. I looked again through the binoculars. It was the three Mexican boys. They must have camped overnight, without a fire.

I slung the rifle over my shoulder and started to walk down towards them. They saw me and stood up as I approached.

"Hello," I said. "Do you speak English?"

The young man in front nodded. "I do, but my brothers do not," he said.

"Okay," I said. "What are you doing here? Do you know that you're trespassing?"

The young man spread his arms out. Without a jacket on, he must have been cold, but I saw the tattoos on his arms. And the small figure on the ground. It was of a skeletal woman in a robe. Same as his tattoos.

"We are like eagles," he said. "We fly where we want. Santa Muerte protects us, from all forms of violence. We listen to her. We worship her. She is our saint." He pointed at my rifle. "Even if you were to shoot us, it would not harm us. She would protect us."

The two guys behind murmured "Santa Muerte" right after he said it.

"This is private property," I said. "La propiedad privada. You can't be here."

The huge high voltage lines ran far up over our heads, spaced evenly on groups of three utility poles, that stretched on forever. The hum of the lines was constant. The young man talked in fast, low Spanish to the other young men. He pointed at one man.

"This is my brother the owl," he said.

The young man he called the owl kept talking in low Spanish that I couldn't make out. The one who spoke English turned back to me. "He says that yesterday, you visited the brother of your father."

I took a step back and swung the rifle up, so it was pointed at them. I pumped a shell into the chamber. "How did you know that?" I said.

The young man pointed all around, at the horizon and at the skeletal woman figure on the ground. "Santa Muerte is everywhere," he said.

The owl was talking in fast low Spanish again and the one that spoke English translated. "You have killed a man. You were protected by Santa Muerte. You know her and she knows you." He reached down and picked up the small skeletal woman, putting the figure in his backpack.

"Don't let me see you around here again," I said. "Now get out of here."

I watched as the three young men walked across the field, to the edge of the far woods and disappeared. I held the rifle on them until they were gone. My skins had goose bumps and the high voltage seemed to have leaked out of the overhead lines and gone into the ground, only to come up through my feet and hair.

As soon as I drove up in front of the main house, Bill came out and stood on the porch. "Did you get anything?" he said.

"No," I said. "I thought I saw a wolf, but it got spooked."

"By what?" he said.

I shook my head. "There were three Mexicans camped at the edge of the field and it must have got wind of them."

"Did you tell 'em to get out of here?" he said.

"Yes," I said. "I did."

"You know, they're actually talking about putting a Mexican consulate in Boise? I read it in the paper the other day," he said. He took a swig from his flask. "Tomorrow, I'll go out with you and if we see them again, we'll escort them to the sheriff."

"If that's what you want to do," I said.

"It is," he said. "I can't have Mexicans on my place. End up with my throat slit and more than just cattle missing."

"They really were just kids," I said.

"Would you want them trespassing on your land? Suppose they started a fire and burned the whole ranch to the ground? Every blade of grass I own, turned into cinders," he said.

"No," I agreed. "You can't have that."

"Right," he said. "Tomorrow, if they're still around, we round 'em up and let the sheriff deal with 'em."

"Have you ever had to do that before?" I said.

"Oh sure. You get all kinds of people that think they can just walk across your land. They don't care," he said.

The next morning, early, Bill and I rode the trails of his property in a Jeep. He stopped at the top of a rise as we headed for the field where I'd seen the Mexicans. From here, most of the ranch property was below us. The view was amazing, under that cold blue sky. The stars were just fading.

"You should have been here when the Teton Dam let loose," he said. "Killed over thirteen hundred head of cattle. It was like somebody took a bottle of cheap whiskey—all that brown water—and poured it right here."

"What did you do?" I said.

"Nothing to do," he said. "My father put in a claim with the government, just like everyone else. I think he eventually got paid." He took out his flask and drank. Then he offered it to me. I had some and handed it back to him. He kept on. "Rebuilt the buildings that got damaged, fix up the house. Went to the auction and bought some new cattle." He shrugged. "What the hell else were we going to do," he said.

We rode in silence to the edge of the woods over the field. Then we got out of the Jeep and positioned ourselves in the same spot I had been the day before. Bill snapped the safety off his Winchester. And we waited. The cattle in the field moved around, away from the woods and the tall grass waved under the high voltage lines. Bill drank from his flask and I did too.

Two hours into the morning, I saw a gray shape at the edge of the woods, moving slowly. I tapped Bill on the knee and he saw it right away through the binoculars. He nodded to me, that I should take the shot. But the shape was gone now. I shrugged at him—nothing to shoot at. He nodded. And that was when he saw the Mexicans.

Coming across the field through the tall grass, the three Mexican boys that I had seen the day before were walking toward us, directly under the electrical lines. Bill fired a shot into the air. His face turned into an ugly mask. He shouted. The boys were running and hid behind a wooden utility pole, on the right side of a group of three, a couple hundred yards out in the field.

"Oh for shit's sake," Bill said. He worked the lever on the Winchester.

"Let's take 'em to the sheriff," I said. "It will get them out of here and off your place for good."

"Yeah, yeah," he said. He took a hit from the flask and put it in his back pocket. "You sabe that Español? Tell 'em to come out, nobody gets hurt. Yell over to 'em," he said. "I hope me firing didn't scare 'em too much." He nodded toward me and the utility pole. "Give 'em a holler," he said.

"Salgan!" I shouted. My voice echoed softly across the field. "Es seguro. El viejo no hará daño!"

The three young men stepped out from behind the utility post.

Bill worked the lever-action. That precise, serious click of metal interlocking with metal, and the sound of the shots threw me off. He fired, four times in quick succession, smoke curling out of the barrel and the sharp echo stinging my ears. The smell of hot metal. I saw the first Mexican go down and as the gunshots cleared. I heard one screaming from the field.

I started to go out into the field. Bill held me back.

"Where are you going?" he said.

"Out there," I pointed.

"To do what?" he said.

"To help them," I said. I could still hear the shots echoing.

"They're dead," he said. "There's no help for them."

"We can't just leave them there," I said.

"I don't know what you're talking about," he said. "You've got the whole thing backwards."

"I've got to report this," I said.

"Report what?" he said. "They'll be gone, tomorrow or the next day. Animals will get at them and take care of it."

"No," I said. "I'm not getting involved in this."

"If you think they're the first Mexicans that have ever been shot on this ranch, you're sorely mistaken," he said.

We walked back to the Jeep and rode to the main house in silence. I immediately gathered my things from my room in the bunkhouse and put them in my truck. Bill was standing on the porch of the main house when I came out.

"Come here," he said. He motioned into the house. "I've got something to show you." I followed him, through the sitting room and living room, straight back to the kitchen. He flipped on one of the burners of massive gas stove. "See that blue flame," he said. "Same color as the sky, right?"

"I suppose," I said.

"What if that sky is fire and this is us, burning in hell? Did you ever think of that? That might not be heaven up there. That blue sky might be eternal fire, just like this gas jet," he said. He had picked up a bottle of bourbon and swigged right off the top.

I drove back to Moscow as fast as I could.

I walked into the office and it was silent. Greg was sitting at his desk. He didn't look up as I came in. It was if a loud noise or incident had just happened and I had missed it.

"You need to tell me what happened out there," Greg said.

"He shot three Mexican kids," I said. "I'm calling them kids, but they might have been in their early twenties. Shot them in one of those back fields."

"He says you shot 'em. I've been on the phone with him for an hour and he says you shot 'em and that he doesn't intend to involve the authorities, but that he doesn't want you down there anymore," he said.

"That isn't true," I said.

"We don't go out like hired guns," Greg said.

"I didn't," I said.

"I don't even know you," he said. "He told me you were drinking on the job. Is that true?"

"Where is this coming from?" I said.

"IS IT TRUE YOU WERE DRINKING ON THE JOB!" he shouted. He slammed his fist on his desk.

"Yes," I said. "I had some drinks. He was drinking too."

"You need to go home," he said. "I have some thinking to do."

"Okay," I said. I stood. "I'll come back tomorrow."

"I don't know why you'd do that," he said. "I certainly won't be done thinking by tomorrow."

I went back the next day, but Greg wasn't there. I walked downtown, ate a couple tacos and walked back. Greg still wasn't there. I don't generally have intuition. But I thought I had some. Greg might have gone to the Steel Dust. Maybe I should go down there too, and talk to him and Bill Warner together.

I sat at my desk in the office and decided to call my Uncle George. I dialed Mercy Hospital and the switchboard connected me to his room. It took him quite a while to answer the phone. He sounded like he was a million miles away.

"Uncle George," I said. "Uncle George its John." I spoke loudly.

"John," he said. I heard the phone receiver touching his plastic tubes. "How are you?"

"Fine," I said. "How are you?"

"I'm alive today," he said. "That's all I can tell you."

"Uncle George," I said. "I have to ask you about Bill Warner."

"Who?" he said.

"Bill Warner, the guy I went over to see in Rexburg," I said.

"Stay away from Bill Warner," he said. "He's crazy."

"Yes," I said. "How is he crazy?"

"Terrible," he said. "Drinks all the time."

"I know that," I said. "Why? Why does he drink all the time?"

There was a pause. "It was his wife," he said. "He came home one day—this was years and years ago—and she was gone. Very pretty girl. So he started blaming people and her mother and said if she ran off, what a piece of crap she was."

"Where did she go?" I said.

"I was working for him at the time and about two weeks later, we found her way in the back of the property, high up in a tree. She'd hung herself," he said.

"Oh," I said.

"But that's not what I'm talking about," he said. "The sheriff said it was suicide but none of us working for him believed it. We all thought he killed her. He claimed Mexicans did it. But I never believed that."

"What did you do?" I said.

He took a deep breath. "I worked for him another four or five years and he was crazy and drunk the whole time. I had a family to support and couldn't afford to make a move." He coughed. "I hope you don't think less of me, John. There was nothing I could do."

"Did you say anything to the sheriff?" I said.

"No," he said. "This is the first I've spoken of it to anybody since it happened."

"I'm sorry, Uncle George," I said.

"I'm sorry, too, John. When you come visit me again, we'll talk about it," he finished.

"Okay," I said. "Take care of yourself."

The receiver clicked on his end. He was already gone.

I walked back across the campus as it grew dark. I locked the door and sat at my kitchen table, drinking beer until I passed out. I don't know how I made it to my bed.

The next day, I opened the front door to sit on my stoop and drink coffee. On the top step, still burning, were two Mexican luck candles. One was colorful, with a painting of an Indian on the outside and lucky symbols and an owl. The other candle was black and white, with a painting of the thin skeletal lady in her veil, holding a scythe. Santa Muerte. Saint

Death. I moved the glass candleholders to one side and sat there drinking my coffee.

Half an hour later, Greg showed up in his truck. He had a coffee in his hand when he got out.

"Hey," he said.

"Hi," I said. "How's it going?"

"Not so great," he said. "Bill Warner's dead."

"How's that," I said.

"Something or someone attacked him behind his house and just about cut him in half," he said.

"Did you go down there?" I said.

"Yes," he said. "I wanted to get some answers."

"Did you get 'em?" I said.

"Not really," he said. "Bill and I went out into the field where you described the Mexicans being shot, but there was nothing there." He paused. "I found a single Winchester piece of brass, that's what I found. Off in the grass."

"Oh," I said. "What do you think happened?"

"I have no idea," he said. He sipped his coffee. He reached into his pocket and came out with three hundred-dollar bills. He put them on the top step. "That's for going down there."

"Thanks," I said.

"Anything else you want to say?" he said.

"No," I said.

He walked toward his truck.

"Yes, there is," I said.

He turned around. "What is it?" he said.

"I'm sorry I shot that guy, but I didn't know what to do fast enough except pull the trigger," I said.

"I know," he said. "Give yourself a little time away from the booze and then come back to work. I think all the news interest has gone away."

"Thanks Greg," I said.

It was almost a month. During that time, every morning, there would be one or two Mexican candles on my stoop. Always lit, burning in the morning when I came out. On the day I stopped drinking, I came out with my coffee under the late fall blue sky and there were three candles, all lit. Two Indians and a Santa Muerte. That was the first day I walked across the campus again, to see Greg and talk about what was next.

ST. GABRIEL

THERE ARE VIOLENT HURRICANES ALL THE TIME, IN my world.

Five men tried to kill my younger brother over some logging rights money, but he lived. By the time I got to the hospital in Spokane, he was sitting up and eating solid food. Recovering. He talked to me about what had happened to him. The five men set him up, to rip him off. They hadn't counted on his dog being so tough. He never went anywhere without his dog and she'd saved his life that night in the woods. She was dead. I got on the phone and the guys I knew in the Pacific Northwest and across Montana, guys who owed me favors, guys who sometimes paid me to move the index finger of my right hand less than an inch, depending on where the barrel was pointing—lots of eyes started to look for this group of five men. I took my brother home to Bozeman, to keep recovering.

The cost of pain and revenge finally dipped into a range I could afford. I got a late-night call, and when it was all said and done, there were Montana state police questions about five men and their sudden death with my name as the answer and the court decided my house should be made of concrete and steel for about eight years or more. That I should wear an orange jumpsuit. Very little proof let me get off light. Three of the men were shot from three football fields away, most likely the result of hunting accidents. Maybe bullets that overreached their animal mark and struck a human. The other two were shot at distances that were deemed impossible by the court forensic expert. No bullet could be accurate, at that range. That's what the forensic expert said. I went to the private prison in Shelby and made my way to Deer Lodge, like everybody in Montana held accountable for their actions. I read the Bible, the most violent story I've ever known—an eye for an eye—and walked the yard when I could. I left when they told me to leave. It had all become one long night to me and that didn't change when I got out. Things didn't seem real to me anymore. My brother met me at my release, eight years and he was doing well, and after a month, we started to talk about money and work and the aspects of the normal world that needed to be attended to.

My brother and I delivered a load of big timber to Lethbridge and a trucker up there put us on to it.

"Biggest storm ever," he said. "Going to wreck the whole Gulf Coast. Hurricanes, the real shit. Lots of work for loggers with their own gear. Big money in the cleanup. You boys headed south?"

My brother nodded. "We are now," he said.

When we got back into Montana, we stopped in a bar in Bozeman and watched the storm develop on the bar TV. Sat drinking and watching those hurricanes sow the seeds of the future for everybody in the Gulf. People abandoning their homes, running to stay alive. For some of those folks, the wind and water would change everything. They'd move, they'd live a life in a part of the country they didn't know existed, or that they hated. They'd be buried in cemeteries that didn't have any stones with their last name already on them, far away from family. The whisper from a voice can make a train jump the rail. And this was a lot more than a whisper. The endless piles of torn trees were sacks of dollars, to me and my brother.

We drove back to our woodlot and rented house and started sharpening saws and collecting equipment into the big pickup truck.

"Do you want to say goodbye to your girl?" my brother asked.

"Not really," I said. I'd been seeing a girl in town for three or four months.

"Okay," he said.

I stood next to the truck. "I don't have anything to say."

"Sure," he nodded.

We packed some guns too, the rifle and ammo, all in the lock box. Just in case trouble knocked and we wanted to knock back. The drive took us through Nevada and Texas. We stopped and drank with a couple of my brother's friends. Driving into East Texas, the disaster started to show and by the time we hit the Louisiana line, it looked like God had been pretty mad that day. Houses torn from foundations, boats in the streets, abandoned cars everywhere, no power, no sewer, no drinking water. We got some papers that allowed us to work, through a connection of my brother's, and we stayed in New Orleans—signed on to cut trees around high voltage at four hundred and fifty a day each, plus food and lodging. Anything we made on the side belonged to us and it was cash paid at the end of each day. It was tragedy for those folks, but it was a license to print money for the contractors. The whole city smelled, when we first got there. I thought of Sodom. And other things.

St. Gabriel only appears four times in the Bible. Some scholars of God say St. Gabriel is an archangel, on the same plane as Michael, and deals in vengeance and death. St. Gabriel is credited with having destroyed Sodom. Others say St. Gabriel is the angel of mercy, one of God's highest, maybe the highest, messenger. I don't claim to know. Somewhere it says that St. Gabriel never really appeared, that all references to St. Gabriel are actually dreams that God had and St. Gabriel is mercy come to life through God's dreams and that mercy isn't what we understand it to be. Dying can be a privilege, I came to understand that in prison, as much as living can be its own gift. Mercy can be flowers, or making sure your aim is true. Dreams die hard. I know mine did. I don't imagine God's died any differently. Maybe St. Gabriel will appear again sometime.

I met her and it was like meeting life for the first time. She opened the eyes of my heart. In any other city she'd have been a model, not a dancer. After, I asked her if she wanted me to go get some cigarettes. So she could smoke and go to sleep.

"Yeah," she said. "That would be nice." She smiled in the dark, hugging the pillow. She was all curves and so alive. Beyond beautiful. A for-real woman. We had talked for hours before this, about everything. She was without a doubt the most beautiful woman I'd ever seen. Inside and out. Her voice wasn't that sweet sickly Southern crap—she was Cajun, spoke her mind and had a good laugh. She lived like she meant it.

I put on jeans, a shirt and my light jacket and walked out into the New Orleans night. The fog was there, the storms had just ended. Crushed cars sat on Canal Street, but on Bourbon it was business as usual. I bought the cigarettes and a lighter and headed back. She was gone when I got back to the room. No note, nothing. The sheets were still warm from her body, the pillow smelled of her. And I tried to take it like a good thing, that maybe she felt like I did and the possibility of getting closer was much more frightening than she could say. Or that she had a man to get home to get home to and leaving was polite—my karma had come back on me from Montana and I put the cigarettes in a drawer with the lighter.

The mess from the destruction went on and on. My brother and I burned through chains and gas and oil. We'd go out and check downed lines or move them with hot-line tools. Then we'd start cutting, so the scoops and chippers could come along and take care of what we left. When the humidity rose, my shirt was wet all day. The sawdust bounced off my safety glasses. We were cutting hundreds of years of growth. It was all the same to us.

She was at the room when I got back that one day. She was a little drunk, high. She had on a blue top and jeans over those long legs. That didn't last. We fucked like champs and kept going. Beyond where we'd been before. She made my cock so hard it hurt and my mouth ached from being on her, everywhere. Hours. We smoked and talked in bed. Drank some beer. She was having problems in town, within the city. The cops were harassing her. Her ex was harassing her. The guy she lived with turned out to be friends with dealers. The cops were watching her. They wanted to kill her, as revenge on her man. And she wanted to leave. She had children, two young boys, and wanted to give them a better life and she wanted a better life for herself. We came up with a plan that fit the hurricane. We made a hurricane of our own.

There is a town in Louisiana called St. Gabriel. It's a new town, only been around a couple years. After the hurricane, it was the morgue for all of New Orleans. The women's prison is in St. Gabriel too, they hold all the security classifications together under one roof. Women from Sodom, you might say, kicked out of New Orleans for their crimes. I doubt that anyone at the prison even knows who St. Gabriel is or was supposed to be. And the number of dreams that have died within those walls, countless thousands, even dying now. It could make your soul cry, if you were a sentimental person.

My brother didn't show two mornings later and when he hadn't come around in the afternoon, I went looking. He wasn't at the bar we hung out at. I finally walked over to the police station, about two in the afternoon and talked to them. They had grabbed him, thinking he was me.

"Who are you again?" the black cop behind the bullet proof glass asked me. He had the NOPD fatigues on and his gun sat smart at his right side.

"I'm his brother," I said. "I'd like to see him."

"We'd all like things," the cop said.

"Can I see him?"

The cop studied the sheet in front of him. "Lots of charges here," he said. People went in and out of the station house with a dazed look.

"What's the bail?"

"No bail," he said. "Just charges."

"What charges?"

He shook his head. "Felonies." Then he went and got the detectives.

They took us in a cop car and another unmarked car out to St. Gabriel prison. Nobody spoke on the way out. We drove around the facility and settled in a parking lot, near the edge of some trees. They had my brother cuffed. We walked out through the mud, until we could see something on the ground in front of us at the very edge of the woods, covered with some dirt and leaves. Half in the woods. It was a woman. In a blue top and jeans. A large caliber shell had passed through her ribcage.

"Do you know her?" the cop asked. The detectives stood back, watching us.

"Not really," I said. It looked like her, but not if you knew her.

Up close, like I did.

"She's been shot at long range. We think she was trying to escape and during the hurricane, someone had it in for her and shot her." He shrugged. "Or something."

"That's a good theory," I agreed.

"You wouldn't happen to know any boys from Montana, that have a reputation as long-shot artists, would you?" he asked with a New Orleans slow drawl.

"No," I said. "I honestly don't."

"That's funny," the one cop said. "Because after we ran your sheet and came up with some facts, we kind of thought it might have been you that pulled the trigger."

"I've never shot a woman," I said in truth.

"People change," the other cop said.

"Not that much," I said.

"We were looking for this woman, in New Orleans," the one cop said. "We were watching you."

"She was here," I said, pointing at the ground.

"You know," the one cop said, "during the hurricane, some bad folks in New Orleans disappeared."

"Must have got caught up in the storm," I reasoned.

"Certainly," the other cop said. "That stuff happens."

"This woman here," the one cop said. "This woman got caught by someone else."

"I don't know anything about it," I said. "I don't know why you have us out here."

The head detective walked over to the corpse and kicked it in the head as hard as he could. He watched me. "I've got y'all out here," he said, "because we think you were together and you're a killer. We have established that. What we haven't established is who this woman is. She was just printed the other day and that got destroyed in the storm. If she's the woman from the prison. On the other hand, if she's this woman we were looking for from New Orleans, the one hooked up with that dealer, then we can call that off, because we'd have done this to her anyways." He drew his foot back and kicked the head of the corpse again as hard as he could. The whole body moved off the ground a foot. "So which is it?"

"I know who it is," I lied. "I know her."

"Why'd you kill her?" the detective asked. "Did she owe you money? Drugs?"

"I didn't," I said.

He kicked the corpse right in the mouth and watched my face the whole time as he did it. "Does that bother you?" he asked. "I'm kicking your girl here." He stared at me. "Play tough guy like it doesn't bother you, but I'm going to kick her again."

"She's not feeling it," I said.

He brought his foot back and kicked the head of the corpse three or four times, hard. The sound was a loud wet smack. The body moved up and down. Mud and fluid mixed on his shoes and the gray cuff of his pants.

"This isn't the man we want," the detective said to the other cops. He motioned at my brother. "Uncuff him and let's go." He walked back through the mud to the unmarked car. I was walking behind him for a couple steps. He turned to me, his face white and puffy. "If that's her, and I think it is, you did us a favor." He kept on walking, toward the cars, alone.

One of the cops came forward with keys and uncuffed my brother. The cops walked back to their car and drove off, leaving me and my brother standing there outside the facility. After we walked for half an hour, we hitched a ride with a guy, back into New Orleans.

The hurricane raged through the night and day. An older man in Southern Louisiana woke up with a straight razor under his bed, with a pink ribbon on it, like someone might use for a little girl's hair. His wife found her gas tank had been filled with pig's blood. A young man in New Orleans who lived with his dad found the locks to the house glued. A guy from Illinois, a DJ, woke up with his shit in the street, and broken ribs. There was mercy all along, no revenge, no vengeance. That's how you know a human did these things and not God. If it was God that had done them, the answer would all be the same. Death, death, death.

The work ended and we drove back to Montana. We hadn't made millions.

I ask myself that now, am I St. Gabriel? Is the mercy that I once had long gone and who will show mercy on me? What a privilege it will be to die. We create ourselves, or so we believe, and we become locked in, we become afraid not to meet the same person each morning in the mirror. I am St. Gabriel and I will stand accountable for what I do and will hold others to account. I am the highest of God's messengers and no Sodom will stand while I live.

Nobody asks a man why he drinks. Mixed in there with the private darkness of reasons, nobody wants to know the answer from the man who is already drunk. I was drinking to get a woman to come back to me, which is the worst reason of all. The cost of pain. When you see someone so bright, such a bright fire, a diamond, it stays with you and their image is on the inside of your eyelids when you close your eyes. I can still see her. She lights up the night of life. Who wouldn't want her back? Her smile alone could cure you of whatever disease had got hold of you. Oceans of booze couldn't put out that fire.

My brother saw her one time, in a bar, on TV, modeling in Milan. I was covered with sawdust and staggered in.

"She's coming," he said. "She'll be in the next clip."

I stared at the screen as it changed. It was her. She walked like a princess and a queen all at once, she fucking owned that crowd and that show and I had to look away. I was proud, so proud of her and all she had done and there was a plan that had worked.

My brother knows better than to ever ask. You don't ask about stuff, because then you can't talk about it on the stand. He asked with his eyes, one night, late. We were standing in the cellar, throwing darts and doing laundry.

"Sure," I said. "Part of it was me. And part of it was her."

"It worked," he said.

"It got her a new life," I said. "She deserved that and more."

"Do you think she misses you?" he asked.

"Not in the way you might think," I said. "Like you might miss an old dog."

"You might be wrong," he said. "I miss my dog every day." He took his shirt off to put it in the wash and even his scars were healing from his trauma. His tattoos always looked amazing. He pulled a clean T-shirt over his head from the dryer. I drank some beer.

"I really think you're wrong," he said. "She's going to come here and be with you."

"Fuck," I said. "I don't want to be with me most days. What would make her want to be with me?"

"Who else would protect her like that?" he asked.

I nodded. "But I would protect her like that and she doesn't have to be around. I'd do it anyway."

"Does she know you feel like this?"

I shook my head. "Look," I said. "I really don't want to get into all this. Somebody who has kids and is living a life, they don't need crap dumped on them. I can handle whatever I feel, regardless of the situation." I drank my beer. "What does it matter what I feel? I'm a grown man."

"What about being happy?" he asked.

"What's that got to do with anything?"

"Are you happy?" he asked. "Without her."

I drank some more beer. "I'm a big boy," I said. "I'm happy for her. That's all that matters." I shook my head again. "She's under enough strain without me being an asshole."

We threw some more darts and I walked upstairs and went to bed. It has been five years and she hasn't shown up. She won't. At first it was hard, but now it's the same. Sometimes, when I'm in a crowd, if we go to Spokane or all the way to Seattle, my eyes hurt and I have a headache. Because I've been looking for her, all day, among the faces. After an eighteen-hour day of cutting and hauling big timber, even the work can't erase her from my mind. Thinking of her keeps me alive some days. Some people would call that sad. They don't know what I'm talking about it. I'm lucky.

When I wake up, I am someplace else in my mind. But she is always there. And I'm happy for her. She died the fake death and will get to live the real life. I will wake up in my coffin underground and be comforted. I'll wait for the hurricane to uproot me from my eternal rest and carry me off. To meet St. Gabriel, to whom I will show no mercy. Even if I am in hell, my aim will be true. Gravity pulls the bullet toward earth. There is friction, recoil energy, computed velocity, measured velocity, freebore travel, resistance, ratio of powder charge. None of it will stop me, it didn't stop me those nights in Montana when I had those five men in my sights and breathed easy and slowly increased the pressure on my finger until that hammer dropped. The cops of heaven can puzzle over the how and why and look for witnesses that don't exist. Maybe she is my St. Gabriel, appearing briefly and now only in my dreams. At least one of us made it out of the night.

If it weren't for her being alive in the world, I'd turn the gun on myself. Show myself the mercy I deserve. The chance to hear her voice keeps me on earth.

JOCKAMO

AFTER PRISON, IT WAS HARD TO GET A JOB. MOST WORK faded if they found out I'd been incarcerated. I left Maine and went down south to look for a construction job. After the hurricanes hit, I found some work in New Orleans. Running heavy equipment and driving truck. Hauling tons of ruined houses to the dump sites. The worst was the kids' toys and the pictures. Moldy, soaked stuffed animals. That really got to me. Pictures so wet you could wring them out. There was other stuff there—dead, bloated pets, and in one house, a dead body. The kitchens were always awful. People don't realize it, the simple danger of what was in some of those refrigerators. The food has sat unprotected for months. The smell of it could kill you. Lethal airborne bacteria. We taped the fridges shut before handling them. We wore masks and breathing tanks. Special hazard suits. We looked like we were still underwater, even though the water had receded. That work ended too. On a Friday, we got back to the big garage where we kept all the equipment and they were handing out the last paychecks. Said the disaster money had run out and good luck to us in finding new work.

I got hold of a buddy of mine, back in Maine. He was part owner of a logging operation. He sent me plane tickets. I'd fly to Cleveland, then to Burlington, Vermont. He'd been awarded a contract to supply a wood-fired power plant. I could run one of his crews, cutting delivered logs from the yard into a usable size for feedstock, and help with that side of the operation.

I was at the New Orleans airport, at the last gate in the terminal. Two hours early for my plane. I sat in the seat closest to the flight attendant's station.

An older man walked by with a small, younger woman. They looked out the floor to ceiling windows at the planes. He was old from work, you could tell that about him. A short man, black and gray short hair cut at home and thick black glasses. Big hands and forearms. He moved stiffly.

The woman was handicapped, from the way she walked and held herself. Her hair was short and uneven. Almost torn, not really cut. She wore denim coverall shorts, a jumper, over a pink short sleeve shirt. Brown corrective shoes. She balled her right hand into a fist and punched her own right thigh. Slowly, she did it again. The bruise on her thigh showed purple and blue from under her shorts and slowly, she punched herself again. She and the man stood there. They looked out the window together.

"There's the plane," the man said. He had a little bit of the bayou in his voice. He looked around and nodded at me. I nodded back. The woman punched herself in the thigh. She said something, but I couldn't hear it.

"They'll take good care of you," he said. "You're going to go on that plane right there." He pointed out the steel and glass window at the runway and the plane closest to the window.

"I can't," she said. She punched her thigh.

The man put his hand on her back. She rested her head on his shoulder and she shook as she cried. His sleeve was wet with her tears when she stood straight.

"We can't drive, honey," he said. "You think about it." He stepped away from the window and walked over and sat one seat away from me. He turned to me, as if we knew each other. "Doctors say she'll kill herself with this," he said and pretended to punch his own thigh. "Give herself a clot and break it loose and float to her heart. Then it's over." He stopped. "She used to do it once in a while, but the hurricanes were too much for her."

The woman spoke. "Since I was eight," she said. "I did this."

He bent forward and looked at the carpet. He lifted his head and we both watched the woman. She was punching herself and softly crying as she looked at the plane. The voice over the loudspeaker system announced flights boarding.

The man got up and guided the woman over to the seat next to me.

"Pardon us," he said.

"No problem," I said.

The woman looked at me and smiled as she cried. Her face was red and streaked.

"I can't," she said to me.

I nodded. "It's fine," I said.

She managed to punch herself even sitting down.

"Just watch her, okay?" the man said. He held out a dollar bill, lengthwise and creased along the center, so it was stiff.

"That's not necessary," I said.

He tucked the single into my front shirt pocket. "Buy yourself a cold beer when you get the chance. You can still get cheap beer in the Quarter, if you look around for it."

"Thanks," I said.

"Do you like the beer down here?" he said. "They used to brew Dixie beer right in the city. It was always pretty good."

"If I'm thirsty, anything cold is good for me."

"I like that beer they got from Abita," he said. "I like Andygator best, and the Jockamo, with the Indian on the bottle." He paused. "I got a cooler with a couple beers in it out in the back of the truck right now. I think I got a bottle of Jockamo in there."

"I like the Andygator," I said. "I've had that."

"Used to drink a lot of Pabst Blue Ribbon," he said. "PBR's, we used to call 'em."

"I like the can," I said. "They're good if they're cold."

"My one cousin—Steve—he got up to Michigan, chasing a woman, a while back. So I'm sittin' down here, sweatin' my potatoes off, and the phone rings. I pick it up—Hello? And the voice says Hey Cousin, it's Steve! And I said Well alright Steve, how's Michigan? And he says I had to call and tell you that the place we're eating at has a drink on the menu called the Johnny Cash and I'm having one, what do you think it is? I said Steve, I have no idea and he said, It's an ice-cold PBR and I thought of you right away. I got a real laugh out of that, both because of the PBR and because I used to be such a big fan of Johnny Cash," he finished. "I was so glad he called me to tell me that."

"That's something," I said.

"It's funny," he said. "You never know when people are thinking of you."

"No," I agreed. "You never do."

"I used to drink a lot of hard liquor," he said. "Now I mostly drink beer, to keep cool."

"I try not to drink when I'm working," I said. "But afterwards I'll have a few."

He nodded. "That's the way to do it," he said. He motioned at the woman. "Sit tight with her for me."

"Okay," I said.

He stood and walked over to the counter and I heard him talking to the woman about his tickets. They wouldn't give him his money back on them.

The punching woman turned and looked at me.

"Were you here for the hurricanes?" she said.

"No," I said. "Right after."

"It scared me," she said.

"I bet," I said.

"We're doing the best we can," she said.

"Sure," I said. "It'll be okay."

He came back over from the ticket counter.

"Nothing doing," he said. He pointed at the punching woman. "She can't fly."

"I can't fly," she repeated.

"What are you going to do?" I said.

"I don't know," he said. His eyes filled up. "This is a hell of a mess." He sat down on the other side of her. The punching woman stared straight ahead.

He kept talking. "Some of the family prays for her, but I don't. Not anymore." He turned to me. "Do you know what God is?" he said.

"No," I said. "I don't."

"God is fear," he said. "Fear that something bad will happen to you, if you don't stay in good with Him." He pointed around, at the whole terminal and the rest of the world beyond. "When you've seen all this," he said, "what is there to be afraid of? There's nothing left to be scared of. When you run out of fear, you stop believing in God."

"These are hard times," I said.

He patted the punching woman on the head. "She's punched herself since she was eight years old. I can't even imagine it anymore." He raised his voice and then lowered it. "God better be afraid of me, that's all I'll say." He looked over his shoulder at a man and woman leaving the terminal. His eyes glistened with water.

"I don't know what to tell you," I said.

He shook his head. "I don't know what to tell myself either."

The punching woman was still staring at the planes. "I can't fly," she said.

"We'll drive," he said. "Tonight we'll drive to Baton Rouge and stay with Aunt Jean." He stopped. "I'll borrow some money from her and see if we can take their truck to Cleveland to drop you off."

The woman shook her head yes.

"Maybe we'll stop to see your cousins in Toledo and get some money there too."

"Yes," she said.

"And then I'll have to leave you," he said.

"No," she said. She put her arms around his neck. And even as she did it, she lifted her arm off to punch herself. They sat there crying and I stood up, as if my plane was boarding.

The man wiped his snot with a stained handkerchief. "Sorry about all this," he said. "We're having a tough day."

"No worries," I said. "I've had my share of those." I nodded. "Good luck to you."

The woman looked up at me. They both stood.

"Luck forgot about us," the man said. He walked a couple steps and turned around. "Can you give us a hand getting out to the parking lot? Have you got time?"

"I've got time," I said. I had already sent my bag through and I hadn't seen any line when I'd come through security. I'd leave myself time and go back through. I took the suitcase out of the punching woman's hand and walked slowly with them, back up the linoleum grade, into the main terminal.

"I'm just right out here in the parking garage," he said as we walked across in front of the ticket counters. We went through the doors and stepped outside.

The three of us walked past the concrete pillars and crossed the street into the first floor of the parking deck. We took an elevator to the second level and got out. There was a concrete deck floor overhead, but it was open-air on the sides of the deck, with some sun coming in. He was walking toward an old pickup truck with Louisiana plates, among the rows of cars and trucks. Sportsman's Paradise it read at the bottom of the plate. The man took a key from his pocket and opened the passenger side first. The punching woman got in. He closed the door behind her. He reached into the bed of the pickup.

"Have a beer," he said. He took the white lid off a cooler, pulled out a brown beer bottle and popped the top with an opener on his key ring. He handed it to me and popped one for himself. He raised his bottle and clinked it against mine. "Here's to you," he said. There was an Indian on the side of the bottle. "I love those Mardis Gras Indians," he said. "With the costumes and big feathers."

I raised my beer bottle. "Better times," I said.

"Here," he said to me. "Take a look over here." He opened a tackle box behind the driver's seat. He lifted out the removable middle and underneath were two flat automatic pistols.

"That small one is a Beretta," he said. "Pain in the ass to load, but it does the job up close. The other one's a Wilson concealed carry .45. That's a manstopper."

"Nice," I said.

"The Beretta is my daddy's pistol," he said. "Kept it in his front pocket, even in church."

"Really?" I said.

"That pistol knows how to do its job," he said. "Let's leave it at that." He drank his beer. "My daddy had a reputation around here and people thought twice before crossing him." He picked up the black Beretta and handed it to me. The metal was cold. It was hard to imagine something so lightweight ever spitting sudden, violent death.

"That's a special heirloom," I said, handing it back to him.

"We could do a private sale right here for say, about four hundred dollars and that would give me gas money to get her out of harm's way," he said. The punching woman sat in the passenger's seat, with her seatbelt on. He talked as if she wasn't there or couldn't hear him. He talked as if I might need to carry a gun. As if he knew who I'd been, years ago.

"I'm flying out in an hour," I said. "I have no way of transporting them."

"You don't have to carry them," he said. "I'll drive with 'em and once you get settled up north, I'll drive 'em right up to you. Keep right on going after I'm done dropping her off." He paused. "Just that I need that gas money to get me on the road today."

"Right," I said.

"You might need a pistol up north," he said. "Never know what might happen up there."

"I thought your truck wouldn't make it up north?" I said.

"That's if I got her," he said, looking at the punching woman. "If it's just me, I can get out and change a tire on the highway, or do whatever's necessary."

I sipped my beer. "No need for that," I said. The planes were loud coming and going and I could see the black tarmac and the sunburned green grass.

"Suit yourself," he said. He had his beer in his hand.

"I can give you about two hundred fifty dollars," I said. "Will that help?"

"Two hundred fifty?" he said. "That's fine. That'll get me started. You can pay me the rest when you see me again." He wrote his number on a piece of paper and handed it to me. "That's my number, for when you come back down."

"That's fair," I said. "I'll probably be back in a month or two. As soon as the snow starts to fly up north." I nodded. I pulled some damp twenties out of my pocket, counted them, and handed him two hundred fifty dollars. I tore the scrap of paper he'd given to me in half and wrote the number of the office number of the wood-burning plant on it. I handed it to him. He handed it back to me.

"Put your name on the back of that," he said. "I'll forget." I did. He shook hands with me. "Good to know you," he said. "I'm Eddie Ourso." He motioned at the punching woman. "This is Lenore."

The phone rang late in the day at the yard and somebody motioned to me. I shut the saw down and took my helmet off. I walked into the office and put the phone to my ear. Snow was starting to come down.

"Yes," I said.

"Hey bud, it's Eddie from New Orleans, how you doin'?"

"Good Eddie, how 'bout yourself?"

"Hell never stops, you know. Just keeps on going. Look, I got a question for you," he said.

"Go ahead," I told him.

"I got to pawn those guns, I need that money," he said. "She's back with me and I got no money for groceries." I could hear the hurt in his voice.

"Pawn 'em, Eddie," I said. "Get whatever you can for 'em."

"You sure?" he said. "I feel bad about doing it, but you understand, I'm in a tight spot here."

"No problem," I said.

"And I can't pay you back that money you gave me for 'em," he said.

"I understand," I said. "Do what you have to do. Buy me a beer when you see me."

"I will do that," he said. "Get some time off and come down and we'll go fishing and drink beer. On me." He paused. "I hate to pawn my father's gun," he said. "Selling it was one thing, but pawning it," he paused, "pawning is bad times."

"He'd understand," I said.

"No," Eddie said. "No, he wouldn't, but it's nice of you to say that. He'd have beaten me to within an inch of my life if he knew about this." He was crying now.

"Take it easy, buddy," I said.

His voice was choked off. "His grave," he said. "His grave was covered by thirty feet of water."

I could hear him crying. "Hang in there," I said.

"I will," he sobbed. "I will."

The cold and snow was everyday in Burlington. Late in the afternoon, on a Friday, I was standing in the loading yard talking to Steve, one of the yard foreman, when a Vermont State Police cruiser eased its way down the sloping entrance ramp and parked in front of the equipment shed. A plain blue cop-sedan followed right behind. A uniformed State Trooper got out of the cruiser. Another State Trooper got out of the passenger's side. He had unclipped the shotgun from inside his car and stood there, watching me and Steve, holding the shotgun. We stopped talking. A cop in street clothes and a heavy jacket got out of the plain sedan. He had pushed his coat back, as if he might need to get at his revolver. Both cars had their engines running.

"Are you armed?" the street clothes cop said to me.

"No," I said.

"Come over here," he said. "Put your hands on my car and spread your legs."

The one uniformed cop spoke to Steve. "Go on about your business," he said.

"What the hell's going on?" Steve said.

"Get out of here or I'll thrown you right in the back in cuffs," the other trooper said. Both troopers were older. Steve walked into the shed, headed back to the fuel and feedstock unit.

The troopers frisked me, took my pocketknife and put cuffs on me. They loaded me in the back of the plain cruiser. The street clothes cop got in and we accelerated out of the yard onto the highway. Headed south as the sun was going down under the snow clouds. He looked in the rearview mirror as he talked to me.

"Do you want to talk?" he said.

"I have no idea why I'm here," I said.

He held a photograph against the dividing grate. It was a still photo from a surveillance camera. It showed me and Eddie Ourso, standing, leaning on his pickup truck. I was handing him the black Beretta.

"What did he do?" I said.

"I'd rather not say," the cop said. "Right now, we're interested in what you did."

I didn't do anything," I said.

"Sure," the cop said. "You think about it. Maybe you'll feel like talking at the station." He drank from a coffee cup. "From the looks of your record, I'd think about talking."

The cuffs were tight on my wrists and every bump hurt, as I rode with my arms behind me. A car went past going north, tires crunching the snow. The uniformed troopers were behind us in their cruiser.

"He's singing his head off down in Louisiana," the cop said.

Lake Champlain was on our right as we drove and the sun shone faintly pink and purple, almost blue onto space between the scattered snow clouds. The colors reminded me of her. I thought of everything all at once—Eddie and Lenore and that we all bruise ourselves constantly and that the time in front of me was just a series of bad things that hadn't happened yet. That my bruise from years ago had broken loose and was floating through me, looking to clog the veins and arteries of my life.

"We know your record," the cop said. "You just found a loophole and got out. Shitty prosecution." He sipped his coffee as he drove. "We'll get you for the full maximum on this one."

"I didn't do anything," I said.

"I doubt that," he said. "Maybe you'll talk at the station. Maybe the smell of that room will remind you of inside."

"I remember what it was like inside," I said.

The cop kept talking, like all cops do. I stopped listening. I wondered what Eddie had done, to get himself into such a jam. I sat cuffed in the back, calm. Waiting for the station and the room and their lies and pressure. And release.

PINWHEEL

EVERY NIGHT THAT JUNE, FROM MY CELL WINDOW IN Orofino, I watched the fireworks color-burn the midnight sky over the Indian reservation across the road. The colors lit up the fields and sometimes the sparks would drift to earth and the old horses the Indians kept would scatter, faster than you would think they were capable of. Speed left from races they never ran, I told myself. I knew horses when I was a kid near Saratoga, in upstate New York. Whole worlds had happened since then. Those horses and fireworks were my only friends at the beginning of that summer.

I wasn't in the race to win anymore. I'd fallen on some hard times in Eastern Washington and a gang that was a branch of the Posse made a deal with me. They'd pay me to finish off another man's time in Idaho. I don't know how they rigged it up, who they paid off. But one day they brought me into a hospital room in Spokane and the deputies that shackled me and took me to Orofino called me by a different name. I was inside under a new name and eight years stood between me and the door.

The Idaho State Correctional Facility at Orofino was an old brick campus, housing twice as many men as it was built for. It was a mixed classification facility, which is the worst, because the killers are in with the guys who forgot a child support payment. The guys doing a decade don't look very kindly on the guy who gets to go home in three months. I was a maximum classification at that time, because the guy I was pretending to be had a record that began in the womb.

The guards came for me early one morning and cuffed me and shackled me for transport. I knew it couldn't be good. Someone had filed a writ with the Federal Circuit Court and the federal judge had ordered that I be brought to his temporary chambers in Boise. They were being forced to produce me, except I wasn't anyone—I wasn't the man they wanted incarcerated and I certainly wasn't going to tell anyone I was working for the Posse. In my own mind, they may as well have been driving a mute to Boise. We passed south through the beautiful Idaho mountains and trees and blue sky. The deputies driving me didn't say a word, just stopped once for coffee and then drove on. We drove into the streets and city of Boise. I slept on a bench overnight in a holding cell and they brought me upstairs into chambers in the morning.

The judge was in robes and seated behind a large desk, with an older woman stenographer in front of the desk. My brother and an Asian man, both impeccably dressed in gray suits, stood in the back of the room. The judge addressed me.

"The court has been made aware of some unusual circumstances surrounding your case." He pointed at my brother and the Asian man. I nodded and the judge continued. "We're convinced…the court has been convinced…". He paused. "The court is convinced that a sealed record and immediate release is the only way you'll be alive at the end of the week. The state of Idaho didn't seem inclined to let you go—so the appeal was passed up to me."

I didn't say anything. The court bailiff came over and unlocked my cuffs and shackles. I rubbed my wrists.

The judge stood. "I'm instructing one of my marshals to escort you to the Nevada border so we don't have a problem. I can't help you if you reenter this state. And you're on your own with the other problems—but we won't hold you here as a stationary target." He handed me some paperwork. "You're free to go, as long as you're leaving the state."

I looked at my brother, who spoke to the judge. "He'll ride with us to Nevada, Your Honor."

"Keep your head down," the judge said. He looked directly at me. "And watch behind you."

My brother shook hands with me, but we didn't say anything, not a word. He drove the new sedan behind the marshal's car, with Mr. Osaka in the back and me in the passenger's seat. It was a long ride, but we finally saw a sign for the Nevada state line. We crossed it and the marshal pulled a U-turn and headed north, back into Idaho.

Mr. Osaka mumbled something and my brother spoke to me.

"I'm sorry we couldn't warn you, but we had a heck of a time finding you. You got yourself in pretty deep."

"What's going on?" I asked.

My brother nodded as he drove. "We'd been looking for you, to come help out with Mr. Osaka's operation. In looking for you, we found out that the man you went in as, the real man, just got arrested in Montana. It was only a matter of time before the Posse tried to get to you on the inside."

Mr. Osaka mumbled to my brother.

"What'd he say?" I said.

"Mr. Osaka doesn't speak," my brother said. "He understands English perfectly well and he probably speaks it, although I've never heard him. I speak for him. Always, for the past five years. He talks in a kind of yakuza dialect—he and I speak it to each other and that's it. Nobody else."

"Handy," I said. I hadn't seen my brother much at the beginning of the last decade and not at all in the past five years, but years didn't come between us. I just figured he had his own job going on, somewhere, and when my plans started to fail, I didn't want to bring him down with me.

He was a couple years younger than me and maybe I felt responsible. He'd gotten bigger since I'd seen him last.

"Do you want to work for Mr. Osaka?" my brother asked.

"What are we doing?" I said.

"Watching whales," my brother said. And as we drove, he detailed the operation to me. In the end, I agreed.

Whales are a select group of Japanese businessmen, probably only two hundred worldwide, who come to the United States to gamble. They're called whales because they bet huge—they're up seven million, they're down thirty million. If one of these guys walks into a small casino on a good night, he can bankrupt the place, or lose enough to let the casino build another club and a hotel.

Whales like bets that other gamblers can't get their hands on and sometimes it can be exotic—betting on street fights, illegal car racing. But the yakuza control the horse racing and that means that the yakuza can sometimes control the whales.

Mr. Osaka bought seven hundred acres of land outside Reno, flattened it all out, put in a private horse racing track and was getting set to lay in a private airfield when some his contractors thought they'd muscle him for more money. Those contractors are gone and now my brother and I are in charge of the operation.

A private racetrack, with all the barns and stables. The whales own stuff all over the world and pretty soon, the private jets are coming in, with the stallions and racehorses the whales have accumulated. A horseman's field of dreams. We've got the compound gated off and the whales arrive, with their limos and their drivers and their party girls. Every morning the races start at eleven and they walk around, drinking, looking at the horses.

Mr. Osaka has only two betting windows open, run by Asian men the same as him. Tattoos on their hands, one guy with a Japanese character right on his throat. These are the honest men, bound to count the money, the take the verbal bets and always pay. No slips, no tickets. These guys are taking bets in the hundreds of thousands and never sweating.

Mr. Osaka walks the compound with us and mumbles to my brother as we pass the honest men by the bet windows.

"As children, they are not taught about wanting. Then, when they learn about money, they are taught it is filthy. The combination makes them honest," my brother translates.

The favorite bet for the whales is the pinwheel. The pinwheel lets the whale run his horse on Mr. Osaka's track, but bet against other horses running at other tracks that come in by satellite feed. Your horse can finish second here but if you've matched it up against the right combo, say from Saratoga, or Pimlico, or Yonkers, you can double or triple your take. Or you can throw your money in a bigger hole. Money is green paper to these people. They give more to the party girls to keep them quiet than I've ever earned in my life. But that ended, too, once I got on Mr. Osaka's payroll.

The horses thundered around the track every day, a different group. Sired by names you'd recognize. The track stayed hard for the rest of the summer and there were winners—Jack Rabbit Fast, Sun Comet, the Last Laugh. Some of the names didn't translate into English.

One morning, my brother and I had to take pistols out to the building where the stable hands slept and escort someone to the gate. We came back by the track and Mr. Osaka stood at the rail, watching the horses take their morning exercise. He mumbled and my brother spoke.

"Do you know the secret of a fast horse?" my brother translated.

"No," I said.

Mr. Osaka mumbled at length and my brother fed me bits and pieces.

"When horses run fast, all four feet leave the ground. They fly. They like to fly. It's their fantasy. But they have to push themselves back down to the ground, so their hooves touch the track again. So when you look at a horse, or watch him in a race, see the look on his face and the jockey's. If they like to fly, that is no good. They must like to push themselves back to the ground, to run."

"Do you bet?" I asked.

Mr. Osaka mumbled. My brother spoke.

"I swore a vow in the beginning never to bet on horses and I have kept that vow. Once, a horse had to be shot in front of me and my father told me, You can see someone's life in the pattern of their death blood. The horse's blood stopped at my feet and it was a sign to me that I should not bet on horses."

I nodded. Mr. Osaka moved his lips and my brother continued.

"If you were shot right now, and we saw your death blood, where would it go?"

I looked at the ground, which sloped slightly onto the track, and Mr. Osaka followed my gaze.

My brother finished. "Stay close to horses, then. Maybe that is your life."

We watched Mr. Osaka walk back to the white clubhouse and he disappeared inside.

They slammed out of the starting gates all summer and soon my brother and I had to make a bank trip to Reno. We didn't go to a bank. It was just a house on the outskirts of the city; it looked like a regular white and blue ranch style. We put the money in the suitcase on the kitchen table and left, as we'd been told to do by Mr. Osaka. I think I saw the blue sedan following us that day, but I'm not sure. We went to the house later in the week, twice, and the second time, I'm sure I saw it. My brother saw it, too.

We had dropped the money off an hour before and were a mile away from the racetrack when the blue sedan pulled in front of us and cut us off. I knew as soon as they got out of the car they were cops. Two cops, undercover. My brother opened the passenger side door and ran up over the bank, as they drew their guns. I slammed them both out of the way with my car and took off. There were shots behind me, and as I looked in the rearview mirror, my brother was getting into the blue sedan, following me.

You've never seen so many people running in such a hurry from anything. Mexican stable boys running into the desert, limos circling around with half-dressed women, and the whales, sunglasses falling off, waving for them to hurry. Planes taking off. My brother watched the gate. Running an illegal racetrack, illegal gambling operation, weapons, now shot cops. We needed to leave.

A fire started near the horse barn. I was still looking for Mr. Osaka, but he was nowhere. There was a bulldozer next to the airfield, left from the contractors. I started it, bulldozed the fence down, got off the rig and opened the stall doors as the flames licked the wood. The horses took off across the field, into the heat. I watched them, shining, maybe three hundred million dollars of property on hooves, running like they wanted to. The owners wouldn't be happy, but I had done it. My brother and I climbed into a new truck and cut the corner of Idaho, before slipping into Montana and up into Canada. We took our pay with us, nothing more—

maybe we hoped that honorable thing would calm Mr. Osaka. The yakuza were like an ocean, deep and violent, and I knew and my brother knew we would live small lives from now on. If we wanted to live life at all.

It was Saratoga that finally called us back. We were there in August on a Sunday, walked down Main Street, bought a racing paper, and then made our way over to the track. Years had passed, we had different names, and we'd just done a big deal in Manhattan. One stop at the track before returning to north of the border. We settled in, examined the sheet with golf pencils and went to the window.

In the third race, we were by the clubhouse rail. There was a tremendous field coming around; the crowd was cheering. It was close. The brown blur of the pack slammed past us to the finish.

A young Asian boy stood in front of us. He'd come out of the crowd; I hadn't seen him till now. He mumbled to my brother and I almost felt bullets piercing my back. Nothing happened. My brother spoke.

"Ms. Osaka says we did the right thing and that we should look for a particular horse in the next race."

The boy bowed and walked into the clubhouse crowd. Sweat ran down my ribs. My brother held up the racing sheet and I looked at it.

It was the maiden race for Komodo Dragon, blinders on, Lasix, and we checked the tote board. Leading off at 85-1. None of the other names could be it. We went to the window and put it all, over seven thousand dollars—that was the lucky limit we'd agreed to bet—on Komodo Dragon. On the nose.

They brought the horses into the starting gate and bang, ring, they're off. Komodo Dragon is at the back of the pack and as they come around the first turn, it can't be. Komodo Dragon is dead last and drifting to the outside. Then it starts. Komodo Dragon passes one, passes two, passes Two-Time Loser, passes Long Johnny. Now it's Komodo Dragon on the outside and the horse starts to fly, to push itself back to the ground, to fly, to push, passing as though the other horses are standing still. You can feel it in the ground and now they're headed for the final turn, it's Komodo Dragon and Rummy, the favorite, Komodo Dragon, Rummy, and the final stretch, Komodo Dragon is flying and pushing and the whip gets him back down to the ground, Komodo Dragon is ahead and farther, by a length, Komodo Dragon.

We're walking up to the window with the ticket and we're not saying anything. But it's there in my head and as soon as we're in the car, safe, moving, back in our own race, we'll talk about it. Beautiful houses in Vancouver and the chance to start over again, a little safer. To run under another name, in a different city, with better chances, another day.

HAMMERLOCK

THEY CAME FOR HIM IN THE SPRING.

The city was newly alive and he was trying to enjoy it. Two men in white shirts and thin jackets, dark hair, walking down Amsterdam Avenue, across from the massive Cathedral of St. John the Divine. He was sitting outside at the coffee shop as the men paused, then crossed West One Eleven. When he saw them, he realized his eyes were tired from years of scanning crowds for them. The one man sat at his table, while the other man went inside the coffee shop to order. The man across from him nodded.

He nodded back. "Are you well?" he said.

"I'm okay," the man said. "I've had my problems. I will have more."

"It's hot this spring," he said.

"Not like our home," the man said. The other man emerged from the coffee shop and mimicked smoking with his hand. Crossed the street, to smoke a cigarette on the sidewalk in front of the park and grotesque statue. Watching.

He looked across the table at the nodding man. "No," he said. "There is a strong winter here on the coast."

"Are we still friends?" the man said. "You are still working at the library?"

"You are sitting here," he said. "Yes. Translation. Foreign collections."

"Good for you," the man said. He tapped the table. "You know what they did to our people," the man said.

"I only know what I read in the papers or see on the computer. I live my life here, not plan my death," he said.

The man across from him pushed several photographs across the table to him. The photos showed a pair of feet, a pair of hands. An empty, dimly-lit kitchen with a sink and a stove. The man pushed a very thin, tiny gold band across the table.

"This is my mother's home in Lima," he said. "These are my mother's hands. This is her ring."

"Yes," the man said. "It is."

He paused. The waitress came out and put a cup of coffee and a pastry in front of the man. The man swallowed some coffee.

"I'm sorry," the man said. "These are serious times." The man tapped the table again. "You have a young son here in the city as well."

"What do you need," he said. "Someone to stay at my house until they are legal. Drugs. What is it."

"No," the man said. He pointed at the photos and the ring. "It is not enough to begin something. Finishing is what we need. What they need."

"Do they have my mother," he said.

"Do you think they don't," the man said.

"What am I to do," he said.

"We will tell you," the man said. "Do you remember the training?"

"I remember," he said. "Do they have your family too," he finished. The man nodded.

"They are going to kill them all," he said.

"They probably already have," the man said. The man looked across the street, at the park and strange statue next to the cathedral. The man looked at his partner smoking a cigarette. "Do you know that when I was in prison, I could not imagine this. Just some vague out, was all I could think of. Maybe a bit of Lima, but not much. In my mind, early, there were women. The fifth year or so, the women faded." The man drank the coffee. "How old is your son?"

"Yes," he said. He ran his hand over his forehead. "Six. My son is six."

The man continued. "There are places I don't wish to return to, but I brought my mind there and so, sometimes, I must return. My mind makes it so, without me wanting that. Often, I return to prison," the man said. "Six is a good age. I cannot return to six, but I wish I could. I wish we all could."

"What will they do to my mother," he said.

"I can't talk about it. You would vomit," the man said.

He paused. "Tell me."

"These are sick people, committed to a cause," the man said.

"Terrorists," he said.

"One man's terrorist is another man's freedom fighter," the man said. "They are devout." The man motioned at the cathedral.

"Tell me," he said.

The man sighed. "I watched them take a woman's eye out with a roofing hammer, then pour acid into the eye socket," the man said. "My own eyes ached as they did it. Every time, they remove all the teeth forcibly, cut off all the fingers and toes. If you have a tattoo, they cut it off. There is no way to identify the body. They make it not be a body anymore."

He was silent. A police car drove past on Amsterdam.

The man motioned at the passing cruiser. "Even if you grabbed an officer and told him, what would they do? What do they know of Peru? The whole world knows and does nothing. When people think of Peru, this is exactly what they think of—corruption, torture—but they do nothing."

"What do I have to do," he said.

"Good," the man said. "This is a good attitude."

He looked at the cathedral. Tourists sat on the steps in the spring sunlight. The partner sat on a bench, looking across the avenue.

"When I was in prison," the man said, "God changed. Can you believe that? God changed. In my mind, there were certain government officials God would not help. The God I formed in my mind as a boy, maybe a six-year-old boy, that God—gray, stern, kindly man in the sky— he was gone. God became a deliverer, someone who would come down and snatch me out of my cell. I was crying to him. Then he became someone who didn't listen, who didn't perform the magic I was asking him to perform. It became very confusing and I recognized it as a lie."

"Yes," he said.

"So who can you pray to? Because you still have to pray, you can't simply not pray. Pray is what comes after begging. So you are stuck, trying to find someone new in the sky to pray-beg to," the man said. "It is not for men."

"Yes," he said.

"Your name is now Guzman. That is what we will call you and what you will call yourself," the man said.

"Guzman is dead," Guzman said.

"He is not dead, but he doesn't need his name anymore. He has a number. That's why we're giving his name to you," the man said.

"What do I do," Guzman said.

"Go to this address," the man said, handing Guzman a set of keys and a piece of paper. The address was on East 47th Street. "And do what we all do. Wait."

The building had no doorman, which was rare on this block. The rusted wrought iron fire escape stairs were on the front of the building. The apartment was small. Two rooms, a galley kitchen and bathroom. Wood floors. One step down into the living room. Windows opened onto the street and fire escape. One window in the back opened to the air shaft. An old flag of Peru hung on the wall of the living room. Guzman sat in the dark and stared at the flag. Listening to the city live through its night.

In the morning, Guzman gets up and takes his pills with a glass of water. He puts on his pants, shirt, and black shoes. Next to the bullets and knife on the nightstand, his cell phone is blinking.

Guzman walks onto the gray stone of Hepburn Park. The mirrored United Nations building sits on the opposite, far right corner. Guzman bought a cup of coffee and stared at the East River, as the steam rises from his cup. He turns back to look at the golden façade of the Trump building. The building reaches to heaven. Guzman crosses in front of it and walks back to the avenue. He walks along 48th Street, gated brownstones on his right. To anyone looking at him, Guzman is a New Yorker, perhaps on his way to work. Enjoying a coffee. No one can see him counting under his breath. Mid-block on 48th, the Consulate of Peru is on the opposite side of the street. Flying flags and with a black iron gate in the front. The seal of Peru on the brownstone, on the right side of the door. Guzman does not look. He walks, counting his steps. When he reaches the cross avenue, he goes left and returns to the apartment. He punches the number of steps into the cell phone.

Guzman repeats this the next day. This time, he drops a small lead weight, the size of a pen cap, on the opposite corner of 48th Street, before crossing. The weight is attached to fishing line, playing out of Guzman's pocket as he walks. When he is directly opposite the Consulate of Peru, the line runs out. Guzman continues to walk with his coffee. The fishing line snags on a car driving down the avenue and is gone forever.

The next morning, early, Guzman walks to East 45th Street. Between the avenues. He stands on the north side of the block.

The men are already there, having coffee.

"I want to show you this," the man says. "It is rare to see a secret in a city."

As the sun rises quickly, the light reflects off the mirrored front of the United Nations building. The clouds of spring pollen dance in the brilliant air, made gold by searing reflected rays. The whole front of the United Nations building is a burning rainbow, and the air is filled with luminous snow of flying pollen. It makes Guzman catch his breath.

"It is one of the most beautiful things I've ever seen," Guzman says.

The man nods. "I come here whenever I am in the city in the spring. It only happens for a couple days."

Guzman stares with wonder.

"This will be in your mind, if we are caught and go to prison," the man says. "This will always be with you. Remember we are giving you this."

That night, Guzman sits at the plaza next to his building, where there are tables, a waterfall and a jazz band. He drinks a single beer, as he listens to the music. The message on the cell phone is terse. Remeasure the distance and angle. No shot can be taken with the numbers provided. Do not forget your mother.

Guzman sobs. He has to come up with a new plan.

Guzman cannot remeasure the distance and angle correctly. The distance and angle is always the same. On his last pass, directly across the street from the Consulate of Peru, Guzman stops and kneels. Puts his coffee on the street. He is pretending to tie his shoe. With a piece of bright white chalk, Guzman draws a circle and small arrow, pointing straight at the consulate. He stands and continues walking.

That evening, Guzman sits at the plaza, listening to the jazz until they close it down.

In his apartment, the bathtub is filled with water. Silver duct tape holds a small vial with a rubber stopper under the water. On the tile floor next to the tub is square glass empty aquarium. In the sink is a large, clear, zip-lock plastic bag and a yellow and red water pistol. A pair of surgical gloves rests on the sink.

Guzman takes off his shirt. Puts on the surgical gloves and flips the empty aquarium upside down in the tub, directly over the vial. The top portion of the aquarium is filled with air, the bottom rests submerged on the ceramic tub. Guzman takes the water pistol and places it inside the aquarium. The plastic gun floats. He reaches under the aquarium and pops the red plastic stopper on the back of the gun. Watches as bubbles trail out of it as is water rushes in. When the gun is almost full, Guzman removes the duct tape from the vial. The vial floats to the surface. Above the water line, Guzman watches his own hands undo the rubber stopper and pour the weaponized powder contents of the vial into the water pistol. He recaps the vial and re-tapes it to the bottom of the tub. He caps the water pistol and coats the red plastic stopper with clear strong glue. Guzman takes the plastic ziplock bag and fills with water from the sink. Then, below the water line, he places the yellow and red plastic water pistol in the water filled ziplock bag and seals it tight. The bag with the pistol sinks to the bottom of the tub, under the aquarium. Guzman tapes the gloves to the bottom of the tub. There are plastic tongs on the floor of the bathroom. He will use them in the morning, to remove the bag containing the gun from the tub.

Early, on East 45th Street between the avenues, Guzman meets a woman and a little boy.

"What are you going to do with him all day," the woman says.

Guzman points at the incredible light reflected off the United Nations building, gold and white pollen burning the air. "I want to show him the city," he says.

The boy smiles. The boy is wearing a windbreaker, with jeans and sneakers. "Ice cream and Chinese food for lunch," the boy says.

"Not too much," the woman says. She bends down to kiss the boy. "Have him back by six," she says to Guzman.

Guzman takes the little boy's hand and they walk together toward Hepburn Park.

They sit on a bench in Hepburn Park, until the boy is done with his ice cream. Guzman talks and the little boy talks back. They are smiling. The man who is Guzman brings a ziplock plastic bag out of his jacket pocket. Inside is a yellow and red water pistol, surrounded with water. The boy is excited. They walk, hand in hand, to the corner of 48th Street. The man who is Guzman kneels down and draws a picture on his hand with his finger, pointing across the avenue, as the boy watches and nods. They look at a photo together. The man who is Guzman takes the water pistol out of the ziplock plastic bag and hands it to the boy. The boy crosses the avenue with the water pistol in his hand and looks back at the man who is Guzman, his father, who is urging him forward. A single drop of water drips from the pistol onto the pavement. The boy walks to mid-block, looks down at his feet and turns to face the consulate. The boy coughs a little. He crosses the street.

The boy is in front of consulate, with the water pistol, waiting.

LA/PARIS

SUBSONIC

THE DRY OCEAN OF SKY OVER LOS ANGELES IS THE clearest it has been in weeks. The most perfect blue. All the way to the airport, I'm thinking about this man, who's in the sky right now. The guy I'm picking up. He left France last night to arrive here today. He's a private investigator from Paris. On the phone, he asked me to get him a gun, so he wouldn't have to hassle with customs. To avoid the usual problems, he said.

I've got on jeans, black shoes and a black short sleeve shirt. Driving a rented Dodge Charger, gray. To impress the man from Paris. I'm watching everything pass. In the cars, we are all speeding on the road, but there are data transmissions, text messages. Everything has its own pace. Children in the back seat. I see it all in the bright afternoon. The earth is moving—the sky—too big for me to see. It is all in motion. All of our lives move at a hundred different speeds all at once. The man from Paris is coming, quickly, to intersect with someone else's life. A criminal's life.

The bullets in my gun don't move yet, and I hope they won't have to.

I'm a private detective in Los Angeles. The type that comes cheap. Digs around in things and finds a case. No license. If anyone asks, I'm just a consultant. My reputation is in the banking community. I track down money that's missing. Forgers, armed robbers. Smash-and-grab crews.

Once in a while, I track down a kid for someone. Or some girl whose come out to Los Angeles with stars in her eyes. I think the people in Paris talked to someone here in the banking industry.

The airport is alive with planes coming and going. Lines of people, walking. Running. Talking on phones. Even when I'm waiting for Air France to land, I feel like I'm moving.

He's on time. Handsome guy, well dressed in sport coat. His English is accented.

"Hello," he says. "I am Francis." He holds his hand out and I shake it.

"John," I say.

We pick up his bag. He would like some coffee, maybe a meal. Sure, I say, and we are driving.

Over the late lunch is when it comes.

"Did you get the gun?" he says.

"No," I say.

He shakes his head. "This is no good."

"We'll have to make due," I say.

"This changes my plans," he says. He eats the beautiful food and drinks a glass of wine. I do the same. As the other diners and wait staff move around the restaurant, in a dance we've all seen before.

The man we're looking for—the criminal—is renting a house on the beach. My friend who works with me—Ray—is at the beach house, holding the man in the house. Ray goes for a walk when Francis and I arrive. It is difficult to understand what the man did. Somehow, he got hold of serial numbers of bills that were supposed to be distributed during the war in Iraq. Bills that supposedly went missing. But no one knew that at the time. He forged US currency with the serial numbers. Later, some of the money was recovered. Somehow, through his criminal activities, a portion of it ended up in a bank in Paris. And French auditors noticed. All of that past movement and action brings us to today. He is sitting on the upstairs bed, smoking a cigarette and talking.

He is claiming to us that he is innocent. It is almost painful. He is an arms dealer, among other things—a known criminal. In Paris, there are other criminals testifying against him even as he talks about his innocence.

"Remember," he says. "You are dust." He is sitting on the bed.

"That may be," Francis says back to him, "but we are in charge now. You will do the remembering." Francis hits him, rocks him off the bed onto the floor. I have to grab Francis, restrain him. He goes downstairs, to ice his hand and wrist. The criminal is bleeding from the mouth and nose. I prop him up on the bed.

"He can't hit me," he says.

"Give me your gun," Francis calls up from the kitchen. I can hear him talking to Ray in the kitchen, asking for Ray's pistol.

"He's serious," I say to the criminal. We look at each other for a minute. I shrug.

"Fine," the criminal says. "I want to live."

"Smart," I say.

Francis is coming up the steps. He has some ice wrapped in a towel on his right hand.

"He'll cooperate," I say.

Francis slows. He looks at me and then at the criminal. "Take him to the marshal's" he says. "They can transport him to Paris."

We secure the criminal in Ray's car and watch them drive off. Then I drive Francis to his hotel and watch him walk into the building.

The blue sky repeats itself. Absolute clear beauty. We are at a sidewalk café, drinking coffee. Watching the world pass by. Men and women walk in and out of the café. Francis is talking.

"You know, there is something I should tell you," he says.

"Yes," I say.

"It is about that man."

"Yes."

"I know that you might think it strange that I came all the way from Paris to track him down." He sips his coffee. "And that I attacked him."

"Maybe," I say. "You are very dedicated."

"This is true. But the case was very personal for me."

"How so?"

He sipped his coffee. He looked around for a minute, as if to light a cigarette. "This is Los Angeles," he says. "I better not smoke."

"It's not allowed," I say.

"Did you ever smoke?" he says.

"Yes," I say. "But it was easy to quit."

"Then you didn't really smoke," he says.

"What were you saying?" I ask. "About the man."

"Oh," he says. "Some years ago, before he was who he is now, he knew my sister."

"Yes," I say.

"She was a young girl, very beautiful. Her modeling career was just starting."

I nod.

"Anyway, he abused her. Hit her. For several years. And before I could get hold of him, before I could become who I am, he was gone."

I nod again. "You tracked him for all this time?"

"There is not a day in my life as an investigator that I have not looked for him. All of his movements—from where he slept and what he ate, to who he knew and associated with—I knew his movements. And I am sure he knew some of mine, absolutely certain of it."

We drive to the airport. The worlds of the other cars were as if in glass balls—in view, but a mystery, the sight of people moving with no sound. Beautiful women, handsome men, gliding along. Going in the same direction and a million different directions at once. The planes climb into the air, as others descend.

"You must come to Paris," Francis says.

"I am sure that I will."

"I will put in a word with my boss and he will have you over to give a key deposition in this case."

I watch him get on his plane.

The next month, an envelope was in my mailbox. A round-trip ticket and a check for €2400. Now I was the man in the plane. Moving, subsonic, through the blue, over the ocean. To Paris.

CITY OF LIGHT

NOW I AM THE MAN IN THE JUNE SKY.

LAX is a place far behind me and as the plane lands at Charles De Gaulle, I think about how much I don't know. The language passes me by and as I make my way through the hustle of the airport, I have the impending sense of a looming, giant mistake. I should have put Francis off, said I couldn't come to be deposed. I have no business being here in Paris.

After the baggage is sorted, I am in a car on the way to the address Francis has given me. The driver speaks perfect English and is full of stories. He tells me how his wife, whom he loved, has become unlovable. She is a burden to him here in Paris. Everything is so expensive and she wants everything and he wishes she would return to Serbia. He has three children, so he has three jobs. One job for each child, I offer. He makes a sound that isn't a laugh. Yes, he says. When I ask him the names of his children, he fades. Look, he says. There is the Eiffel Tower. I was being lied to. There is no formerly beautiful Serbian nag-wife, no three children. This is the story he has invented to get better tips from customers. He begins to talk about food and the weather, as if the conversation about his wife and children never happened. He starts to talk about religion. Let's ride in silence, I say. He looks at me in the mirror, as Paris traffic circles all around us in the bright light, as the filthy beauty of the city comes fully to life. Turning, braking, moving, past all the buildings until a stop in front of the address. I don't say a word as I get out and walk away.

I text Francis and he is at the door, ushering me into his building. We walk up to the second floor.

"This is both my office and apartment," he says. "Thank you for coming."

We sit a small conference table and he brings out some water, wine, cheese, charcuterie, olives, wrapped grape leaves. Pate, bread, crackers. He sits across from me as we drink the Pinot.

"How is this deposition going to work," I say.

He takes a Manila envelope from a low shelf behind him and pushes it across the table toward me. I look into the open end. There are two stacks of US cash inside. I pat the envelope and look back at him.

"Things have changed," he says. "We would like you not to testify."

"Who is we," I say.

"Myself," he says. He shrugs. "Plans have changed." Outside, cars go past and a siren comes close and continues on. Distant.

"What happened," I say.

Francis nods. "These are bad people," he says. "Enjoy yourself here, I'll take you out and we'll see Paris and then return to Los Angeles and forget all of this." He gestures at the Manila envelope. "A quarter of a million dollars to forget something. It seems fair. Do you agree?"

"I'm not really sure what I'm agreeing to yet," I say. I taste the wine. "What happened to the case?"

"The man you tracked in Los Angeles, that I came from France to apprehend, he is long gone. Vanished. And the prosecutor here in Paris, who was going to make the international case, he is gone. So last week, as I'm sitting here, my sister is at the door. I hadn't seen her in a year. You remember that she had known the man I tracked to Los Angeles, that he had beaten her, years ago." Francis takes a drink of wine.

"Yes," I say. "I remember."

"I let my sister up and she gives me all this money—all US cash. She is being used by them, to get to me. If I don't cooperate, if you don't cooperate—they will kill her. Then they will kill us. They have started a new gang, a new crime syndicate and that man I tracked to Los Angeles is the brain. My sister left in tears, begging me."

He eats some bread and cheese. An olive. I do the same.

"You could have sent me an email," I say. "You could have phoned."

Francis nods. "I feared an email or call would have made you curious and suspicious. And you are good at what you do—you tracked him down in Los Angeles no problem. I was afraid you would begin to investigate." He points at the envelope. "A face-to-face talk and some money might convince you not to."

"Who are these people?" I say. "What's to say they won't kill us anyway?"

"They call themselves Opinel, after the French folding knife. More commonly they use the phrase Number Twelve, which refers to the largest Opinel knife. Big enough to kill a man, but fold it and it slips right into your pocket. Unseen. Sometimes they use The Crowned Hand as a symbol." He drank some water and another sip of wine. "They are gypsies. French Travellers. But they have gone from stealing chickens to being an international syndicate, based in France." He shrugs. "Very bad people."

I nod. "What about your sister?" I say.

He puts his hands on the table and lets out a big breath. "I want to help her. It seems impossible, but I want to help her." He shakes his head. "I simply don't know how to do that yet." He stands up and walks away for a minute and I hear a door open and close. A toilet. Water running. He returns.

"So what would you like to see in Paris?" He indicates the envelope. "Are we agreed? About the forgetting?"

I need the money. My apartment in Los Feliz is steep and clients are spotty. This could float things for a while. I nod.

"I was nervous you would say no," Francis says.

I shrug. "I live in the real world," I say. "Like you."

"I hoped that was true," Francis says.

"Let's see Paris tonight," I say. "Give me a minute on my phone and I'll change return ticket to late tomorrow or the next day. Whatever I can find."

"That's fine," Francis says.

I managed to get a return flight for the next day and we went out. To restaurants, in the beauty of the neighborhood and the city. Drinking, eating. We laughed and told stories about the past. Francis thanked me for coming. I said it was nothing. We listened to music, went to a club. Drank more. Saw the women and men of Paris, so alive and moving.

As a million cars flew on the streets. It was well after midnight when we walked back to the apartment, up to the second floor.

There are two men seated at the table, drinking wine, when we enter. They nod at Francis.

"Sit down," the one man says to me.

There are no sharp knives on the table; nothing that could be used as a weapon. So I sit down.

"John," the one man says to me. "You work for us now."

"You accepted payment, in fact stolen funds, from a foreign agent," he says. "That's ten years in French prison."

"Not to mention having your US passport revoked, then serving twenty years in US prison when they extradite you back after you've finished your sentence here," the other man says.

"Who are you," I say.

The larger man speaks. "You can call me Alpha." He points at the other man. "And call him Beta." He takes a drink of wine. "We're with the DGSE—the French secret police."

"Yeah," I say. I'd had a fair amount to drink. "I don't work for anybody."

"Well, you may want to rethink that, because you can't get home right now," Beta said. "Check your phone."

I look at my phone. I have emails indicating the ticket I had purchased had been canceled. When I tried to go into my travel app, the app won't open.

"What's this about," I say.

"You and Francis lucked out in Los Angeles," Alpha says. "We'd been trying to locate the brain of The Crowned Hand for over a year. Somehow you managed it. And brought him back to France, which is even more astounding. He lasted in custody about an hour, when he vanished."

Beta takes over the story. "We have to cut off the head of that gang. No matter what it takes. We got Francis to get you to come over here, because they know what both of you look like and if they think you're looking for them, they'll come out of the woodwork to kill you."

"I'm supposed to go around looking for them, but really I'm your decoy," I say.

"Under the guise of looking for his sister," Alpha says, nodding at Francis. "They'll be watching you while we're watching you. And when they come out, we'll arrest them."

"How come you don't have some secret agents do this," I say.

"Opinel is everywhere," Beta says. "We can't trust our own field agents."

"I'm not doing this," I say.

Alpha backhands me a lot faster than I thought he could move and I am on the floor, bleeding from my mouth and slightly from my one ear. I am seeing stars. He already has a pistol out and I feel the cold metal of the barrel on my temple, pressing.

"Grande puissance," Alpha says. "The brand-new Browning Hi-Power. I have an old one too, which I treasure. You would be my first kill with this new one. Are you going to relax and accept the future or is this your end?"

I think of everything. All of my life surges through me, as if to tell me what it would be like if all of that was missing. Gone, with a bullet through my skull, blood leaking onto the floor and never coming back. I remember something my father had said to me. Patience will take you where emotions cannot. If I am patient, I might gain enough time to live to see another day. And another.

"I'm sorry," Francis says. "They already had me. They made me bring you here."

Alpha takes the Browning off my head and I right my chair and sit down. "Do you really have a sister?" I say to Francis.

"Yes," Francis says. "But the DGSE provided the US cash. To entrap you and make you work for them."

"Entrap is a nasty word," Beta says. "You're dirty. If it wasn't this, it would have been something else."

"I guess I'll be in Paris for a while," I say.

"It could go fast, it could go slow," Alpha says. "How good are you at finding people?"

I nod. Drink some wine from the bottle. Drain it in one long drag. "I'm the fucking best," I say.

"Let's just see if you can stay alive long enough for us to arrest them," Alpha says.

"The fucking best," I say. "The best of the worst."

As all of Paris moves outside, the lights, the people, June itself and my life taking a direction that doesn't exist in a city I don't know.

EIGHT BALL

THAT AUGUST, AS SOON AS THE WORD CAME THAT Ackerly had been spotted in Texas, we moved fast. Jimmy Work and I drove my blue pickup truck the three days from New York to El Paso— my brother was already there, waiting out the blistering Texas heat inside a diner north of the city. Jimmy Work was glad to be on the road. He'd been doing time at McNeil, the federal joint in Puget Sound, for about seven years. He didn't say much during the ride, just looked out the window and enjoyed the highway view and the sky. We met my brother at the diner.

"Are you sure it's him?" I asked. The three of us were sitting in a red fake leather plastic booth, eating egg breakfasts with coffee and breathing cool conditioned air.

"I'm sure," my brother said, nodding. "I checked it out myself." He took a swallow of coffee. "He's hustling pool games down at the Exchange Hotel."

"It makes sense," I said, pointing my chin at the diner windows and further toward El Paso itself. "I think he's originally from here."

We finished and I paid and tipped and the three of us walked across the hot parking lot and got into my brother's full-sized black Ford Bronco. The air above the macadam shimmered with heat demons. Jimmy Work climbed into the backseat and checked the gun, a pump-action three-oh-eight—short-barreled, with a black, Parkerized finish that, from a distance, you might mistake for a shotgun.

My brother was sitting behind the wheel. "What's he calling himself?" I asked.

"Al," my brother said. "He says he's Al Broughton from back east. I heard him say that to a couple guys before he won their money."

"Well if he can't pay me when we get there, he's all done," I said.

There was a metallic snap from the backseat as Jimmy Work clipped the three-shell magazine to the underside of the three-oh-eight. "He'll pay," he said. "One way or another." Jimmy Work pulled a pack of Camels out of his shirt pocket, shook one loose, lit it and took a drag. He rested the rifle on the seat next to him. He talked around the cigarette. "I forgot Texas was this hot," he said. He wiped his brow with a red kerchief and stuck it in his back pocket. "Hotter than the steam off my piss," he finished. His denim work shirt was soaked through with sweat. "Did I ever tell you about Bob Luce?" he asked me.

"No," I shook my head. "You didn't." My brother turned to look at us.

Jimmy Work nodded. "Bob Luce was the first guy from Texas I ever knew. Don't mess with Texas was about the first thing he ever said to me. He was a big guy, maybe six nine, close to three hundred pounds. He was at McNeil."

My brother started the truck and flipped on the air conditioning.

Jimmy Work talked. It was as if he wasn't in the back of that Ford anymore.

"Right next to McNeil was another small island. After I'd been there about two years, the feds built another smaller facility on the other island. A couple of us got transferred over—they took us there shackled and cuffed in a boat—and Luce was one of us.

"The smaller joint they called the island workhouse and it was less restrictive, lower security. We'd go out and cut trees and dig holes—it was all fenced in and guarded and where the hell were we going to go?" He took a long drag off his cigarette and kept on.

"Luce, he looks over to the shore of the backside of the peninsula and see's Indians fishing. You could tell they were Indians because their trucks didn't have plates and they looked dark, with long black hair, just like Indians. There must have been a reservation there. Usually there were at least ten Indians, fishing and drinking beer.

"Luce starts to yell over, every day. He's a big guy, loudmouthed, so his voice carries—'Hey Chiefy' he yells over one day. 'I want to scalp your squaw.'

"He keeps it up, every day. Maybe half an hour a day. 'Hey Big Chief' and 'Hey Red Man!' And the Indians on the shore would give him the finger, but they never yelled back.

"He kept it up right through the fall into the winter. Snow came and one of the guards told Luce to shovel off the basketball court. Luce separated off from the rest of us, he went over to the court area to shovel. There was this crack!" Jimmy Work smacked his hands together. "Luce fell down and the snow was all bloody around him. Those Indians blew the back of his head off with a high-powered rifle. We scrambled around for a minute and got back inside the facility. No other shots came." He looked at me and my brother. "I don't think they looked too hard for who did it," he said. It was the most I heard him talk. Ever.

"Can you blame them?" my brother said.

"No, no," Jimmy Work said. "People get what they deserve."

"What did you miss most while you were in?" I said.

"I thought I missed being out," Jimmy Work said. "But it all seems the same to me now."

"Let's go," I motioned my brother.

Jimmy Work ended up slamming the truck door closed on Ackerly's head before it became clear that we were serious, not just pool players who would fold up and fade away. Jimmy Work grabbed Ackerly in a headlock, took him kicking and yelling through the back door, into a paved alley behind the Exchange Hotel. My brother opened the door on the big Bronco and Jimmy Work shoved Ackerly headfirst onto the driver's seat, then yanked him back a little by the seat of his jeans and his belt and slammed that door for all he was worth. Akerly's knees buckled, his legs went soft. Jimmy Work slammed the door again and then again, harder. Ackerly's voice was muffled, because he was screaming into the truck, so it didn't sound as loud as you might think. Then Jimmy Work hauled Ackerly out onto the black top. Blood was all over Ackerly's head and he was in a fog.

"It's in my trunk," he said. He weakly flipped a set of keys out of his pocket. My brother went over and picked them up. "The Barracuda out front," Ackerly finished.

We stood there while my brother walked down the alley toward the street. Ackerly sat on his ass bleeding. My brother came back down the alley with a green gym bag and gave us the thumbs up.

Fast, Jimmy Work reached into the backseat of the Bronco and came out with the gun. He brought it up to his shoulder and drew a bead on Ackerly's left leg, the upper thigh. Jimmy Work took two steps forward and fired and Ackerly rolled around on the ground. Then he passed out. I watched Jimmy Work's eyes as he did it all and if he blinked or looked away, I didn't see it. He wanted to leave a reminder, a warning for others. People don't limp for no reason and especially around a pool hall or a bar—you notice those things, if money's involved.

ACES BEAT KINGS

OUTSIDE MY BEDROOM WINDOW, IT IS BITTER DARK AND the snow is falling. Middle of February and deep into New Hampshire winter that never ends. The clock shows 4 a.m. I sit on the edge of my bed, sweating. Every night, at four a.m., I wake up from a nightmare. Four a.m. is the most recorded time of death in the world. People go to sleep and never wake. Their lives end as they lay dreaming and they stay in eternal darkness. Maybe everyone that has horrible dreams goes through a cycle of increasingly terrible visions, until their hearts give out, aneurysms burst and maybe that cycle culminates collectively at 4 a.m. Maybe the vivid horror of the dreams drives life away, and death comes in, providing the peace and calm that life never can. Life generates dreams, makes a second life happen in the sleeping mind. A second life that intrudes and feeds off the first.

This time, my dream was about a friend from childhood—Marty DeMeo, lived a few doors down from me where I grew up—in the upstate New York hamlet of Cementon, two hours north of Manhattan on the Hudson River—Marty was cut in half from a double-barrel, over-and-under shotgun blast as his father mistakenly handed him the loaded rifle from the trunk of their car, parked in their own driveway after duck hunting. Five years later, Mister DeMeo hooked a hose up to the tailpipe of his running car, sat in the driver's seat and sucked on the hose, killing himself in his own garage. He missed Marty and felt guilty. Thirty years later, Marty's mother took the same shotgun, tried to put her mouth over the barrels, broke a tooth, must have found she couldn't reach the trigger, set the loaded gun in the corner and stepped away, presumably to get a wire coat hanger to rig up a trigger pull. She did not apply the safety as she stepped away. The rifle fell and discharged, blowing off her right leg at the hip and wounding much of her lower back. She lived alone, in their old house, and it was about a month later that her sister took the train up from Manhattan and found Marty's mother—her sister—blown to pieces, dead on the floor, covered with dried blood. In my nightmare, I was a doctor and they brought the three bodies to me and wanted me to sew them together, to make one living being, that could walk and talk and be alive—only I wasn't a very good doctor and the monstrosity I created wouldn't come to life. It just lay on the operating table, moaning and gasping for breath.

I go downstairs, into the small kitchen of my rented house, to make some coffee and try to shake it off. I have to drive north to Haverhill, New Hampshire, around noon. To meet two guys coming down from Canada with five pounds of ecstasy and some MDMA, along with ten pounds of phenylacetone, so I can start my meth cook. I have all the rest of the precursor chemicals and titrates hidden in my basement. I normally set my cook up in the garage, to help vent the fumes and so if the thing exploded violently, I might be able to prevent the house from catching fire. If everything went well, I'd be ready to sell it all off in a week. I sipped my coffee and watched darkness and the snow.

The snow is still falling at five a.m. when the officers came to get me. There is no blaze of glory. Three cars pull up, uniforms get out, guns drawn.

They handcuffed me, put the leg shackles on and stuffed me into the back seat of a state police cruiser. We drove north and east through the snow, skirting the White Mountains. Clouds covered the sky as we pulled up to the Federal Correctional Institute near Berlin, New Hampshire. It is two facilities—the large, medium security penitentiary and the much smaller, maximum facility. We pull through two gated fences, next to the maximum.

My friend Michael is lying naked in the snow. He was doing three to eight at FCI Berlin. He looks so much different. The back of his head has been blown off, so he no longer has ears. His blood is outside of his body, scattered all around him against the white of the snow. He looks frozen to me. The officers take me inside and cuff me to a table. An administrative officer comes in, holding a letter with my handwriting on it.

"We found this letter in his things, in his cell," the administrative officer says. "Former inmate Michael Bennet. Do you know him, did you correspond with him?"

I shrug.

He points at the letter. "Is that you—JT? Is that what they call you? Your name is John Thorn."

"I don't know what you're talking about," I say.

"I think you do," he says. "I think you do know what I'm talking about." He calls out to the guard. "Bring Frederic in here," he says.

"Hello," Frederic says. He wears his hair in a crew cut. He's smoking a cigarette. Short, muscular build, with thick hands. Dark brown jacket, dark pants, black work boots. "I am Frederic MacMillan. We're going to talk now."

"I doubt that," I say.

He hits me in the face. Probably not as hard as he could. Hard enough to make my lips bleed. My head rings. I see floaters.

"Do you know what the difference between your death and mine will be," Frederic says.

"No," I say. I spit a little blood.

"At my funeral, there will be medals placed at my grave. Flags lowered out of respect. Rifles fired as a salute. My wife will sob. My mistress will sob. And I will be proclaimed as having been justice in the great Province of Quebec. All of Montreal will be in mourning and glasses will be raised and my name will be inscribed in stone. And the following year, they will celebrate my greatness on the anniversary of my passing." He takes a drag off his cigarette. "You will evolve from a missing person to a cadaver dog discovery in the woods, two years after you died. Some remains in an evidence bag and a two-sentence note in the newspaper about human bones and the police are looking into it. And no one wants to find you, so the file will be shuffled and stacked and you will become deader. A dead leaf—bright for a season, falling from the tree, drifting on the wind, dead by the time you hit the ground."

I nod.

"So you tried to warn your friend about Operation Wendigo," Frederic says.

I shake my head. "I don't know what that is."

Frederic points to the letter in my handwriting. "It says here—Beware The Wendigo. Quebec police have a border-jumping unit in the woods. Trust nothing. Will say more when I see you. Think of ninety times seven minus the four is danger. Aces beat kings. JT."

I shrug.

"Ninety times seven is six hundred thirty—six thirty, in terms of hours. Minus four hours is two thirty. We had set up a meeting at the house for two thirty in the morning—which the letter says 'is danger'.

No one showed up at the meeting. So your message must have been passed on. What is 'aces beat kings'." He stares at me.

I sit there.

"What does 'aces beat kings' mean," Frederic repeats.

I sit there.

"Well, if you won't tell me, I will tell you what the Wendigo is. The Wendigo is a beast, a creature of the north woods. It is a cannibal. It eats, but is always hungry. It is a way of life, for some. In Quebec, in Montreal, we police ourselves—we don't have the Royal Mounties. We don't allow them in the province. So when the drugs in Montreal became a problem, we came up with our own solution. Lure the drug dealers over the border, into New Hampshire. Into abandoned houses and farms. And kill as many of them as we could. Make it look like there had been a dispute with someone they had met in the US. As if their Wendigo lifestyle had eaten them. I coined the Operation Wendigo name myself."

I sit there.

Frederic gestures around, at the prison. "Sometimes, people work with us here, in the great Northeast Kingdom," he says. "So now, you will work for us."

"I won't do it," I say.

He whispers to me. "Then lie down in the snow outside next to your scumbag friend so we can shoot you too," he says.

I sit there.

He draws his pistol and racks the slide. Puts the cool barrel on my forehead. "You'll be dead before you hear the sound of the shot," he says.

"I'll do it," I say.

"Yes?" Frederic says.

"Yes," I say.

"Oh," Frederic says. "I love yes." He holsters his pistol. "Wonderful choice." He stands and hits me as hard as he can and I fall over onto the concrete floor, taking the chair with me. "You will stay here tonight," he says. "Tomorrow we will begin working."

I know it's four a.m. when I sit up in the holding cell.

In my dream, I was sixteen and sleeping. In my dream, I awoke when I felt a piece of paper under my green plastic jail pillow. I pull the piece of paper out. It was a note from Alvin, the kid who occupied the same bed before I was assigned to it at the detention house in Buffalo. Earlier that day, Alvin had been found hanging in the basement. He had put the seat of his jeans over a beam in the basement and hung himself by tying the pant legs around his own neck and jumping off the washing machine. He had tied a plastic bag over his head, in case the jeans didn't work. His note read "Tell Mom and Sister I love them. Tell Dad I don't. Tell Grandma I love her. Tell Aunt Heidi I don't. Tell them all I can't take it." He had signed his name.

I was nervous. Should I take the piece of paper downstairs. No one was supposed to leave their room at night. It was against house rules. I walked into the dark hallway. I got to the landing and top step and called out "Prospect on the stairs." The house manager motioned for me to come down into the main house. He took the note from me, as the other house staff surrounded me.

"Why didn't you bring us this right away?" the house manager said.

"I did," I said. "I just found it."

"Maybe someone killed him and fabricated this note and you're in on it," the house manager said.

"That's insane," I said.

"Lock him in the outer room," the house manager said to the staff. And five staff carried me outside, behind the house, to the trailer that served as the outer room. The light was on inside the trailer and they locked the door behind me.

There was Alvin, laying on the couch. His face was slightly blue and his neck was severely bruised. The detention house was waiting for his body to be picked up by the cops—his family wouldn't be allowed to do it, no family could come into the detention house and the department of corrections was understaffed, so it had to be the cops for the body pickup—and the staff made me sit with his body all the rest of that next day into the night. I just sat there staring at him. I don't know how long I'd been in the trailer when there was an awful noise from inside Alvin, a loud groan and his mouth opened to release air that smelled and his one arm shook and moved.

I'm awake in the holding cell when the officers come and take me through the concrete halls, outside to Frederic. Michael's body is gone and new snow covers the spot where he was. The officers cuff me and put me in the back seat of Frederic's four-door Jeep. He begins to drive and I know the way. He is headed to Montreal. We cross the border at the Pittsburg, New Hampshire—Chartierville, Quebec border station, where Frederic shows his badge and papers identifying him as a Quebec detective. No one asks who I am. The road signs are in French and the distance given in kilometers, as we head for Montreal.

Frederic pulls out a phone as he drives and holds it back towards me, so I can speak into it. "I am going to dial a number. These are people you know—Martan and that gypsy piece of shit Hudz—have them meet you at Atwater Market. Tell them you have twenty thousand US dollars and want to do a deal. But you only have half the money on you—they have to come meet you tomorrow to pick up the rest. The address is Sixty-two Meadow View Drive, Pittsburg, New Hampshire. It's a log cabin. They can drive across the top of Vermont to reenter."

"They won't do that," I say.

"Make them do it," Frederic says.

"What if I can't," I say.

"Then I will make you stop breathing," he says. Frederic dials the phone.

The phone is ringing and I recognize Martan's voice. "Yes."

"Martan, it's John," I say.

"This is good," Martan says. "You were a no-show in Haverhill yesterday."

"Too much storm," I say. "I am in Montreal right now, headed to Atwater Market. I have 20K."

"Same order as yesterday?" Martan asks.

"Same," I say.

"Go to the butcher stall where Hudz's brother works. He will give you a box of meat," Martan says.

"Okay," I say. "But I only have half on me."

"Fuck, John, what the fuck," Martan says. He is talking to someone in the background. I hear Hudz's accent. "Fucking asshole," Hudz says. Martan gets back on. "We need the whole thing."

"I didn't bring it all across in case I got stopped," I say. "You come across tomorrow—you and Hudz—and get it from me."

"Where," Martan says.

I say the address Frederic has given me. "Sixty-two Meadow View Drive, Pittsburg, New Hampshire. It's a log cabin. Then you can drive across the top of Vermont and re-enter there."

Silence. "Make the pick up at Atwater Market from Hudz' brother. If that goes smooth, see you tomorrow." Martan clicks off.

We enter Montreal on the highway and drive to Little Burgundy, where I can see the art deco tower of Atwater Market from the street. We pull into the parking lot and Frederic gives me an envelope—ten thousand dollars—and slowly, I walk inside the massive building, as shoppers go past, with bags and carts, filled with the best produce and meat and fish Montreal has to offer. On the second floor, I walk past the vendor's counters and stalls, lining both sides of the great hall. All the meat and sausage under glass—cut, prepared, ready—and I stop at the counter where Hudz' brother works. He looks like Hudz—half gypsy, half Ukrainian, wearing a hair net and gloves and a bloody white butcher's coat—and he puts a large cardboard box on the counter. When I lay down the envelope, it vanishes into his butcher's coat and he goes back to cutting meat, as if I am a real customer who just received my order and he is a real butcher, with a job to do.

I carry the box outside to the Jeep, where Frederic is waiting. We drive a block, to the Super C, and he stops the Jeep, gets out to open the box on the passenger's seat. Under two cuts of meat, there are other wrapped packages. Frederic pulls a knife out of his pocket, flips the blade and slices the butcher's paper. Pills—ecstasy, mostly—and several packages of phenylacetone. There is another plain clothes car in the Super C parking lot and two men come over to Frederic and take the box with them. One of the men walks back to the Jeep, with two long rifle cases, which he puts in the rear of the Jeep. He sits in the passenger seat, with a black ski cap on and a gray jacket, sipping a cup of coffee.

"This is Dennis," Frederic says to me. "He's coming with us." He turns to Dennis. "And this is John the informant."

"Hello, John," Dennis says.

We get back on the highway and follow the same route, to the Chartierville-Pittsburg crossing. The snow has stopped and it's getting dark as Frederic drives the Jeep down a long, plowed tree-lined driveway and up a slope and stops in front of a log cabin, invisible from the road.

"Sixty-two Meadow View Drive, Pittsburg, New Hampshire," Frederic says. He and Dennis get out and unload the rifles. They put a blanket around me in the back seat and lock the doors of the Jeep— there are no rear interior door handles. It's black as Dennis vanishes into the woods with a blunt, Honey Badger semiautomatic rifle and I can see Frederic has started a fire inside the log cabin. My breath is fogging the windows of the Jeep as I drift off to sleep.

Sitting here in the snow. Watching the cabin through the dark. I smell wood smoke and I know it's four a.m., because I'm awake.

In my dream, I'm five years old and locked in the small, cinder block ice house. Each of the men in the neighborhood had shot a deer that week and six deer were hung inside the ice house, to let the blood drain. They were going to save money by having the game butcher come and butcher all the deer at once. For that day and night, all I could do was sit inside the ice house—the smell was awful, I could hear the blood dripping. Brushing up against stiff fur. An eye peering out of the black. Flies buzzing in the dark. The men had accused me of opening the door to the icehouse while I was outside playing and leaving it open. This had let flies get on the deer and now there were maggots. The money they were going to save was gone, due to a careless five-year-old boy. Without telling my parents, one of the men locked me in the ice house. No one found me for a day and a half. I am breathing so fast, my ribs hurt from own heart.

I watch the cabin.

Maybe death was coming out of me. I was generating it. Maybe that's what happens to everyone. We're seeing it backward. We think that people and things die independently of us, but they don't. The person generating the death looks at them and then they die. Each of us has a certain number of deaths inside us. Almost everyone we see will die before we do. Have we done that to them, in some way. We had a hand in it. All the animals I've ever known are dead. Many of the people. I was part of it all. We live as we dream. Alone. Trapped inside our life, to be tortured by our dream life. Unable to get out or stop the cycle.

The snow is still falling here. It should be getting lighter outside, but it isn't. It's getting darker.

It is too late. And I have failed to live.

There is a man coming out of the woods. It's Martan, dragging Dennis' body. Holding Dennis's Honey Badger rifle. Hudz is behind him and now they're firing through the cabin windows at Frederic, who is firing back and the gunshots echo into the closed Jeep. Hudz empties a clip into a cabin window and no more shots come from the cabin. Hudz and Martan approach the Jeep. Hudz is tapping on the passenger's side rear window with the barrel of his pistol. Metal on glass. Tink tink tink. He is speaking now. I hear him through the glass, with his heavy accent.

"Aces beat kings," Hudz says.

LOS MILLONARIOS

THE LATE JANUARY STORM SETTLED OVER THE CANADIAN Maritimes for a few days, then slowly drifted west to Moncton and Fredrickton, covering the weekend with snow and freezing rain. Midnight Monday, it moved across the Eastern Maine border. Right after lunch, snow started to fall again in Bangor and up north. To where I was working, a couple miles outside of Lincoln.

Old Henry Warner, the shift foreman, walked around and told us they were closing the pulp mill early, because of an accident in the loading yard. My brother and I saw the ambulance in the parking lot as we walked to my truck.

"Who was it?" my brother asked.

"Pete Bartell," Henry said. He was wearing a blaze orange safety ski hat, work jacket and coveralls. Brown steel-toed thermal work boots.

"What happened?" my brother asked.

"I don't know," Henry said. He pointed his chin at the group of illegals huddled together, smoking, near the chain link fence entrance to the yard. "Ask them." He spit. "They come up from Portland. I don't even know how they get up here. Some of them have never even seen snow before."

"How bad was Pete hurt?" I said.

"As bad as you can get," Henry said. He watched the ambulance as it sped out of the parking lot. "No lights, no sirens. It's just a white hearse, is all it is."

We stood there for a minute as the snow came down and Henry looked at my brother.

"You guys were friends with Pete, right?" Henry said.

My brother nodded and shrugged. "Sure. I knew him a little."

I nodded too.

"With this snow, we'll be plowing the lot all day and his truck is just going to get in the way. Can you drive it to his brother's house? He lived across the street from his brother Dave," Henry said. "I think he leaves his keys in it."

My brother thought for a minute. "Sure," he said. "I'll do it. I know where he lives."

"Thanks," Henry said. "I'm sure that would help Dave a lot. He's going to have enough to deal with."

"You got a brother?" I asked Henry.

"Yes," he said. He took a cigarette out of a pack from his jacket pocket and lit it.

"Where is he?" I said.

"In a halfway house in Oklahoma," Henry said. He took a drag on the cigarette.

"How'd he get there?" I said.

"Don't ask," Henry said. He turned to my brother. "Thanks for doing this."

"Sure thing," my brother said.

My brother climbed into Pete's old pickup, gave a thumb's up that he had the keys, and followed me out of the mill parking lot. It was beyond strange to have my brother behind me driving Pete's truck. We drove about twenty minutes. Out of town and into the woods. The snow was coming down. We turned down the dead-end dirt road where Pete had lived, in a converted barn across from his older brother Dave's trailer. It looked like Pete was behind me the whole way.

When we drove up, it must have fooled the dog too. The big husky shepherd mix—Pete's dog—ran around and then went after my brother when he started to get out.

Dave was sitting on his porch and called the dog off. "What's this?" he said, pointing at the truck. "Where's Pete?" Dave walked off the porch toward us.

"There was an accident at the mill," I said.

Dave squatted like a catcher, sitting on his heels, looking down at the dirty snow and ice of his dooryard. Finally, he stood. There were tears on his face. He reached out and shook my brother's hand. Then he shook my hand.

"I'm sorry," I said.

Dave nodded. "Why don't you leave me alone for about half an hour, okay? Go get some beer and sandwiches. You got money?"

"I've got it," I said.

"I don't care what kind of beer, but get it in bottles. I hate cans," he said.

"Okay," I said. "Do you want any hard liquor?"

Dave pointed toward the trailer. "Thanks," he said. "I got some inside and that's where I'm headed." He walked back toward his porch.

My brother got into my truck and we drove to the store. They had twelve packs of bottles in the cold case and my brother grabbed one.

When we got back, Dave was there with the dog. The dog was running circles are Pete's truck in the snow.

He took the bottle of beer and the sandwich I gave him. He set his bottle of beer on the porch railing and started to unwrap the sandwich. He watched the dog—still running circles—as he ate. He took a swallow of beer and set the bottle back on the porch rail. "I can't have this," he said. He stepped into the trailer and came out carrying a short-barrel guide gun, a bolt-action magnum. "Get hold of him," he said.

I tried and the dog bit through my sleeve.

"Oh for Christ's sake," he said. "Hit him with something."

Neither of us moved.

Dave raised his voice. "Hit him. I'm putting him down, so hit him with something."

My brother pulled a four-foot piece of stiff steel electrical conduit out of the truck. It was silver and hollow and whistled as he swung it. He hit the dog three times. The two other dogs ran behind the trailer. Pete's dog lay in the snow, unable to move.

Dave drew the bolt back, took a round out of his pocket and slid the bolt home. He took two quick steps up to the dog, bent slightly as he put the short barrel near the dog's head and pulled the trigger. The dog's head jumped off the snow and blood and dirt flew out from underneath.

"That's the end of him," Dave said.

"Yes," I said.

"Always a fair amount of recoil on this one," Dave said.

"I saw that," I said.

He looked down at the dog. "Don't worry about it," he said, talking to me. "I've lived in Maine my whole life. There's places inside of me that'll never get warm. Not here. Not in hell either."

I nodded.

"Better for the dog," he said. "He loved Pete and he never would have come around."

Dave took a rope leash off a hook on the porch. He hooked it onto the dog's collar and dragged the dead animal across the snow, behind the trailer. He came back out, brushing his hands on his coat.

"So, what did you used to do, with my brother?" Dave said. He drew a small flask bottle from his coat and took a drink. Then he picked up his beer off the railing and drained it. He opened another and drank from it.

"What do you mean?" I said.

"He used to come back from hanging around with you guys and he'd have money." He put the beer to his lips.

"Do you mean from work?" I said. "We took a few trees down, once in a while."

"No," Dave said. He sipped his beer. "No, I don't mean from work." He shook his head. "This wasn't tree-work money."

"He came up north a couple times," my brother said.

"What happened up north?" Dave said.

"We found an unmarked road," I said. I swallowed some beer.

"No shit," Dave said.

"Sometimes…" I shrugged. "Some of the stuff coming across the road got taxed."

"Let's take a ride up there," Dave said. "How do you know what you're going to find up there?"

"You don't," my brother said. "Might be nothing."

"Might be ten grand," I said.

"Might be more," Dave said. "Let's go." He tossed his beer bottle into the snow.

It took us two hours in the snow, on logging roads the last half hour, to get into position and sit tight. We left the truck three miles back and climbed up behind the old dam keeper's house. We had a clear view of the structure and the ice and flowing water on the other side. We stayed till the sun started to come up, in the freezing cold. Drinking the beer and whiskey. Dave's rifle was coated with frost.

"That was a waste of time," Dave said. "I'm frozen."

"Sometimes it's like that," my brother said.

"Is this what Pete used to do?" Dave said.

"Yeah," I said. "Pretty much. We used to visit Tevez, sometimes. Pete liked him."

"Who's Tevez?" Dave said.

There was a very small island, a hundred yards off shore and close to the dam. My brother pointed at it. "Tevez lives there," my brother said. "We used to ask him if there had been much activity on the dam."

"And my brother talked to him?" Dave said.

"Yes," I said.

"Let's see if he's there," Dave said.

We walked through the snow, to the edge of the massive frozen lake.

"Tevez!" my brother called, toward the island.

"Come on!" a Hispanic voice answered.

"How does he live out there?" Dave said. We started to walk across the snow-covered ice.

"You'll see," I said.

The ice was slippery under the snow and we moved slowly. Tevez stood on the frozen island shore, ready to greet us. He was small with a dark complexion, wearing a full insulated camo suit and a camo ski cap.

"Welcome," he said.

"This is Pete's brother, Dave," I said.

Tevez nodded. "Where is Pete?"

Dave spoke. "He's dead."

I could smell the whiskey of Dave's breath.

"Let's go inside, so no one sees us," Tevez said. "And so I can express my sympathy."

The island was very small, maybe fifty yards all around. Heavily wooded, trees growing out of the stone and dirt. As if someone had cut a circle of the Maine forest and just put it in the lake. Tevez led us to his small insulated building, which was probably eight by twenty. It was painted camo, same as his suit. He left the door open as we went in. He had a heater going inside, burning some type of fuel, with an attachment through the wall to vent any fumes. All around the walls of the small single room were blue and white flags and blue and white soccer jerseys. We sat at four folding chairs around a small table.

"What's all this?" Dave said.

"I am from Bogotá," Tevez said. His accent was thick with South America. "I was born there, in the slums. The Assassin's Cradle, they call it." He smiled proudly and pointed at the flags and jerseys. "I support Los Millonarios, the most important football club in Columbia."

Dave looked at him.

"Soccer," Tevez said. "You call it soccer. I call it football."

"Oh," Dave said.

"I am so sorry to hear of your loss," Tevez said. "Pete and I worked together many times." He was heating some coffee on a camp stove right outside the door. "Do you want hot coffee?"

"Yes," Dave said. "Thanks."

My brother and I both nodded.

Tevez came back in with three cups of steaming hot coffee, then got one for himself and sat back down. He drank from the steaming black cup. "Pete and I became friends," he said.

"How?" Dave said.

"I am here for an organization that runs in and out of Portland and up to Canada. They put a lot of time and money into this, including this building. But other people, they have discovered this way to get across the border. I can't have that disrupting what I'm doing," Tevez said.

"So where there was activity that wasn't yours . . .?" Dave said.

"Yes," Tevez said. "I would call Pete or one of these gentlemen and it would get taken care of. They got to keep whatever they found. Sometimes I paid them. It doesn't matter to me. I have a business to run and what they say about Columbians and drugs—it's much worse than what they show on TV, so I make sure I do my job. They could hurt my family back in Bogotá."

Dave took a drink of coffee. "Do you still need things taken care of?"

"Always," Tevez said. "It will be almost impossible to replace your brother."

"What if I did it?" Dave said. "Along with these two guys," he indicated my brother and me.

Tevez took his gloves off and held out his hand. "It's more than I hoped for," he said. "I lost two of my brothers, in the drug wars. You have my sympathy."

Dave shook his hand. "Okay," he said. A pen and notepad sat on the counter and he wrote on it and handed a sheet of paper to Tevez. "That's my number," he said.

Tevez looked around. "Men like us, we are not welcome in heaven. I love my family, but if I do not provide, they will be dead. So I have to love money and I have to love those things I have to do to get money." He paused. "And I love football," he said. "To watch Los Millonarios on a bright, sunny day at El Campín. Screaming and cheering—it is as if everyone in the stands who is wearing the white and blue is my brother and for that moment, that is my heaven. Men like us, we make our own heaven and go there while we are alive." He drank his coffee.

Dave stood. "We better head back. I've got a lot to take care of."

My brother and I shook hands with Tevez. "I will walk behind you," Tevez said. "Then I will walk backwards to the island, covering the tracks as I go."

We walked back across the ice, with Tevez following us and waved at him as we started the walk to the truck.

Dave didn't say much on the way back. We dropped him at his place and then went back to the rental cabin we shared, on the other side of town.

"Do you think he was pissed?" my brother said as we drove.

"About what?" I said.

"That Pete used to do that," he said.

"I don't know," I said. "Too late to fix it now if he was."

There was no funeral for Pete. Most of the members of the family lived in Florida and they weren't going to come up in the middle of Maine winter. We saw Dave once in town, getting groceries and he said he'd had Pete cremated. Dave looked like he'd been on quite a bender when we saw him and his cart was full of booze.

"Having company?" my brother said.

"Just me," Dave said. "And it's barely enough."

Two weeks later and Dave showed up outside, almost at dark. My brother and I were outside, bringing in some wood.

"Hey," Dave said. "What are you doing?"

"Just got off work," I said.

"Let's go up again," he said.

"When?" I said.

"Today. Right now, come on. I just got a call," he said.

I looked at my brother and he nodded. "Okay," I said. "Give me a minute to get ready."

"Take your time," he said. "I'll wait out here." He took a drink from a beer bottle and put it back down between his legs. "Bring something to shoot with."

The dam was the same as we'd left it. East Grand Lake stretched to the Canadian shore. An ocean of ice. We got into position in the woods and had a perfect view of the dam. Dave pulled out a pocket-size bottle of whiskey and we each had a slug. Around midnight, a motor and a single light appeared to be coming through the woods toward the dam. It was a snowmobile with a single rider.

Dave poked me and pointed in the direction of the snow machine. The rider stopped in the shadows before the dam. He had a bag on the back and he opened it and looked inside.

Now there were other snowmobiles, coming from the Canadian side. Two machines. Parked on the Canadian side of the dam. The men, two from the Canada side and one from the Maine side, walked on the snow to the middle of the dam.

"Who do we shoot?" my brother breathed.

"Shoot 'em all," Dave said.

"You sure?" I said.

"Yes I'm sure," he said.

We opened fire at the same time and the three men on the dam went down in a heap. The shots echoed deep into the night for an instant, and it was over.

"Leave them," Dave said. He walked through the woods and took the duffel bag off the snow machine on the Maine side. "This is ours. Now let's get out of here."

When we got back to Dave's trailer, he opened the duffel bag. There were a bunch of bags of whitish crystal powder—meth—and five thousand dollars in small US bills. Dave counted out twenty-five hundred and gave that to me and my brother.

"You want any of that?" Dave pointed at the meth.

"No," I said. "Thanks."

"Not me," my brother said.

"Maybe I'll do some and sell some," Dave said. He looked at both of us. "Did Pete do meth?"

"Yes," I said.

"A lot?" Dave said.

My brother pointed at the bag. "Pete would have done half of that," he said.

"What does it do to you?" Dave said.

"Gets you high," I said.

"Makes you crazy," my brother said.

"Did it make Pete crazy?" Dave said.

"I couldn't say really," I said.

"How many times did he go up to see Tevez?" Dave said.

My brother shrugged. "I don't know."

"Okay," Dave said.

Two days later, the fire company responded out to Dave Bartell's trailer. He was sitting on the porch, drinking beer and hard liquor. He had his rifle with him, so they couldn't do anything except stand there and watch him burn. He sat right on the porch, even though the flames were over fifty feet high. One of the dogs jumped off, fully engulfed in flame, towards the firemen. Dave shot the dog in midair and started laughing as the firemen scrambled around in the snow with an extinguisher. They couldn't put the fire on Pete's truck out, either. It was burning across the street. Dave had rubbed it with some chemical compound and the fire wouldn't go out. The converted barn that Pete had lived in caught and turned into a full structure fire within minutes. The explosions from propane tanks behind the trailer was so violent, it lifted the burning trailer off the cinder block foundation and then it slammed back down. The fire units had to back up, from the heat of the flames. As the wind shifted, the whole town of Lincoln smelled for a minute like Dave Bartell burning—it overshadowed the smell of the pulp plant. The firemen claimed they heard him laughing, right up till the flames finally burned themselves out, and everything was glowing hot cinders.

My brother and I went up to East Grand Lake early in the spring. The ice was still on the water, but it was thin. We stood on the shore, late at night, and my brother called over to the island.

"Tevez!" my brother said. His voice echoed across the lake, into the depth of the crisp night.

"Tevez!" I called.

We stood, waiting. The sounds of the lake and the woods were all that was alive in the dark.

I talked to my brother on the ride home. "You want to go back up later this week?" I said.

"No," he said. "Let's find something else."

"Like what?" I said.

"I don't know," he said. "Let me think about it."

"Okay," I said.

We drove over to Dave Bartell's place once, but you could hardly recognize anything. It almost still seemed warm, although that would have been impossible. There was a big black spot where the trailer had been. It was hard to believe people had ever lived there. It was as if all the booze and meth that had ever been consumed on that spot had somehow come into contact with rage and ignited. All at once, into an ever-clear, white-hot intensity.

NOTHING BUT ENEMIES

1.

THIS IS THE LAST JOB.

He can't count how many times he's said that to himself. Driving through the morning heat to tell her. To walk the edge of a lie in front of her. The road goes by and he punches the Charger and he goes through the scenarios. In less than an hour, he'll be driving up in front of the little house she rents outside Austin.

"Sandy," he starts.

She's in a towel, just out of the shower. So many curves. Tattoos on the inside of both her arms. "Baby, tell me after," she says. The air conditioning is a low hum and she drops the towel. Her damp footprints seem to vanish behind her as she walks to the bedroom. He's seen men follow her ass for a whole Sixth Street block in Austin. When he tells her after, she slaps him.

"Sandy," he starts. "This is the last job."

"John," she says. "I won't be there on visiting day." She hits her cigarette. "No guard is frisking me because of something stupid you did."

"Sandy," he starts. "This is the last job. Enough money to get away."

Slowly, she nods. She stands up from the kitchen table, and goes to the front door. Opens it. "Get out," she says. "Don't come back."

"Sandy," he starts. "This is the last job. Enough money to get away. Half a million dollars in cash."

She's wearing underwear and no top. No bra. She could date, fuck, go to dinner with any man in Austin. She's ruined marriages just by walking past couples on the sidewalk. She's blonde and tan from the Texas sun. "Are you sure, John? Because you've said this before and then almost ended up in Huntsville."

"I'm sure," he says.

"Do it, then. Do it and let's get the hell out of here," she finishes.

"Sandy," he starts. "This is the last job. Enough money to get away. Half a million dollars in cash. Jimmy put me onto it."

They're sitting on the back porch in the morning sun, drinking coffee. She's smoking a cigarette. "How did Jimmy hear about it?" she says.

"I don't want to get into all that," he says. A car passes on the street and he follows it with his eyes. "It's a big job."

"Is he helping you with it?" she says.

"Yes," he says. A car door closes somewhere up the block. There's a distant siren fading.

"Fine," she says. "But let's never go through this again. Ever."

"Ever," he says.

"Don't lie to me, John," she says. "Tell me the truth if it kills you."

He nods. "I don't know if we can actually do it."

She nods back. "I know," she says. "And I'm not waiting while you do time. Again." She sips her coffee and crosses her perfect legs. "Other men will be fucking me and I'll love it." She takes a drag off her cigarette. "Men with money you don't have."

He gets off the highway and turns. Waits for the light and turns again. Ten minutes north of Austin, he turns off the street onto the hot macadam of her driveway.

"Hi, Sandy," he says. "I've got something to do with Jimmy."

She's getting a cup of coffee in the kitchen. "Want coffee?"

"No thanks," he says.

She sits on the couch in the living room, across from him. Her star tattoos sparkle. Her hair shines. "What's up?"

"We're going to hit someone on the highway. Jimmy's got it planned."

She looks at the rug. Back at him and shrugs. "What's this got to do with me?"

"Do you want to come with me? When the job is done?"

She leans back on the couch. "Come with you where, John?"

"Out of here. We'll have half a million dollars."

"I'm not going to ask my life to do tricks anymore," she says. "You're a fucking asshole if you think that."

He shook his head. "This is legit, Sandy. Jimmy's got it all worked out."

"I'm not going back to stripping and hustling drinks and bullshit. With you locked up. I want a better life. Is this crap you're doing going to get me a better life?"

He paused. "Yes," he says.

She looks at the digital clock on the cable box, next to the TV. "It's 8:15 a.m. If you're not back here by 6:00 p.m. tonight with that bag of cash, don't come here anymore. Because if this is as big as you say it is, it will mean you either blew it or lied to me or some shit fucked up somewhere and I swear to God, I'll make this the last job. By my call. The clock is ticking on you right now."

"That's fine," he says. "Be ready to leave when I get here."

"John," she says. "I've been ready to leave for five years."

2.

COOK IS SIPPING COFFEE AS HE'S DRIVING. LENARES IS keeping an eye on the suspect's vehicle. They're in a plain black Mercury Marauder, with a cop dash array and a riot shotgun clip-mounted on the center console. They pass a sign on the highway that says they're entering Texas.

"Far away from home now," Cook says.

"Yes," Lenares says.

"Beats working some stupid house-sit in Portland for a pin joint," Cook says.

"I'm so tired of hippies," Lenares says. "Who the fuck ever thought they'd all settle in Oregon."

Cook changes lanes to keep the car in view. "How much do you think they have in there?"

"It's hard to say. You know how that goes," Lenares says. "Could be as much as five million, depending on what other drugs they got from those bikers.

Cook whistles. "Five million is a lot."

Lenares nods. "It ain't bad." He sips his coffee. "I better check in with Dave. Let him know we're in Texas."

"Good idea," Cook says.

Lenares gets on his cell phone. "Dave, I wanted to let you know we just crossed into Texas following the suspects. Our position is mile marker one-eight-five on Highway 83 headed south toward Abilene." He nods as he talks and clicks off.

"What did he say?" Cook asks.

"Check in with him every hour to give a progress update," Lenares says.

"Think anybody else knows about this besides Dave?" Cook asks.

Lenares shakes his head. "No," he says. "Why should they? Dave's supervising detective for the whole of Clackamas County. If he wants to pursue a bust and let cooperating jurisdictional agencies know at the time of apprehension, that's totally his call."

Cook changes lanes. "So we could shoot these guys and take the drugs and tell Dave they got away. Like you and he did on that meth bust last summer."

"When we went back to that house," Lenares says, "someone had killed those guys and taken their bodies."

Cook smiles as he presses the accelerator. "Yeah," he says. "Someone who had a decent knowledge of forensic technique, rubber gloves, body bags, and was so careful they didn't leave a piece of hair or a print at the scene." He laughs. "That was a phantom cop job if I ever saw one. The dark blue ghost."

Lenares stares straight ahead, at the road and the cars. He drinks his coffee.

"We could do the same thing here," Cook says.

Lenares stares ahead.

"We could do the same thing here," Cook says. "Or I could go to IA when we get back to Portland and talk to them, since nobody seems to want to talk to me."

Lenares sips his coffee. "You're fucking around with heavyweight people, you know that, right?" The traffic is around them, people in cars, all in their own little moving worlds.

"Am I?" Cook says.

"Why do you think we're out here?" Lenares says.

"Following a carload of drugs," Cook says.

Lenares nods. "You think what we want you to think."

"What are we really doing?" Cook says.

"Following a carload of drugs driven by people who didn't give Dave Beck his cut before they split town," Lenares finishes.

"So nobody knows about this," Cook says.

Lenares points with his chin at the car they are following. "They know. Those people. They fucked Dave. They didn't pay him like they were supposed to."

"We can do it," Cook says.

"I think as long as Dave gets his cut," Lenares says, "it will go fine." He sips his coffee. "When they pull over, let me drive a little. I'm falling asleep over here."

"Okay," Cook says.

3.

OLIVAS SITS SHACKLED TO A STAINLESS STEEL TABLE that is bolted to the floor. The table has four, round, stainless steel seats that are welded to round beams that are welded to the center column of the table, which is held to the concrete floor by a square stainless steel pressure plate and twelve hex bolts, three on each side of the plate. Olivas is focused on the television that hangs from four steel suspension arms, ten inches below the ceiling in the corner of the room. He is watching a black and white surveillance tape of himself.

On the tape, Olivas is in the yard, lifting the whole stack effortlessly on a weight machine. Several inmates are in the frame, one Mexican acting as a spotter and two others, smoking. A corrections officer walks past the group and out of frame. As the officer crosses, for a second, something flutters out of his hand to the ground. The inmates nod at him. Olivas stands, immense press bar in his hands loaded with plates at both ends. He tosses it in the direction of the guard as if it was made of tissue paper. The impact makes a sickening noise on the tape. Olivas watches himself rip a round plate off the end of the bar that's still in the frame and he's beating someone with it. The noise is inhuman. The tape ends and is replaced by the face of an administrative law judge.

Two guards and a corrections administrator enter the room behind Olivas.

"Gentlemen," the administrative law judge says. "I have watched the evidence tape and am ready to render a decision in this matter." The men all watch the screen as the administrative law judge shifts his papers. "Given the violent nature of Mr. Olivas, I am ordering that he be transferred into the custody of the maximum security holding unit at El Campo, Texas. Transfer to take place immediately and I'll follow up with El Campo on the paperwork." He pauses. "Do you understand Mr. Olivas? If you do not, I speak fluent Spanish."

"I understand, your honor," Olivas says.

The corrections administrator clears his throat. "Your honor, I don't understand. The guard he assaulted is in a coma and could die at any minute. This is clearly grounds for an in-house resentencing."

The administrative law judge adjusts his tie on screen. "You don't need to instruct this court on how to be a court, Lieutenant. The prisoner will be moved first, for his own safety, so that no facility personnel retaliate on behalf of their brother officer. Once he has been moved, the court may reconsider imposing sentence. That's all." The monitor shuts off from the court's end.

The Lieutenant shakes his head and talks to the guards. "Get him down to booking, they're probably already waiting for him."

Olivas stands as the guards unshackle and then re-shackle him. They shuffle with him, through the open steel door and down the concrete halls toward booking. As they pass a plexiglass holding area, several Mexican inmates start applauding and cheering.

"Olivas es el jefe del infierno!!"

It echoes in the facility. As the boss of hell is led to booking.

4.

LENARES IS DRIVING WITH COOK AND THEY'RE KEEPING the vehicle—a black Ford Taurus SHO with Louisiana plates—in sight. All the way from Oregon. They just crossed into northern Texas an hour ago and now, the vehicle parks outside a diner, on Route 183. An hour outside of Austin.

"Who's this?" Cook said. A pickup truck slides in directly behind the Taurus.

Two men, both in baseball caps and sunglasses, get out of the pickup truck. Two other men, dressed the same way, get out of the Taurus. Another car, an Audi four-door coupe, pulls up next to the pickup truck and two more men get out. Other cars are entering and exiting the parking lot. The men in baseball hats are all carrying gym bags. They move quickly, getting into different cars than the ones they got out of. And start to head onto the road south to Austin again.

"Oh fuck!" Lenares says.

Lenares steers their car back onto the highway and accelerates.

"That was smart," Cook said. "Too smart for these guys to just randomly think of."

"Do you think somebody tipped them to us?" Lenares says. He's steering through morning traffic at sixty-five, trying to keep the cars in sight.

"Who?" Cook says.

"Some neighbor from Oregon?"

"I doubt that," Cook says.

"Which car should I follow?" Lenares says.

"Follow the one we came down here after," Cook says.

"One's got the drugs and the other is an empty fake?" Lenares says. "Who's in the third car?

Cook shakes his head. "I don't even see how that's possible. That they thought to switch like that."

"Should we put the flashers on?" Lenares says.

Cook is already on the phone. "Dave, it's Joe Cook and I'm in the car with Roberto Lenares. We're still following the car. It just entered Texas, about an hour ago."

A voice comes through the speakerphone. "Okay. Everything all right?"

"Not really," Cook says. "They stopped at a diner here below the state line. The driver of the car got into a truck that was parked in the lot and an unknown male is now driving the car. A third car is involved as well."

"Joe, you broke up a little. Repeat that for me."

"The Oregon vehicle with Louisiana plates stopped in a diner south of the state line. The suspect exited his vehicle with a passenger and when he came out, he was met by a group of other white males. The suspect did not reenter his own vehicle. He got into a Ford pickup truck and waited for the unknown male to get into the Oregon car and get back onto the highway. A third vehicle, an Audi, is also involved."

"I got it now. Which vehicle are you following?"

"We are five car-lengths behind the Oregon vehicle with Louisiana plates."

"Did you get the plate from the Ford?"

"No," Cook says. "It looked like it had been purposefully obscured with mud."

"How about the Audi?"

"No, it moved too quickly," Cook says.

Lenares fights the traffic to stay in sight.

There is a pause over the speakerphone. "Okay. Let the Ford go. Let the Audi go. I want what's in the car, not the guy driving it. We can get him later. Update me in an hour." He clicks off.

"Maybe the plan just got easier," Cook says.

"Maybe," Lenares agrees.

5.

THE JOB COMES FROM JIMMY WORK EARLY THAT MORNING. They are talking at the old cinderblock garage and junkyard, as they sit around drinking coffee. The sun is just coming up.

"There's something coming down the pike," Jimmy says.

"Is it worth going after?" he asks.

"Let me ask you something," Jimmy says. "How much money do you have right now, total, cash, that you can put your hands on?"

He thinks for a minute. "Maybe two grand. Maybe."

Jimmy looks up at the ceiling. "In other words, one false move—which could be two flat tires, an old debt that comes back, a broken hand at work—and you're flat broke."

"Probably."

"And you wanted to know what again?" Jimmy says.

"Is it worth going after? I don't think I could last, doing more time," he says.

"I don't know yet," Jimmy said. He was covered in tattoos. "For you, almost anything is worth going after."

"Okay," he says.

"People can get arrogant and foolish," Jimmy says. "In terms of information. But in this case, it's somebody who turned on them."

"From the inside?" he says.

"Prison does different things to different people," Jimmy says. "Some people get scared. Some people get brave." Jimmy spits. "It's hard to say."

"Was this somebody you know?" he asks.

Jimmy nods. "I used to know them."

"Could be on the level," he says.

"It's not the information that I'm questioning," Jimmy Work says. "It's why the information was told to me."

"Sure," he says.

"I'm a very specific person," Jimmy Work says. "You would only tell me something if you had a specific reason."

"Right," he says.

Jimmy keeps on. "Because you have to know that I'm going to set my network in motion, I'm going to send kites out to the end of my web and see what comes back."

"Right," he says.

"And if you're bullshit, I'll know in about a day," Jimmy says.

"Yeah," he says.

"That's the thing about an echo," Jimmy says. "It will tell you about the person who let out the scream in the first place. Even if it comes back a whisper." He sips his coffee.

"How did this come back?" he says.

"It all checked out," Jimmy says.

"What do you want to do?" he says.

"I want you to help me do one last job and then ghost it out of here," Jimmy says.

"I'm all for it," he says. "When?"

"Now. Today."

John looks at the concrete floor of the garage. "Seriously?"

Jimmy Work stretches his hands around at the garage. "All of this," he points at himself, "is going to be gone. The smoke of money is going to provide the cover."

"Think we can do it?" he says.

"I don't really give a fuck," Jimmy says. "If we get caught, doing time will beat sitting here every day." He tossed his cigarette in the dirt. "They gave me time when they locked me up and now I'm doing time out here. It's all the same to me."

"I'd rather stay out," he says.

"That's because you hated it inside," Jimmy says. "I got so I liked it."

"How long were you in?" he says.

"Over eighteen years, all together," Jimmy says.

"That's a long time," he says.

"It was like one long, shitty day," Jimmy says. "Something so big, you can't imagine it. I can't even tell you about it, that's how big it was." He shook another cigarette loose from his pack. "Do you have problems waiting for you back on the inside?"

"Maybe," he allows.

"I was the problem," Jimmy says. "And now, all I want to do is erase myself."

"That would suit me fine," he says.

6.

RAZOR WIRE SITS IN COILS ON TOP OF ALL THREE FENCES leading into the private prison south of Interstate Ten near El Campo. Belgian guard dogs patrol between the second and third fence. The prison itself is a squat, red brick and concrete structure. The heat waves come off the bricks and metal fences as the sun rises. Like a piece of hell that crawled up to the earth's surface.

The two guards handcuff Olivas to a solid metal ring that is cemented into the wall of the interrogation room. They bring him a folding chair and he sits there, his right hand held slightly above his head because of the cuff in the ring. A white man in a sport coat and slacks with a tie and shiny shoes comes into the interrogation room.

"Good morning, Mr. Olivas," the man says.

"Good morning, sir," Olivas answers.

"I met some people yesterday who know you," the man says.

"Yes," Olivas says.

"And they told me you could identify the man I'm looking for," the man says.

"Yes," Olivas says. "I know him."

"How do you know him?" the man says.

"From New Orleans," Olivas says.

"The people I met yesterday are very interested in seeing you get to Mexico safely," the man says.

Olivas nods.

The man continues. "If you can do this one thing for us, I think we can do something for you."

"I'll do it," Olivas says. "Get me close enough."

The man nods. "You'll be close enough. We're doing it today."

"Today?" Olivas says.

"Right now," the man says. He knocks on the inside of the interrogation room door and the two guards come in. The man speaks to them. "Inmate Olivas needs medical attention, so bring the hospital van around. We're taking him out of the facility."

"Yes sir," the one guard responds. As the man leaves the interrogation room, the guards uncuff Olivas from the wall and he shuffles along with them, his shackles jingling against the concrete floor.

7.

"THAT'S THE WHOLE THOUGHT," JIMMY SAYS. HE POURS himself another cup of coffee. They are sitting on green lawn furniture, in back of the garage.

"What's that," he says.

"Life and death are linked, no matter how you look at it," Jimmy says.

"I don't follow you," he says.

"Life is the reason you're going to die," Jimmy says. "It's your own life that ultimately kills you."

"Okay," he says.

"So the trick is to die inside your own life and live again," Jimmy finishes.

"Is that what we're going to try to do here?" he says.

"Do you know what a tanda is?" Jimmy says.

"No," he says.

"It's like a tiny cooperative bank, where everybody puts money in," Jimmy says.

"Okay," he says.

"A bunch of people in the French Quarter got together, over the years, and came up with a way to get their drugs using that theory," Jimmy says.

"How's that?" he says.

"They bought this abandoned piece of property in Oregon and they grow some of the best weed in the country there," Jimmy says. "And they cook up too—meth and coke. From the raw to the ready useable."

"Okay," he says.

"So they put their money in when they're in the French Quarter, then every year, one of the group goes out and makes sure it's all cool out in Oregon," Jimmy says.

"I follow you," he says.

"And they bring back a full year's worth of drugs into the Quarter, to split among the cooperative."

"How much?" he says.

Jimmy sips his coffee. "They sell some of the week to bikers in Oregon and some of the meth too, so about two million dollars' worth of shit makes the trip back from Oregon."

"Wow," he says.

"An entire carload," Jimmy says.

"Holy shit," he says.

"That ride back must be white-knuckle," Jimmy says.

"Sure," he says.

"But then, if you're in on it and you live in the French Quarter, you don't have to buy drugs for a year," Jimmy says. "You can just get high and throw beads off your balcony. No more risks, no dealing with dirtbags."

"I can see that," he says.

Jimmy finishes his coffee. "And we're going to take it from them."

"I'm in," John says. "What's the split?"

"Half a million in cash," Jimmy says.

"I'll do it," he says.

"People are going to die," Jimmy says. "Just remember it's their own life that killed them."

"As long as it isn't me," he says.

"Then kill the other guy first," Jimmy says. "Do you think she'll come with you when it's done?"

"I don't know," he says. "But I'll tell her and see what she says."

"Don't tell her too much," Jimmy says. "In case she doesn't want to come."

"Okay," he says.

"There are a lot of eyes on this one," Jimmy says. "Be high-level careful."

"Okay," he says. He walks out of the garage and gets into his Charger.

8.

ATF AGENT PHILIP DELACROIX KNEW THAT MORNING how he was going to handle it. He is already working at his air-conditioned office in Houston and has dispatched two field agents—Ben Conklin and Arnold Peters—to track the vehicle even before it reaches Interstate Ten. He is in contact with the field agents on his push-to-talk. He'll leave the office at 11:00 a.m. and drive north, to take charge of the situation once they detain the vehicle. He checked and loaded his weapons the night before. A Sig Sauer that he wears under his sport coat in a custom shoulder holster and a Benelli shotgun in his personal SUV. A .44 Magnum Smith & Wesson Mountain Gun is strapped under his driver's seat. Once they've secured the suspects and transferred the drugs to his personal vehicle, he will shoot the agents and the suspects and dump the bodies in the Gulf of Mexico at night. There are already a dozen of his bodies in the Gulf. It is a plan he'd used before and this was too good a haul to let slip past. When the heat dies down, he'll go into the French Quarter and take the money and drugs from those people as well. What the hell were they going to do—report stolen drugs to the New Orleans Police Department?

9.

THE TWO AUSTIN UNDERCOVER COPS DRIVE DOWN THE block again, past her house. They see the Charger in the driveway and take down the plate number as they pass.

"I got to get back," the one cop says. "My overtime is done."

"We'll head back right now," the other cop says. The one driving. "I'll come back with whoever just came on duty."

"What are we watching her for?" the other cop asks.

"She's connected with some heavy hitters, some guys who occasionally work with the Aryan Brotherhood."

The cop shakes his head. "Really? Her?" He shakes his head again. "I don't see it."

The other cop shrugs. "Maybe that's why we're watching her. You'd come back for her, wouldn't you?"

"I'd be fucking her right now," the cop finishes. "I'd call my wife and say we were all done. Take the kids and get out."

"Jesus," the other cop says.

Sandy had been sitting on the back porch the last time they drove down the block. Smoking a cigarette in the shade of the eaves of her small rental.

10.

COOK KEYS HIS PUSH-TO-TALK AS LENARES FIGHTS TO keep all the vehicles in sight.

"Dave, we can't do this. I think you have to ask for backup here in Texas."

Lenares speaks up. "They're getting off."

Cook talks louder. "Dave, it looks like the vehicle from Oregon with Louisiana plates is getting off into a truck stop weigh station, prior to Interstate Ten."

The voice comes back over the phone. "I'm informing Texas right now of the situation. This may take half an hour or so before backup is at your location. Keep the suspect vehicle under surveillance. Lenares, make sure it goes smooth."

Lenares and Cook drive slowly through the maze of parked big rigs. Then they spot the vehicle.

"Dave, be advised, there is a Texas DOT operative talking to the men in the car. He has them off to one side of the weigh station, with his DOT flashers on behind them."

The voice crackles back. "He's probably just advising them to leave the weigh station. Do you think you can apprehend the car safely?"

Cook looks at Lenares, who nods. "Yes," Cook says into the air.

"Proceed as if you are helping the DOT officer and I will try to get a DOT supervisor on the line. What is your mile marker location?"

Cook and Lenares never hear him. Cook shuts the phone off as soon as Lenares drives up, to block the vehicle they had been following all this time in.

"This is it," Cook says.

"Don't panic and don't rush it," Lenares says.

 They both get out of the car.

"Can we assist you, Officer?" Cook says. He has his badge out. Lenares holds his badge out as well. They are close to the car now. The man behind the wheel has a ball cap and sunglasses on and so does the guy in the passenger's seat. They don't look familiar to Cook.

The man in the DOT uniform turns and shoots Lenares first. His first shot strikes Lenares in the shoulder, spinning him, so the second shot goes through his back and shoves him over the trunk of his own car. The third and fourth shots go through his spine and lungs. Cut through his life like heat lightning. He spills to the road surface, leaving a wet carpet of red blood everywhere.

Cook takes the shotgun blast from the driver full-on in the face. The shot drives through his skull, splintering bone, driving shards of himself into his brain. He stopped breathing before he hits the ground.

The man in the DOT uniform gets into his DOT pickup, shuts the flashers off and speeds back onto the highway. The two men in the car drive onto a waiting ramp at the back of a big rig. Once inside, they secure the car with rachet chains. They get out, pull the solid door gate down on the truck, closing the car off, and put a lock on it. Once they are in the cab, John starts the big rig up and steers onto the highway. At the first opportunity, he takes an exit and gets back on. Going north, away from Louisiana and Austin. Back the way they had come.

11.

JIMMY GOES TO THE BATHROOM IN THE GARAGE AND comes out. He pours himself another cup of coffee and sits down next to John.

"How are we going to sell the drugs?" John says.

"I've got connections," Jimmy says. "You'll bring the car back in a big rig to a truck stop near Abilene and then you can leave. It will all be taken care of."

John nods.

Jimmy keeps on. "But you've got to have your eyes open. There will be a lot of people out sniffing around for this thing."

"What makes you say that?" John says.

"You know about it. I know about it. What makes you think other people don't know about it?" Jimmy says.

"I guess I thought it was a secret," John says.

"You need to grow up," Jimmy says. "No adult talks about secrets. That's shit you say when you're a kid." He puffs a cigarette. "There's no secrets."

12.

"WE'VE GOT THEM ALL IN SIGHT RIGHT NOW. THE occupants of the vehicles all have baseball hats and sunglasses on."

Delacroix keys the radio again. "Repeat that, fifteen." He is already on the road from Houston in his personal SUV. He was having them use a private ATF frequency. It would eliminate suspicion afterward.

The voice comes over the radio again. "All the occupants of all three cars are wearing baseball caps and sunglasses. We cannot identify the people inside the vehicles."

Delacroix makes up his mind. "Pull them over for something," he says.

"Sir, the vehicle with Louisiana plates has exited the highway. We have lost visual."

"Pull the pickup truck over," Delcroix orders.

The response comes back. "They are not in violation."

"Make some shit up!" Delacroix says. "Pull the big Ford pickup over. I want to know the identity of the occupants right now."

He hears the sirens go on. He'd been in cars enough. He knew how the routine was going to go. He hears both cruiser doors open and close. He could hear the ghost whoosh of cars speeding past the undercover cruiser. Then he hears gunfire.

The radio stays in Delacroix's hand. "Respond fifteen." Crackling static. "Respond fifteen." Nothing. "Respond fifteen."

If he called the state police, that would give away his position. And let them know that he'd been following the drug car without telling them. And thinking that he was going to take the drug car for his own.

"Respond fifteen." He tries again. Nothing comes back.

Delacroix makes an illegal U-turn with his SUV and starts south, back toward Houston. Men smart enough to run a three-car switch were probably smart enough to know someone was watching them. He hopes the two agents were dead. That would eliminate any problems he might have.

13.

IT HAPPENS AS THE BIG RIG IS EASING INTO THE LOT OF the truck stop. Two Mexicans get out of a Toyota SUV and open up, full-bore with an automatic shotgun, on the cab of the rig. People in the lot are screaming and diving for cover. The auto shotgun tears up the windshield, tears a door off, tears part of the hood cowling away, as John and the guy inside with him return fire with pistols and a shotgun of their own. The auto shotgun goes on and on and on. As if a small army is shooting. Finally the guy next to John comes out with a machine pistol and sprays the Toyota, rakes it with lead, and then hits it again. The shotgun stops. The guy next to John reloads and sprays the Toyota again, as the Mexicans sag out the doors. John isn't firing anymore.

14.

THE TWO DETECTIVES WATCH HER COME OUT OF THE house late that afternoon and get into her car, a black Honda coupe. She is wearing a bright red sundress and carrying a small gym bag.

"Jesus," the one cop says. "That's some body she's got."

The Honda backs out of the driveway onto the street and pulls away.

"Just follow her so she doesn't make us," the other cop says. "When was the last time John was up here?"

"The other team spotted him this morning," the cop says. "He stayed for about half an hour."

"She's probably going to get groceries, but follow her anyway," the lead cop says.

"I'd follow her anywhere," the other cop says.

The Honda heads toward Austin and the cops follow.

She parks at Whole Foods and goes inside. The parking lot is almost full of cars and the cops wait in the heat.

"Wish I had something to drink," the one says.

"Go in and get something," the other one says.

"Nah. I'll just wait," the one says.

15.

JIMMY LOOKS AT JOHN. "HAVE YOU EVER BEEN IN a gunfight?"

"No," John says.

"Well it's a hell of a thing," Jimmy says. "Everything breaks around you and if you're hit, it's like somebody took a scalding thick knitting needle and ran it through you. You'll get hit in the leg and your back will spasm, because you're all connected and don't realize it. A gunfight will make you know you're alive, at least for a second."

"How fast does it happen?" John says.

"Faster than I can tell you," Jimmy says.

"What's the best thing to do?" John says.

"Don't be outgunned," Jimmy says. "That's the worst."

16.

THE PRISON VAN GOES THROUGH EACH GATE AS IT opens and closes. The guards enter in the codes and show their cards to each other. Olivas sits on a bench seat in the back, closed off from the drivers. The man in the suit sits in the rear passenger's seat. Sweat forms on his brow. The two guards up front are heavily armed.

"Mr. Olivas," the man says. "We will let you off in the park up here, out of view of the facility."

"Okay," Olivas says.

They drive in silence for half an hour, on the highway. Below Interstate Ten, they exit near Eagle Lake. Down into a small park and wooded area. There is a big Ford pickup truck in the parking area.

The prison van stops and the guard driving pops the lock on the back door.

"Don't forget your debt to us, Mr. Olivas," the man says.

There is no answer. Jimmy Work had already got out of the big Ford and Olivas is riddled from his machine pistol. Jimmy Work flips three grenades into the prison van and slams the back door shut as he runs toward his Ford.

The concussive blast lifts the prison van off the ground. It blows the windows, the doors, the panels. It flips the flaming prison van onto its side and the gas catches fire and something else explodes. Jimmy

Work runs over Olivas' body as he drives out of the park and back to the highway. An arm lies forty feet away from the prison van as he drives away.

17.

THE SUN BEATS DOWN ON THE COPS WATCHING SANDY from the parking lot. Finally they see her bright sundress come out. She is carrying a cloth grocery bag and wearing a straw sunhat.

"What the hell was she buying?" the one cop said.

"I have no idea," the other cop said.

They follow the black Honda back out of town. It parks in the driveway at Sandy's house and the cops keep a distance, moving slowly down the block.

18.

IN THE DEAD WHITE OF WINTER, A BIG MAN IS DRINKING a beer in Portland, Maine. He pays cash and walks out, onto the hard-packed snow and ice. He walks through a decent neighborhood to an older brick building. Two story, with a light in the window. With gloves on, he works the lock with a universal pick and the door whispers open. There's a noise coming from the roof. He keeps going up, inside, silent in his boots and jacket. He goes up spiral stairs to the roof. Sandy's in the hot tub. She looks at him.

"Where's John?" she says.

"He's gone," the man says.

"Do you mean dead?" she says. "Where's Jimmy?"

The man takes ten rubber-banded rolls of bills out of his jacket pocket and spills them onto the roof. "We're all dead," he says. "We use paper made of dead stuff, to print pictures of dead people on, to try to pretend we're alive." He walks back through the roof door, heading down the stairs.

Sandy wraps in a towel and gets out of the hot tub. She calls down the stairs. "Where are John and Jimmy?"

The man keeps walking. "Nowhere and everywhere," he says as he walks. "Make that last, because there isn't any more." He stops, but doesn't turn. "Smart people don't ask questions," he says. "Smart people know when they're been lucky." And he's out the front door.

19.

JOHN DRINKS HIS COFFEE. "HOW CLOSE HAVE YOU BEEN to dying?"

"Close," Jimmy says. "Over the edge and pulled back."

"What's that like?" John says.

"What do I give a fuck? Do you think death wouldn't just be some other kind of sentence for me? And then I'd just figure out ways to fuck the devil," Jimmy says. "People think crazy shit about gangs. I'm my own gang, that's why they could never figure out what I was doing, that's why I survived. I'm not the dog that drools when you ring that bell. I'm the dog that tears your throat out when you bend down to see why I didn't answer the bell."

"I hear you," John says.

"I know you do brother, because if you pull this off with me, you'll be just like me. And free. Gone, for the first time," Jimmy finishes.

"I want it bad, Jimmy, but I'm nervous to reach for it."

"Grab it," Jimmy says. "Don't let it grab you."

20.

THE COPS BURST INTO SANDY'S HOUSE IN TEXAS AND there's a woman in a sundress, making dinner. It isn't Sandy.

21.

SANDY, STILL IN HER TOWEL, PICKS UP ONE OF THE BUN-dles of money. It's hundred-dollar bills, in bunches bigger than her fist.

22.

TWO NEW ORLEANS COPS, WALKING AT NIGHT, THROUGH pedestrian Exchange Alley in the French Quarter.

"Why you so jumpy tonight?" the one says.

"Something's going on," the other one says.

"What?" the one asks.

"I'll tell you after," the other one says.

They pass the Pelican Club and a small group of people come out. From an upstairs balcony across the street, some beads get tossed.

"Tell me now," the cop says.

"Tomorrow," the other cop says. "Might be an opportunity."

STRAIGHT RAZOR

THEY MUST HAVE STARTED EARLY, DRIVING NORTH FROM Manhattan, because around seven a.m. my dogs perked up and let me know that a vehicle had turned off the main road onto the gravel and dirt of my driveway. I gave the dogs—Goliath, the mastiff and Hank, the Belgium Malinois—the word to stay put. A quick whistle out the back door and Hank's brother Ty bounded into the house. He responded to my command to lay on the kitchen floor. I left the back door cracked. In case I needed three friends with teeth fast.

There were four men. Two in each truck. We talked on the gravel circle behind the house. Looking over the field I used as a part-time woodlot and workshop. It was all a work in progress. I had only lived here for three years.

It wasn't good to see any of them. We talked about death happening in far-off places. About a new, sealed silencer that was available for the .17HMR and how it was as quiet as a pellet gun. The notion of the reverse sniper. About not taking a tactical and often impossible position nine-hundred yards away, but setting up in the middle, with camouflage, and using quiet, up-close headshots.

"Getting hit with a .17HMR is like being stung by a bee," McMurdo said.

"A bee moving at over two thousand five hundred feet per second," I said.

"I could see it working," the one man said. He was staring at the tree line.

"In a crowd, it's headshot, headshot, headshot, and then nothing," I said. "No misses, minimal noise. Very little ballistic evidence."

"I think you have a point," the other man said. "There are social engineering aspects to this. How many world leaders and rebel generals are going to appear in front of troops or public situations wearing a full-on Kevlar helmet and face shield? They'd seem scared, if they did that." He adjusted his sunglasses. "I think you're onto something."

"What's the protection ballistics on those shields?" McMurdo said.

"All protection can be defeated at the right velocity," I said. "Most of those clear, mutant plastic barriers give way at over a thousand feet per second."

"Shoot 'em in the eye and what's left of the round will ricochet and splash-fragment back into their brainpan off the inside of their own helmet," McMurdo said.

The first man laughed and I nodded in agreement. The other man nodded too—he heard it and approved. He never looked away from the trees that bordered the field.

The fourth man was totally silent. He stood away from us, in front of the two trucks. I could see the outline of a shoulder holster under his light black jacket.

I think this is why I don't do it anymore. Everything becomes a killing machine. Normal people think that death is loss. Life is gain. My thoughts don't work that way, after more than a decade of working in the shadows. I am always in situations that have been misrepresented. In unfriendly geographies, in whatever most-recently-created hell has cropped up.

In the end, we talked about Daniel Woodson. I listened and they told. This was an extreme situation and they had a plan, about what I was going to do. Or try to do. I'd go in as an observer, using the Woodson killing as a talking point. If I found any agency men or operatives, try to bring them home alive. Bribe whoever needed to be bribed to do it.

In any given plan, there are a variety of holes. The one man was calling these known unknowns. The other man, the one who wouldn't stop watching the trees, talked about unknown unknowns. The jargon in shadow work just makes the shadows darker. It doesn't illuminate anything. It's just a different way of saying that the field operative on the ground could easily be fucked beyond belief. My cover was thin, but acceptable. I was paid in cash, given cash to spread around, and given the appropriate papers. They got back into the trucks and drove back down the driveway, onto the main road. I walked into the kitchen and the dogs were still on high alert. I told them to relax. I had the cash and my papers in a small black duffel bag.

"The bills are paid for a year, boys," I said. "Steak tonight." Goliath knows the word steak, so his tail patted the floor for a minute. Hank and Ty have more of a work ethic than Goliath. They were still listening, in hopes that something would move outside and I'd release them to tear it apart.

I started to prepare to leave the next morning. My brother would come over and take care of the dogs and house for me. They got along well with him. In the morning, I'd be a different person. Every time I went into the field, I was a different person. I'd be Sam Matthews, flying to Jamaica. The murder capital of the world. And out of the over sixteen hundred unsolved murders that had taken place on the island during the last twelve months, I was going to focus in on a single victim. A seven-year-old boy named Daniel Woodson. I'd be a forty-something white guy, looking for a seven-year-old black kid who'd been supposedly shot in the head, while a sea of black island faces looked on. Worse, little Daniel Woodson had been shot by a cop. In the past two years, over seven hundred Jamaicans had been shot by their own police force. And no cop in Jamaica had ever been charged with murder. Woodson was just a conversation piece for me. Enough of a breeze to keep my paper-airplane-of-a-cover-story flying. While I looked for operatives being held. That's how ugly things are in the land of shadows. Murdered little boys are window dressing for other operations.

The approach and departure of Norman Manley International Airport always bothered me and this time was no exception. Beads of sweat on my forehead and once I got off the plane, the minute the humid, stifling air from outside hit me, my shirt was soaked. The good-time reggae music was drifting in the boiling atmosphere, as a bunch of islanders hawked rum to the arriving tourists.

Inside the terminal, a police officer in a white shirt and blue dress pants with a red piping and dark blue cap—the duty uniform of the Jamaican Constabulary Force—held a hand-printed sign with my name on it. Matthews. The officer's skin was the color of straight coffee. I followed him through the terminal to the front exit. There was a thin boy, selling bottled water to anyone who didn't look Jamaican, but I brushed him aside. We got into the back seat of a tan sedan, with a driver in similar uniform and a man in the passenger's seat in a khaki uniform.

"Go," the man in the khaki uniform said. The driver flipped the lights twice and moved into the flow of traffic. The man in the khaki uniform spoke without looking at me. "I'm Inspector Martins. We will take you to see the Senior Superintendent."

"Good," I said. "Did you bring me a weapon?"

Martins lit a cigarette and blew smoke out his open window as we drove. "What would you need a weapon for?" he said. "You are an observer. A controller. You are not JCF."

"No," I said. "That's true. But I was told I would be provided with a sidearm. Given the nature of my business and my standing." We passed some men, cooking on the side of the road on barrel grills. The smell of street food mixed with the steamy air and traffic noise that drifted into the car. Island women in colorful fabric head wraps walked in groups among the tourists.

Martins did not turn to face me. He smoked his cigarette out the window. "I do not think your standing has been determined yet. Your new standing is ahead of us—as yet a mystery. Who you are and who you know when you are off this island—that doesn't concern me," he finished. A huge graffiti mural proclaimed the War was not the Answer, on the side of a falling brick wall.

"Okay," I said.

"We have been long used here," Martins said.

"I understand," I said.

"No," Martins said. "But you will in time." He drew on his cigarette. "You will."

The sedan made its way through the crowded hot streets of Kingston. The slums, the notorious killing fields, were in the distance. Nobody wanted to kill off the tourist trade by scaring people as soon as they got off their airplane. Take the white wallets directly to their enclosed hotel compounds and pray that the storm of violence claimed only local, Jamaican lives. The gold, black, and green flag was everywhere. Gold is the sun shining. Green is the land. Black is hardship. It might be the truest flag I know.

We arrived at a Jamaican Constabulary Force building and got out. I went up the steps and Martins ushered me into the Senior Superintendent's office. He got up from behind his desk and shook hands with me. I sat in the chair in front of his desk. Photos and award plaques decorated the plain gray walls.

"What can we do for you, Mister Matthews?" he said. "I'm Senior Superintendent Trilling."

I reached into my briefcase and produced a letter. "I have a letter here requesting that I be given a weapon from the JCF armory. To use for the length of my stay." I put the letter on his desk.

Trilling didn't touch the letter. "Who is this letter from?"

"The Scotland Yard liaison to the JCF," I said.

"You see," he said, "there is a problem with letters. You might have a letter signed by God himself, but what if it was written by the Devil? I'll look into it." He punched a button on his phone and spoke. "Come to my office Wilson."

There was a knock on the door and an older white man wearing a suit appeared.

"This is Captain Wilson. He is here to aid in communications to Scotland Yard. Captain, were you made aware that Mister Matthews would be visiting us and needed a weapon?"

Wilson shook his head. "No sir. I don't believe I was sir. Do you want me to provide him with one from the building armory?"

Trilling shook his head. "No. I don't think that will be necessary."

"Anything else sir?" Wilson said.

"No, Wilson. Dismissed."

Wilson quietly closed the door as he left.

Trilling held his hands out. "Our Captain Wilson is uninformed on this matter. I would certainly be willing to search for a weapon for you to use, but as you can imagine, my time is quite valuable."

I took the letter off the desk and put it into my briefcase. I brought out a manila envelope and set it on the desk. "This might be of interest," I said. "These will be available shortly in the US, but I can provide this sample for your department right now. They're the new one hundred-dollar bills issued by the Treasury. Some are in circulation now."

Trilling opened the thick envelope and stared at me and then at the bills.

"They have some new security features," I said.

"This interests me a great deal," Trilling said. "I'll make sure these get into the right hands. And will put a pistol in yours."

"Thank you," I said.

"Except that our Captain Wilson doesn't know who you are," Trilling said. "And Captain Wilson is a very smart man."

"I'm going to be in charge of the mentoring operation," I said. "Operational Mentoring Liaison Teams. OMLT."

Trilling nodded. "Now this I have heard of," he said. "Tell me, what are we like to you? In the US? Some kind of island Afghanistan?"

"No," I said.

"Everybody sees opportunities in our problems," Trilling said. "Opportunities for themselves. Drug runners. Killers. Flesh-traders. The United States." The traffic noise from outside was like a distant heartbeat. Kingston was alive, no matter how many people were trying to kill it.

"It's not like that for us," I said.

Trilling nodded again. "Tomorrow we will introduce you to one of our Assistant Commissioners. He will talk to you."

"Thank you," I said. "And I need to talk to you about Daniel Woodson."

"Who is he?" Trilling said.

"Seven-year-old boy, native of the island. He was shot and killed last December, near his home," I said.

"I'm sure the investigation is ongoing," Trilling said.

"Well, there are people in the US who would like an update," I said.

"Certainly," Trilling said. "Let me prepare an official update for you." He brought out a cigar, clipped the end with a cutter and lit it with a butane lighter. "The investigation into the death of Daniel Woodson is ongoing and the Jamaican Constabulary Force, especially Senior Superintendent Emerson Trilling, are searching round the clock to solve this most grievous of crimes. All God's sympathy to his family, especially his mother." He blew a smoke ring up to the ceiling.

"Supposedly," I said, "the Assistant Commissioner was personally present when the boy was shot."

Trilling shook his head. "No," he said. "I accompany the AC on all investigations. He was not present at that time."

"Were you?" I said.

"Mister Matthews," Trilling said. "Myself and my fellow officers are often accused of things when we are not present. Murders. Rapes. Accusing is one thing—proof is another. No officer in Jamaica has ever been convicted of murder. The people here are liars and I say that, born and bred on this island."

I nodded. "The Woodson case is a priority. And in my role as observer, I'm supposed to check in on any Americans being held prior to sentencing."

Tilling nodded back. "The Assistant Commissioner will handle all that with you."

"Yes," I said.

"Martins will take you to your quarters for the night and place a guard with you," Trilling said.

"I thought you were going to get me a pistol?" I said.

"That will not happen today, Mister Matthews," Trilling said. "Nothing happens on any one, given day in Jamaica. Island time is different."

"When do you think you'll be able to get it to me?" I said.

Trilling thickened his accent as he smiled. "Soon coming, mon," he said. "Soon come." He was laughing as I left the office. Martins was waiting for me outside and drove me to a small cottage on the edge of a hotel complex. A uniformed JCF officer stayed on the porch after I shut the door. A shot from the bottle of rum on the dresser and I was asleep before I knew it.

In the morning, Martins and I walked to the hotel lobby for coffee and breakfast. I ate the ackee and salt fish, with sides of fresh fruit. More of the coffee. Martins ate a little and sipped tea.

"Let's go," he said. Two other officers were waiting for us in the car. I picked up my briefcase and followed.

Assistant Commissioner Hill met us on the steps of another JCF complex, not far from the hotel. Kingston was in the distance. The complex was surrounded with the green, lush jungle-forest associated with Jamaica. AC Hill was a big man—six four with a massive chest and arms. Coal-black skin and slightly graying hair under his officers cap. He wore his 9mm at his right hip, ready to draw. The humidity was already working on me.

"Mister Matthews," Hill said. "You are here to fulfill your forward observer role." He didn't extend his hand to me.

"Yes," I said. "I spoke with Senior Superintendent Trilling yesterday…"

AC Hill cut me off. "He and I spoke this morning," Hill said. "He will handle the Woodson inquiry for you. I have one man being detained here right now. He might fall under your authority."

"What's he been charged with?" I said.

AC Hill laughed. "A variety of things," Hill said. "Come. You can talk to him."

Hill led me down a corridor with holding cells on each side. Officers saluted Hill as we passed. Martins trailed us. At the end, there was a solid cell door with a guard stationed outside it. Hill motioned and the guard produced a key, and opened the steel door.

There was a large, muscular white man tied to a metal chair that was bolted to the floor. The man could barely look up at me.

"Do you know each other?" Hill said.

I shook my head. "No," I said. "I've never seen this man."

"Are you certain?" Hill said.

"Absolutely," I said.

"Very well. I will leave you alone to talk to him, since you are observing here. Maybe he will talk to a countryman." Hill stepped out of the door and I heard the lock click.

The man on the chair looked up slightly. "I think my collarbones are broken and possibly my arms. My neck might be fractured and some ribs are cracked," he said.

"Christ's sake," I said. "I really don't know what I can do."

"Don't worry about it," he said. "The whole place is bugged anyway."

I shook my head.

"What are you here for?" he said.

"To observe," I said. "And to find out what happened to a little boy. I'll see what I can do."

"Try to get me home," he said.

I nodded and knocked on the inside of the steel door. The guard opened it and let me out, closing and re-locking the door as I left. Martins was standing there. He led me through, out the back to a makeshift airplane hangar. Hill was there, smoking a cigar with another officer.

"Did he speak with you?" Hill said. He let a smoke ring float into the stifling wet air.

"Not really," I said. "He's injured and needs treatment."

"Yes," Hill said. "These things can be costly." He shifted on his feet.

I reached into my soft briefcase and drew out an envelope. I handed it to Hill. He opened it and counted the bills. He took several out and handed them to the officer next to him. Then he handed some to Martins.

"This is good," Hill said. "Tomorrow you can take him home." He counted the remaining bills. "But we would like his name. So that if we ever catch him stealing half a ton of marijuana from us again, we'll have something else to call him besides CIA man."

I shrugged. "I don't know his name," I said.

Hill shrugged back. "That's okay," he said. "Try to find out by tomorrow."

"Yes," I said. "But he goes with me tomorrow."

Hill held his palms up. "One way or another, he will go with you tomorrow." He walked away from me, with the other officer. Martins and I headed back through the complex, to the car and the burning humid sun. Back to the hotel and my cottage. The JCF officers left me there and I had a drink next to the pool. Watching the sunburned tourists get in and out of the tepid water. There was a private security officer on my tiny porch when I walked back to my room. He stood straight as I walked past him and entered my room. I saw him smoking a cigarette before I went to sleep.

I was driven back to the compound in the morning. The guards took me behind the airplane hangar. There was the white man I had met the previous day, lying on the ground in a pool of his own blood. One of the guards was lying face down on the ground and appeared to be unconscious or dead. Another one of the guards was holding his right arm and sobbing. From the look of it, his arm was severely dislocated—out of the shoulder socket and perhaps broken. He had grappled with someone and lost.

"What happened here?" I said.

"The prisoner asked to shave," the one guard said. "We gave him this basin of water and soap and like gentlemen, we gave him a straight razor. He cut his own throat and we tried to stop him, but he did it too quickly."

"That's impossible," I said.

The guard took two fast steps toward me. "It's right here, man!" he said. "Do you want to see it?!" He brought the razor up in his hand, flashing the blade in the sunlight.

"It looks as if there was a fight," I said.

"There was," the guard said. "We tried to stop your friend from cutting his throat."

I shook my head. "He was no friend of mine."

"Then why do you care if he's dead," the man said.

"I just want to know the truth of what happened," I said.

AC Hill came out from the back of the complex and caught the end of my conversation. "Ah, yes," he said. "The great American search for truth. You lie to the entire world and now you are here, on my island, and suddenly, I am somehow denying you the truth." He puffed his cigar. "If I were the truth, I would run from you, so that you could never find me."

"Can I take his body back with me?" I said.

"Are you prepared to pay for it?" he said.

"Why would I have to pay?" I said. "I paid yesterday."

"Because we think you can afford to pay," he said. "Maybe if you make me happy, Trilling will find out about that boy for you." He pointed at the dead operative on the ground. "Did you get his name for me?"

"No," I said.

"It is deadly business to try to steal from us," Hill said. "We will kill anyone we catch doing it."

"Understood," I said.

"Tell that to anyone who will listen," Hill said.

I nodded.

I'm in the terminal when two JCF officers come up behind me.

"Sir, you are coming with us," the one said.

Outside, in a car, sits Senior Superintendent Emerson Trilling. He doesn't speak as I enter and sit. Once I close the door, we're speeding through the heat and the stench, into the slums. Graffiti and murals cover the concrete walls along the streets and the car turns and turns. Gunshots in the distance to the right, but it's as if they have all heard it before. No one even recognizes it's happening. Slamming through the streets. Past the cart vendors, the shops, the burned-out buildings, the piles of trash, the goats, the abandoned cars, the pounding music, the crowds, the houses. The smell of food. The blazing sun and soaking heat. The stench.

We stop in front of an alley and the officers and Senior Superintendent Trilling exit. The alley is blocked off, by two jeeps and JCF officers armed with M-16s. They salute the Senior Superintendent and make a path for him. He strides up the alley like a dark king and stops in front of an open door.

"You coming?" Trilling said.

"Yes," I said. I'm sweating from the waves of humidity.

Trilling enters the room and I follow. There are two bodies, covered with flies, in the room. A black man and a black woman. The flies are buzzing. Both individuals have been shot multiple times. There is a pistol on the floor next to the woman.

"Do you know who that is?" Trilling said.

"No," I said.

"That is Valerie Woodson. The mother of Daniel Woodson," Trilling said.

I stare. The cover story I was told—grieving, inconsolable mother, relatives in the United States—didn't mention that she might be armed or involved with the police.

"Now," Trilling says, "let me tell you something. A year ago, on December the second, my men respond to this block. We get a tip that this man," he points to the body on the floor, "a known drug dealer is hiding here. We are looking for this man, for reasons I will tell you in a moment."

Trilling reaches down next to the man and brings up a small knapsack. He shakes it and shakes it. Until something falls onto the floor. It's a human hand, severed at the wrist and caked with dried blood.

Trilling keeps on. "This man, what he does, when he kills someone, he has a hand with him, slashed off from another crime he has committed. So he takes these hands and puts the fingerprints on guns and crime scenes and spreads the blood and DNA around. Then, after a while, he throws this one out and gets another hand. He does it to confuse us—and it works." He stares at me. "But on that night, for Lord knows the reason—Daniel Woodson ran from this house after we had it surrounded. He ran so fast, Mister Matthews, with no shoes, just wearing shorts and a Harbor View FC shirt—because of Gardner, the footballer."

"Yes," I said. "I know."

"He had a bag he was carrying. And I thought to myself, what could be in that bag? I knew the officers at the end of the alley would stop him," Trilling said.

"You were here, personally?" I said.

"LET ME SPEAK!" Trilling yelled. "Before he reached the end of the alley, she shot him. His own mother shot him and in the confusion that followed, she managed to hide that weapon and her drug dealer boyfriend got away. They made him run with a human hand in a bag, Mister Matthews, do you see what we're dealing with here?" Trilling said.

I shook my head. "You shot him," I said. "And you just drove up here and shot this woman, whoever she is."

"Pay me again," Trilling said. "More than you paid Hill." He reached for his pistol.

I hit him, with my right elbow in his face and twisted his wrist and arm. I had his pistol now. I clear the chamber and removed the magazine, scattering the shells on the floor of the room. Next to the bodies.

Trilling was stopping the blood coming out of his nose with a white handkerchief. He came close to me. "I tell you," he said. "If you come back on this island, you will not leave it. Do you understand me?"

I wiped the gun down with my shirttail and dropped it on the floor as we walked out.

The drive back to the airport was uneventful and the flight back to New York was smooth. I was feeding the dogs that evening, when my cell rang. It was McMurdo.

"How was the weather?" he said.

"There was a killer storm when I was over there," I said.

There was a silence. "One storm only?" he said.

"That's all I saw," I said.

"Any luck with Daniel Woodson?" he said.

"No luck," I said. "Let's not do that again."

"I'll talk to you soon," he said.

I hung up.

That night, I had a dream about a little boy who ran all the way across my field. When he reached my house, he showed me a paper bag he was carrying. I opened it. It was a hand. It was my hand.

PLAYBOY

I HEARD SOBBING THAT SPRING SATURDAY AFTERNOON and walked down the back stairs to see who was crying. My downstairs neighbor—Jane—was sitting on the wood picnic table, bawling her eyes out and smoking a cigarette.

"What's wrong," I said.

"Oh Jesus, John," she said. I had startled her, by accident, coming through the back door. "He went to that funeral and now he's at the wake and it's horrible." Jane's ex-husband, Frank, lived next door in a separate building that had been converted into four apartments. Frank lived in the rear apartment on the ground floor, with a view of the old apple orchard. Jane and Frank had been divorced for about ten years. They made an arrangement to live near each other to help raise their sixteen-year-old daughter, Jenny. The court had determined that Jenny should live with Jane. Frank was a biker and a concrete worker, probably in his early sixties.

Jane held up her cell phone. "One of the cousins just called me. She said it's awful."

"Where's the wake?" I said.

"After the funeral, they all went to The Blue Flame," she said.

I nodded.

"Can you go get him?" she said. "Make him come home." She took a drag on her cigarette.

"Is he drunk?" I said.

"Well what the hell do you think," she said, through the tears and the smoke.

"Last time he was drunk," I said, "it was hard to handle him." There had been an incident in the yard, where Frank had touched some woman's ass and that woman's husband had hit Frank with a two-by-four twice, once in the ribs and once in the head. Frank had come out of his apartment with a short, single-shot, break-barrel .22 and pulled the trigger, starring the other man's windshield and sending a ricochet whizzing through the apartment parking lot. When the cops showed up, nobody said anything and eventually, they went away. I knew Frank owned several hunting rifles, so it could have been worse.

"Do you think it's easy to deal with you, when you're drunk?" she said. A couple of times, I'd been really lit in the backyard, around the grill. This was my first apartment since my divorce and I had managed to get a decent job, running heavy equipment at the timber yard. Somewhere in my mind, I held the idea that I would be seeing a lot of women in and out of this apartment, but it never happened and I think it came out when I got drunk.

"Fair enough," I said. "I'll go talk to him. But no promises."

The bar was only five miles down the road. The parking lot was full, probably twenty or so cars. I picked out Frank's big blue van right away. I was glad to only see a couple motorcycles. I had trouble picturing guys navigating the bikes after a full day of drinking.

It was loud inside. People were wandering around, drinking and talking in groups of twos and threes. Some laughing, some crying. Frank was sitting at the bar when I went in, talking to a young couple. A girl with long straight brown hair and a guy with a home crew cut. It was strange to see Frank in a tan sport coat and shiny black slacks, with a thin, black shiny tie.

"Yeah," Frank was saying. "I just wanted to get right in there with him."

"I bet," the crew cut guy said.

"Do you know how light that coffin was?" Frank said to the girl. "And he was a damn big guy. Bust you right in two."

Her eyes widened.

"But that cancer," Frank kept on, "cancer ate him from the inside. Hollowed him out. He could have fought six men by himself, before he got sick."

"Sure," the crew cut guy said. "I bet he would have. I only knew him as an old man."

"He was never an old man," Frank corrected. "My father, God rest his soul, was an old man. Couldn't fucking feed himself. Richie was no old man."

"Sure," the crew cut guy said, sipping a beer. "Sure."

"You should come for a ride on my bike," Frank said to the girl.

She smiled. "What kind of bike is it?" she said. She tossed her hair over her right shoulder.

"Harley Shovelhead," Frank said. "Nineteen seventy-nine."

Before the crew cut guy could say anything, Frank saw me. "Johnny my boy," he said. He clapped his hand on my shoulder. He loud-whispered in my ear. "Do you know," he said, "that his wife had the nerve to come over here and demand that table saw back from me. She wants me to deliver it to her house right after this." He took a slug of whiskey and beer.

"Maybe she wants to give it to his son," I said.

"Then how come his son couldn't come over here and ask for it?" Frank said. "He knows me—hell, his father and I took him fishing and hunting more times than I could tell you. He cost me a buck one year, wouldn't shut up out in the woods and then cried once we got up in the tree stand. Richie had to take him back home."

"I don't know about any of this," I said. "Can you keep it down? You're really doing a number on these people."

"Did she send you here?" he said. "Did Jane send you? To shut me up?"

"No," I lied. "I came here on my own."

"He and I were closer than brothers. Closer than brothers. Used to shoot dope, screw women—everything." He jerked his thumb at Richie's wife. "Lot more action than she ever showed him."

"A little respect would go a long way here," I said.

"Do you see her?" Frank said, still looking at Ritchie's wife. "She's not beautiful. Do you think she's beautiful?" People turned toward Frank, as he raised his voice.

"No," I admitted. "I don't."

"Nobody here is beautiful or handsome," Frank said. "Fucking fooling yourself. But that doesn't mean you can't smile. Doesn't mean you can't screw." He downed his whiskey in one gulp and signaled for another. "John," he continued, "she used to wait up at night to yell at him, when we'd come in. Awful stuff, just awful."

"You want to know what I did?" he shout-whispered.

"What's that," I said.

"I put a Playboy under his jacket," he said.

"You did what," I said.

"I got there early and when the funeral director left the room, I opened the casket and moved Richie's arm and put a Playboy under his jacket."

"Where did you get it from?"

"I stopped at the gas station on 209 and got some beer. There was a guy getting a sandwich for his kid, so I had to wait and I started looking at the rack of magazines and thought of Richie. He and I had been in that gas station lots of times. So I grabbed him a Playboy."

"Did you really put it in the casket?" I said.

"Yes," he said. He finished his whiskey. "I did."

Richie's wife was standing about five feet away, with her brother. She was dressed entirely in black, as was her brother. I had seen him around before, an ex-prison guard. Most of those guys can retire early. He was a big man, but it had gone to fat and you could see it was hard for him to get around.

"You defiled Richie's casket?" the wife said. "Did you really do that?"

Frank nodded and drank. "I did it," he said. "Wanted my brother to enjoy himself in eternity."

I thought she'd slap him. She turned away and her brother followed her. The whole mood at the bar changed.

The conversation was so loud that people came over. Ritchie's wife's brother had three sons and they, in turn, had four sons between them.

"Frank," her brother said, "you're out of line."

"Fuck you, Melvin," Frank said. "You're too used to dealing with those cons. I speak my mind." The bartender set a shot glass full of whiskey and a beer on the wood bar in front of Frank. "Here's to Ritchie," he said, raising both the shot glass and the beer bottle and winking at the young woman with straight brown hair. People on the other side of the room, who weren't paying attention to the conversation, raised their glasses as well.

For a minute, the men seemed to back away from Frank. I relaxed a little, too. But several of them came back, including Melvin and suddenly grabbed Frank, dragging him off the barstool and headed for the parking lot.

"Don't get involved, John," one of them said. "We know he's your friend."

"Six on one isn't fair," I said.

Outside, they were punching Frank in the face and when he finally got up, he punched a couple of them even harder. One young guy fell to the macadam and didn't move. They tried to tackle him, but Frank kicked his way free and made it to his van. Already, his eyes were almost puffed closed and there was blood on his face. In one motion, he opened the driver's side door to the van and came out with a flat, black, semiautomatic pistol. He fired a shot in the air and everything stopped.

The men stood about ten feet away from him, staring at him.

"You need to leave," Melvin said. "This has been a mess, but if you go, we'll forget about it."

"Are you going home with me?" I said.

"No," he said. "I'm staying right here." He reached back into the van and pulled out a beer and twisted the cap off. Held the bottle up to his lips and took a long drink. "I belong here," he said. "With my brother Ritchie."

I looked at Melvin.

"He can stay in the parking lot," Melvin said. "But if he does anything more, I'm calling the cops."

"Okay," I said.

Frank looked at everyone. "Those people that want to celebrate Ritchie will find that the ceremony has moved to the van," he said. "I will share my beer, with all you ugly people."

The men moved back inside and I started to walk away, toward my truck.

"Hey, John," Frank said.

"Yes," I said.

"I just wanted my brother to have some beauty and get some action. At least those women in those pictures smile," he said.

"They do," I agreed.

"Because it's their job to smile," he said. He pulled another beer out of the van and twisted the top off. "Nobody's beautiful like those women are beautiful," he said, "because it's not their fucking job to be beautiful."

"Right," I said.

"Ritchie deserved that," he said.

"I'll see you at the house," I said.

"Jane's not beautiful," he said, "but that doesn't matter to me. She never knew that."

"Tell her," I said.

He nodded and kept drinking. I walked to my truck and pulled onto the highway.

Jane was still sitting on the picnic table, smoking a cigarette, when I drove in.

"Where is he?" she said.

"He's still there," I said. "He wouldn't come with me."

"Was he okay?" she said.

"Not really," I said. "Nothing I could do."

"How's he going to get home?" she said.

"I don't know," I said. "People will probably give him a ride." I walked back upstairs and turned the TV on. Sat watching the ballgame, drinking a beer.

Deep in the night, I woke up to the sound of Frank's motorcycle. He was riding around the parking lot in a slow circle. On the back of the bike was the young woman he'd been talking to at the bar. She had no shirt on. I could see, as he passed under the street light, his eyes were blackened. He pulled the bike out onto the main road and must have given the throttle a real shove, because the bike took off, load as thunder, carrying him and the half-naked girl off into the night. I heard the bike breathe as he paused for the light at 209 and then make the left turn and head up the hill, onto the miles of straight road that stretched to southern Ulster County and into Catskill Park. The roar of the bike was still clear, still screaming into the night, defiant. I listened to the roar for several minutes before going back to bed. From downstairs, there were faint noises and soft footsteps away from their front window. I didn't know if it was Jane or her daughter. Someone had watched Frank take off.

The next morning, someone was knocking on my door. I opened it. Frank was standing there, wearing a T-shirt, leather jacket and jeans. Both of his eyes were black underneath and there was a small cut covered with dried blood on the right side of his face. The knuckles of his right hand were skinned and raw.

"Hey," he said. "We've got to go do something."

"What," I said.

"Get that backhoe off your site and take it over to cemetery for me," he said.

"You can't be serious," I said.

He drank his coffee. "Look, it's all legit. Her brother's going to be there and we talked to the cemetery groundskeeper, he understands. It'll be fine. Shouldn't be more than three swipes with the hoe, I'll jump down into the grave, open the casket, take it out and we'll be done. Then just shove the dirt back in the hole." He took another sip. "You're pretty good with that thing, right?"

"Yeah," I said. "I'm good with it. I don't know Frank. This sounds crazy."

"Well, we all agreed to it yesterday, after you left." He motioned to his black eyes and his hand. "There was a little scuffle in the parking lot and we got it sorted out."

"I was there," I said.

"There was a little bit after that too," he said.

"Did you take her the table saw?" I said.

"Already dropped it off this morning and got a coffee for you on the way back. Come on, let's get it over with," he said.

"Alright," I said. "Let me put my work boots on."

Frank drove us over to the timber yard. It took me three tries, but finally the backhoe started. I pulled it up onto the lowboy and shut it down. Then I took the rachet chains and locked the wheels in place for the ride to the cemetery. I backed the cab up and hooked onto the lowboy. I followed Frank to the cemetery.

My main concern was leaving ruts in the cemetery. Fortunately, Richie's gravesite was on the edge of the cemetery, where new plots were being laid out. There were only three headstones in this section. I removed the rachet chains and drove the backhoe off the lowboy.

Her brother was standing next to the grave. The earth on top was fresh, brown soil. I pulled the hoe up to it and deployed the hydraulic pads. Frank stood close to it, drinking his coffee. The first bite of the hoe's teeth was a little hesitant. I came away with half a shovel full of soil. The second pass, I made sure to get a full load.

"Can you see anything?" I yelled to Frank, over the machine.

Both Frank and her brother stepped to the edge of the grave. I saw Frank shake his head and give me the thumbs up. Her brother looked briefly at me and shook his head. They couldn't see anything. I worked the controls and moved the hoe for another pass.

I heard the scrape and Frank screaming at the same time and immediately raised the bucket. Her brother was standing at the edge of the grave and shaking his head, holding his head in his hands, kneeling. I shut the machine down, got out and walked to the grave.

Frank had already jumped down into the grave, on top of the casket. He was holding a large field stone, which he tossed onto the fresh grass. It was the size of a small toolbox.

"Who the fuck backfills a grave with rocks?" Frank screamed.

Her brother was crying.

"What happened?" I said.

"You hit that stone," Frank said, pointing at the stone, "and it pushed through the dirt and scratched the casket lid."

He carefully brushed some dirt away with his hand, revealing gray metal beneath the dirt. There was a white metal scar, about ten inches in length, down the face of the metal. A tiny dent ran the length of the white scar.

Her brother was up. "Get the hell off the casket," he said to Frank. Frank hoisted himself back up onto the turf. The brother's face was red with tears. "I want you to drive to the gas station right now and bring me back a Playboy magazine right here." He turned to me. "Fill that fucking hole and don't fuck anything else up." He ran his hands over his eyes. "I'm going to tell her we got it and it's over, is that clear?" He looked at both of us. "Never talk about this again, to anyone."

Frank took off in his van. I started the machine up and put the dirt back in the hole, without digging up too much turf. I raised the pads and drove the back hoe onto the lowboy. I secured it with the chains. There were ruts where I had driven the machine onto the grass and depressions where I had put the stabilizing pads down. The brother was walking around, trying to smooth the ground with his feet. He wasn't doing anything, wasn't affecting the torn earth.

I pulled the lowboy down the cemetery road and back onto the highway. Dropped it off at the timber yard, exactly as I had found it. The rain had just started to fall and as I walked along the highway, it increased and the clouds became thicker and darker. I didn't know what I would do if Frank pulled up behind me in his van. I hoped I could just walk home, soaked. I kept walking, as the rain came down harder. Soaking the ground and everything, as cars and trucks passed. It was a longer walk home than I thought it would be.

CALIFORNIA

THIS HOT, AUGUST MORNING, THE OCEAN SMASHES against the black, Maine shore rocks, as it has forever. Long before any of this was introduced. Before the time change. Years ago, if something happened in Maine, it happened at the same time in California. It was simply dark on the far coast. There was no three-hour difference. The salt spray from the ocean wets my face and I walk away from the rocks, back to my truck. To go to work. I have to cut some wood.

It's easy for me to travel in my mind. Got used to doing it when I was locked up for the first time. If I wanted to be out of my cell, I'd imagine someplace else. I've been everywhere in the world without ever leaving a facility.

Today is the day. I got a letter from you that said even if you survived, you could lose the use of your left arm. In California, they are going to put you almost naked on a stainless steel table, pierce your chest cavity, and go hunting for the small black death that grows inside you.

I'm here in Maine. I could pierce my own chest with the saw, in solidarity. A chainsaw is an imprecise tool, not like the silver surgical blades and bone spreaders the doctors will be using on you.

What do doctors do, in California, in the morning? They are not doctors yet, are they, while they are sleeping? Or do they dream the special dreams of doctors, different from me and you? Dreams of the health they so rarely get to see. Is every human sick, to them? I wonder if the lobstermen I see are the same while sleeping, dreaming of their boats and their traps and their life on the ocean.

The trees I cut here in Maine are not as big as the trees I could cut in California. Most are healthy, grown for the purpose of being cut. A tree tells the story of itself through the rings inside its trunk. A thin ring might mean a fire, or a year when there was a drought. When they open you up this morning, they will see your rings and the rings of those five years we were together. One thick ring and four very thin ones. Fires and droughts combined. You were right to leave me, Ann. I still smell like gasoline and oil. I am still here and will never be able to get to your there. You were right. I have not seen you in over a decade, but you were right.

How will I know when you've entered heaven. I used to think I would know somehow, but I won't. In your letter, you asked me to pray for you. I don't even know if I believe in heaven anymore. I am no good to you and you are right to be away from me.

I am still on parole here. I don't know when my last day will be, since I have done things I wasn't supposed to. I drank cheap whiskey. I'm drinking it this morning. It keeps me from going places in my mind. I will always drink, Ann. My days are different than yours. Than other people's. One day does not fall after the next, with a new chance for hope and happiness. It is all one, long, never-ending day to me, with no let up. It wasn't that way when I was a kid, but now, since I was in that last time, things haven't been good. My kindness doesn't shine through anymore. I've worn thin—internally—and I would fail you, Ann. As I did. I'm failing myself even now.

Have you ever pretended to walk somewhere far in your mind? To the east of here is the wild ocean and it would scare me to go that route. I would start out going west from my apartment, across the street, through the park, to the bridge. Up the long, winding ramp, onto the bridge. Up High Street, over Congress. There's the Eastland Hotel on the right. Down the hill, past the Y and the sketchy gas station. Through the big park. Walking on the highway. I think the easiest way for me to go would be Burlington. On the highways and through the forests of Canada. South into Washington, Seattle and along the beautiful coast of Oregon. Into California. Going other ways makes it get fuzzy and I fall off the edge of the earth.

I want to be there right now. While the doctors are still sleeping. I want to be the night janitor, polishing the floor of the hospital entrance for you. I want to be the gas station attendant, filling the doctor's car, the man who put up the cell towers to carry their calls, the groundskeeper putting up the reserved parking sign for the doctors, the Mexican guy on the mower making the grass perfect, the road crew putting the lines on the highway, the intern sanitizing the surgical instruments, the nurse putting the surgical mask and gown on the doctor. I want to be the sprinkler man, the guy smoothing the macadam. All of it done while the doctor was sleeping, so that he wakes up in a world so fresh and bright that he is filled with hope and love and joy and clarity and precision and success.

And that he is not like me. Overweight, failing, depressed beyond measure. Filled with hate. Running a chainsaw because I can't do any-thing else.

I would wear a clean shirt and meet him at the front door of the hospital.

"Good morning," I would say.

"Good morning," he would say.

"You seem out of breath," he'd say.

"I just walked here from Maine," I say.

"That's a long way," he'd say. "Take it easy."

"Please save Ann," I'd say. "Did you get a good night's sleep?"

"Yes," he'd say. "I always sleep well. But today is a different day. I can't make any promises."

"Why not," I'd say.

"Doctors don't make promises," he'd say.

"But I made a promise to her," I'd say.

"Did you keep it?" he'd ask.

"No," I'd say.

"That's why we don't make them," he'd say.

"But you slept well, doctor?" I'd ask.

"Yes," he'd say. "I always do. You don't understand, do you."

"Oh," I'd say. "I don't think I do."

So let's pretend this is not the end. Let's pretend this an endless beginning and you're happy. You're healthy. Take yourself back to before cancer. For me, that's a long time. Before my great-grandparents died. On Christmas. Martina passed away—she had both breasts removed—but no one told me. They didn't want to ruin my Christmas morning. Can you believe that. How kind people were to me then and what a kid I was. Please, take yourself back to before cancer. Take yourself back to before me. I think that's what you were trying to do in California, before all of this. Keep doing it, Ann. I do not know where I will be when you die. Let's hope I'm not around and you are soaring through life and we tackle the problem that way.

I'm cutting trees here today. Fifty acres to clear by the end of the month, if my parole officer lets me stay out. I work with three other guys and none of us are really worth anything. Just some guys with saws and trucks. We're not doctors, or physicians. We're not special or good.

But you are, Ann. In my mind, I wish I could walk to you today. I wish I could get there this morning.

What do doctors do, in California, in the morning? Where is the doctor who is going to save you, in the darkness of that early hour.

ACKNOWLEDGEMENTS

I'm very lucky to be married to the amazing writer and artist Shanna McNair. Thank you, Shanna!! None of this would have been possible without you and your tremendous efforts. Much love and thanks—you're the very brightest star.

Nothing But Enemies is dedicated to my good friend—writer/ executive producer/showrunner—Tim Walsh. Huge debt of gratitude— thank you Tim, for all you do.

Thanks to Gary Lennon—playwright/writer/executive producer/ showrunner—for being absolutely wonderful and generous. Thank you, Gary.

Thank you to Antonio D'Intino for all your support, effort, and good cheer.

Thanks to my brother, the artist Will Wolven, for such a great cover photo.

And to the great Johan Cruyff for inspiration. You have to shoot to score.

Scott Wolven is the author of the short story collection *Controlled Burn*. The title story was included in *The Best American Noir of the Century*. His story "The Copper Kings" appears in *20 + 1*, an anthology of 21 short stories "by emblematic American authors" (Albin Michel). His stories were selected for seven consecutive volumes of The Best American Mystery Stories Series and his story "Playboy" was featured in *Playboy Magazine*. He has published widely in online and print journals. He wrote on the TV series "Hightown" (STARZ /Bruckheimer) and his story "Hammerlock" ("Hepburn") screened at the 52nd New York Film Festival. More at scottwolven.com.

www.ingramcontent.com/pod-product-compliance
Lightning Source LLC
Chambersburg PA
CBHW051109300726

48981CB00001B/65